Mike -3

THE McKENNAS

by Virgil S. Cross

E.M. Press, Inc.
Manassas, VA

This is an original work of literature.

Cover illustration and design by Kevin B. Spain

ISBN: 1-880664-22-4
Library of Congress Catalog Card Number: 97-675

E.M. Press, Inc.
P.O. Box 4057
Manassas, VA 20108

The Boise Basin Country

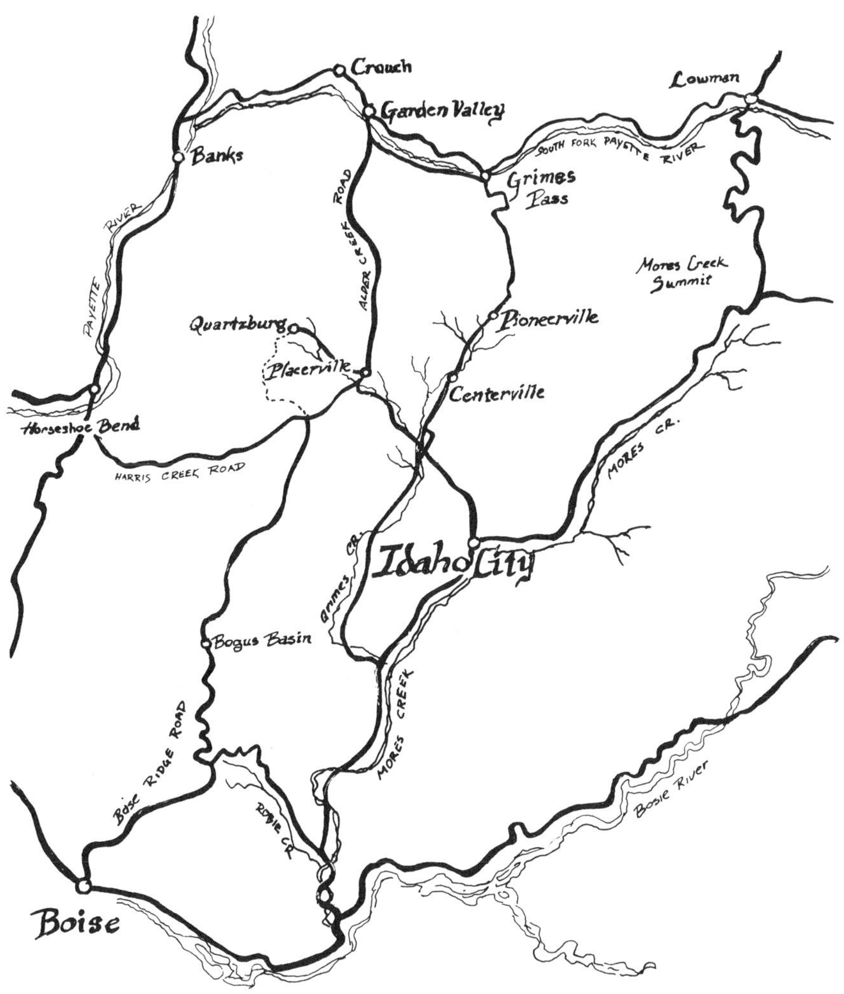

PROLOGUE

As I was growing up in sparsely settled south and central Idaho, rumors and gossip were a means of entertainment. There were many versions of stories concerning the owner of the big ranch. All were undoubtedly embellished from teller to teller. They all had three things in common. The owner, very well liked and highly respected, was a wealthy man who had hit it rich in the gold fields. He had been saved from hanging by an Indian and had adopted an orphan boy. It was after I had finished college and started teaching school that I had the idea of writing the story someday.

I wanted to fish the wonderful trout stream that ran through the ranch. When I drove up to the large, white ranch house to ask permission to fish, I saw an elderly lady stooped over in her rose bed. When she stood up, she was trim, straight, and tall. From her classic facial features, crowned by a mass of grey hair and startling blue eyes, I could tell she had been a beautiful woman.

After exchanging greetings, I said, "I would like permission to fish. I will close the gates, and I want only four fish." She smiled.

"It is nice of you to ask permission and to limit the fish you take. So many people are just plain game hogs."

I touched a yellow rose leaf and said, "They need iron."

"So that's what ails them. What shall I do?"

"If you put a heaping tablespoonful of iron chelate in a gallon of water and spray them while the sun is not shining, they will green up in a few days."

"My memory isn't so good. Would you come into the house and write it down for me?"

After we entered the house and were seated at the table in the kitchen, she asked, "Would you like a cup of coffee? The pot is on the stove and is hot. I'm a little lonesome and it's nice to have someone to talk to. Everyone is busy haying."

"Were you one of the first settlers here?"

"My husband was one of the first. He came here from Idaho City in 1863 and I came here in 1864."

"Where did you meet him?"

"I met him in Boise. He came from Kansas and drove a team of four mules to California in 1850."

I told her that was quite a story and someday I would write it up.

She said, "My goodness. You'll have to change the names." She hesitated, as if in thought, and added, "And change the location of the ranch to another area."

I said I surely would.

To depict the events of the period required research in libraries in Salt Lake City, Boise Public Library, and the Idaho Historical Society. I also visited the Boise Basin and Idaho City, where more gold was taken from an eighteen-square-mile area than from all of Alaska. Diaries of people who made the trek to California, and diaries of early settlers furnished a wealth of information. The story covers Greg McKenna's journey from Kansas City to California gold fields, to Idaho City, and finally to his ranch in southern Idaho.

Being reared in Idaho and well acquainted with most areas, and my own mining and prospecting experience, helped to write this story.

I hope you like Harry. I did.

CHAPTER 1

THE EARLY YEARS

The blinding flash of lightning, followed by the sharp deafening sound of rolling thunder, split a tall tree a few feet to the right of the team of bays that were hitched to the buggy. As the tree burst into flame, they bolted, completely out of control in spite of the frantic efforts of the driver to turn them away from a grove of large poplar trees. The woman in the buggy bent over to shield the well-wrapped baby clutched in her arms. As the horses swerved to avoid a large tree, the linchpin broke and the buggy rolled off the tongue, crashing into the trees. Gregory McKenna's parents were killed, leaving him an orphan at one year old. Gregory was bundled tightly in a blanket and miraculously escaped injury.

The McKenna farm in Kansas adjoined the farm of Helen and Carl Fletcher, a well-thought-of, kindly, churchgoing couple who had been childless for four years and yearned for a child. The families had been close friends, and Helen had taken care of Greg on several occasions. She immediately took the baby into her care, regarding him as a gift from heaven. Carl approved because Helen was happy, and he thought the boy would be help on the farm.

Carl was an intelligent schemer and planner. He asked Helen, "Would you like to adopt the boy?"

She gave him a hug and while still holding him, said, "That would be wonderful. I love Greg very much and feel that he is my own son!"

"I'll check with Judge Bishop and see what can be done."

The judge was a kindly man who thought that Carl was a good citizen, hard working, honest, and solid.

"If you will have the boy baptized as Gregory McKenna Fletcher, I'll sign the adoption papers."

"All right, Judge, we'll have him baptized next Sunday."

When he returned home, Helen was feeding Gregory, who was vigorously enjoying his milk.

"Helen, we are not going to have any trouble adopting him. The judge said that if we have him baptized Gregory McKenna Fletcher, he will sign the adoption papers. I stopped by the minister's house on the way home and he will baptize Greg right after the hymn next Sunday. He said that if he cries we can take him out so he won't interrupt the service."

"He is such a darling child and you are a wonderful husband!"

The minister was pleased about the baptism as the Fletchers were good churchgoers and contributed their share toward the upkeep of the church. Also, it would shorten his sermon.

Greg only made a face and shook his head when the water was sprinkled on him. The minister said a prayer asking for the happiness and welfare of the child. The Fletchers beamed when he praised them for taking a homeless orphan into their home as a son.

Judge Bishop looked over the baptismal certificate.

"This is fine, Carl. I congratulate you for taking in this orphan. It shows what fine people you are. I will fill out the legal adoption certificate and it will be in the mail tomorrow. There is quite a bit of talk about what will happen to the McKenna farm."

This gave Carl a chance to say what he had been carefully thinking about: how to get the McKenna farm, which was eighty acres of prime bottom land adjoining his farm, without paying for it.

"Judge, the McKennas were immigrants. The farm isn't mortgaged and Greg is their heir."

"Is there any information as to their relatives overseas?"

"We have gone through their effects and found no correspondence with anyone."

"You are right in that Greg is the legal heir. We can draw up a trust paper so he will inherit when he comes of age. You will be the trustee."

"Judge, we haven't been able to have any children. Since he is our son, he will inherit everything anyway."

"Carl, this may not be entirely legal, but I'll tell the recorder to make the deed over to you."

"Judge, if you think that is right, it is fine with me. We couldn't love him more if he was our own child."

Under the loving care of Helen, the youngster soon stopped crying for his mama. Carl was pleased because the happiness of Helen filled their life. By the time Greg was five, he was called at times to give the family blessing. He also knew his alphabet and could count. Helen frequently pointed out how smart he was. She found a copy of *McGuffy's Reader* for him and, by the time the blue-eyed, sandy-haired six-year-old started the first grade, he could read surprisingly well. Arithmetic came easily to him.

Mrs. Crawford, the middle-aged school teacher, was a strict disciplinarian, frequently using a ruler on the knuckles. In the small country school with eight grades in one room, she had only nine pupils and could give individual attention. She taught manners and conduct as well as the alphabet. She also read the Bible to them and stressed the creation of man by the Lord in Adam and Eve. Greg wondered about that and asked his parents how man got on earth. He thought they had to be babies first.

His parents didn't contradict the teacher, saying, "That is what the Bible says. The Bible is a history of what happened a long time ago. These stories were passed only from person to person and maybe there were some changes in the telling. God made man and woman and they had babies: Cain and Abel."

Mrs. Crawford caught one of the pupils lying and lectured the class. She read the Ten Commandments to them and said, "Lying is a sin. You can go to hell for it! If you lie, you are always a liar. No one will believe you from then on."

Greg was glad that it was Percy who was getting the tongue-lashing. At supper, Helen asked, "What happened at school today?"

"Percy lied, and Mrs. Crawford gave him what-for and told us that it is a sin to lie."

Carl said, "She is right, it is a sin. If a man's word is good, it is priceless. If you always tell the truth, you have nothing to remember. We will never spank you for telling the truth."

Greg started helping his mother at a very early age. At six he was feeding the chickens and carrying water from the well, which had a chain and cog wheel for drawing water. When he was almost seven, he was a big, strong boy, larger than the other second-graders. His parents had both been large.

"Helen, there is no use in sending Greg to school anymore. He can read, write, and figure better than any of the pupils in that school." Helen wanted Greg to graduate from the eighth grade and get a diploma, but she gave way to her husband.

Helen and Carl were close together in bed on a Sunday evening. They often talked in bed about matters they didn't want Greg to hear.

"Carl, we are going to have a baby! I'm sure. You should have noticed that I missed my last monthly flow, and now I have missed another. This morning after breakfast I almost threw up."

During the next eight years, Helen had five children, three boys and twin girls. Greg helped the overburdened mother, even feeding the babies and changing diapers. The years from thirteen to seventeen were pleasant for Greg, in spite of the fact that Carl had the six-foot-two-inch, two-hundred-pound boy/man do almost the work of two men. But Greg knew about his parents' farm, and thought it would be his when he turned twenty.

Carl was shrewd. When the migration started westward, he was able to envision what would happen and what the needs of the immigrants would be. He started to raise draft horses. Using a Percheron stallion and small mares, he could raise horses of fifteen-hundred pounds, large enough so four of them could pull a covered wagon. St. Louis, only a short distance away, and Kansas City, farther west, were gathering places for caravans, and there was a large demand for good horses. Greg had a knack for gentling and breaking horses, which he enjoyed doing.

Carl would buy clothes for him and occasionally give him a miserly dollar. Greg protested about how little he was getting when the hired man got three dollars a week, milk and meat, and a house to live in. To appease Greg, Carl gave him a grey colt from one of his brood mares that was bred accidentally by an Arabian stallion. It turned out to be a big, long-legged, grey gelding, with high withers and a strong back. The flared nostrils, short head, and ears showed its Arab ancestry. It wasn't the fastest horse, but as Carl said, "It will take you there and get you back." Greg named him Star. His other possession was a cap-and-ball squirrel rifle with which he had killed numerous squirrels and prairie chickens.

Greg had been working around the barnyard, training the new teams to drive. The Fletchers, with their five children, had gone to town. When he slipped and fell on a pile of soft, watery horse manure and really messed up his pants and shirt, he went to the house to wash up and change clothes. He was upstairs in his room and had just started to dress when the Fletchers came home. The children stopped to go to the two-holer and play in the yard. Carl and Helen were arguing. Greg listened.

"We have enough to buy the Pickens farm. We need three farms—one for each of our boys when we die."

"Carl, we need four farms. The McKenna place belongs to Greg."

"He isn't really our son, Helen. We took him in and raised him and gave him a good home. We don't owe him anything. The McKenna farm is legally in my name and that's where I am going to keep it."

"You know Greg loves farming and talks about having a farm of his own."

Carl was adamant. Greg was shocked that he was being cheated and that Carl didn't consider him a son. He slipped out the door quietly. At supper that night he ate silently.

"What are you thinking about, Greg? Has a cat got your tongue?"

"What did you say, Mother?" Helen repeated her question.

"I was wondering why all the people are going west."

Carl said, "People are migrating because there are large numbers coming from Europe. They settle in a place like we have here and have children. Soon there isn't enough land or work for them, so they move on. The people with money buy up the farms and become richer and richer."

"Is that what you are doing, Father?"

"I've been smarter than most. Raising horses is a very good business now. People are going west because so much land is available for the filing. Now that gold has been discovered in California, they think all they have to do to get rich is go to there."

"You mean that all you have to do is to go west to Oregon or California, find a piece of farm land, file on it, and it is yours?"

"Yes. It is a hell of a long way and a hard trip of almost a year to get there. People who have made the trip report that the route is lined with graves. When you get there, you have to clear the land and wait for it to produce. It is a great opportunity for a young person who has enough money to last several years until his farm starts paying off. But if I were going west, I would still raise horses. The Army will need them as there is going to be more trouble with the Indians. The North and South could fight a war. A farmer would have trouble selling farm crops out west because there are not too many people to buy them."

Greg interrupted, "It would take several years before you would have enough horses to sell."

"You are right. It would take a lot of money to finance such an operation."

Greg was confused and deeply hurt as he could not understand Carl's actions and attitude toward him. He had always considered Carl and Helen to be his parents. Helen especially had been everything a loving mother could be. He bitterly resented the fact that Carl had cheated him out of his inheritance. He decided to see a lawyer.

When the uncertain eighteen-year-old entered the lawyer's office, the friendly man greeted him with, "Sit down, Greg. I'll be with you in a few minutes." A little later he summoned Greg into his office. "Have a chair and tell me all about it."

After hearing about Carl and the former McKenna farm, he told Greg, "I'll check the court records and let you know what can be done."

The lawyer's report a few days later was almost without hope. Greg could sue when he was twenty-one. The cost would be very high and even then he might lose the case. It would be difficult to change court records. After several days of deliberation, Greg decided to leave for California and look for gold. There would be no way for him to accumulate enough money to sue.

CHAPTER 2

THE WAY WEST

In March of 1850, Greg and his horse, Star, both tired and hungry, arrived in Kansas City. His only possessions were his clothes, two blankets, a small canvas tarp, an old McClellan saddle, his squirrel rifle, and seven dollars of the eleven that he had saved. Although it was late in the year, many caravans were scattered miles from town to let their stock graze.

He rode up to a sign saying, "LIVERY STABLE". The proprietor, Ben Miller, said, "I charge fifty cents a night, and that includes a quart of oats and hay."

"Can I sleep in the barn?"

"Only if you don't smoke."

"I chew a little, but I don't smoke."

The thirty-cent stew at the small restaurant was filling. Greg thought that if he got a good night's sleep he could find work and keep Star. The bed in the straw was warm and comfortable. He was used to the smell of hay, horses, and manure. The owner had said, "Sonny, you watch for me and if anyone tries to take a horse out, call me. I live next door."

Greg didn't go to sleep immediately. He was wondering if he should have left the comforts of his home with the Fletchers. He had left a note for Helen saying, "I am going west. There is no future for me here. I thank you for all you have done for me. Love, Greg."

He was almost asleep when he heard the barn door squeak. There were light footsteps and a muffled voice saying, "We can saddle up and get out of here before he wakes up." Hurriedly putting on his pants and boots, Greg slipped out the door away from the men. He was panting as he pounded on the door to awaken the proprietor, who answered quickly.

"Two men are saddling up horses!" The proprietor was in his long red underwear. He put on a pair of boots, reached for his double-barreled cap-and-ball shotgun, and ran toward the barn with Greg right behind him. The two men were just starting to lead their horses out of the stalls.

"What the hell do you two mean by trying to sneak out without paying your bill?"

The two men were surprised and speechless for the moment. Greg lit a lantern. Both men wore guns, but the cocked shotgun trained on them made them keep their hands up. The shorter one said, "We were only getting an early start. We were going to stop at your house to pay you."

"Like hell you were. You are a pair of cheap deadbeats. You owe three dollars and fifty cents each. Pay up or I'll sell the horses. If I report you to the sheriff you'll end up in jail. Sonny, stay clear." The proprietor pointed the shotgun at one of the two. "Pay up first. Put your money on top of that feed box and step back to where you were."

The man complied.

"Sonny, go and count the money. Walk to the side so I can kill them if they make a move."

"There is three dollars and fifty cents here."

The same procedure was repeated.

"Now, you two turn around slowly and walk out the door. If you put your hand anywhere near your gun, I'll blow you in two with buckshot." He followed the two cursing men with his shotgun and watched them ride away.

"What is your name?"

"They call me Greg. I am Gregory McKenna."

"Greg, I sure thank you. You just can't take a chance on people in this town. They will slit your throat for your boots. Go back to sleep and I will call you for breakfast."

The breakfast was a hearty meal of sausage, biscuits, and gravy. The livery owner asked Greg, "What are you planning to do?"

"I'm going west to see if I can get a farm."

"You can't get there by yourself. Can you drive a four-horse team?"

"Mr. Miller, I've been driving four horses since I was thirteen."

"There is a demand for drivers for caravans. You have to be careful about who you hire out to. Many of the outfits are very poorly planned and have horses and mules that can't stand the trip. The wheels and axles will wear out before they get there. Do you have any money?"

"I have seven dollars and forty-five cents."

"That isn't going to last very long with prices the way they are. If you want to, you can sleep in the barn and I will feed your horse. I can see that you will be able to keep people from skipping out without paying. I've been losing a lot of money that way. If you will help take care of the horses, I'll feed you. This will give you time to find a job driving with a caravan. It is a month late for caravans to be going to California, as they are apt to get caught in deep snow in the Sierra Nevada Mountains. If they are going to Oregon, which is a much shorter trip, they might make it. Before you take a job, let me look over the outfit."

Greg was overwhelmed by the offer.

"Thank you, Mr. Miller. You won't be sorry. I'll show you how much I can help." He didn't try to contact any caravans for three days. He worked at cleaning up the livery stable and grounds. He fed, watered, and curried the horses.

Ben Miller was very pleased and complimented Greg, saying, "You sure have been handy and more than earned your keep. To find a job, inquire at the saloons and leave word there. Ask people around town. Some will be nasty but most are helpful. You could leave word at the other livery stables because we all sell oats to the settlers.

Greg listened carefully as he rubbed Star's nose. Ben eyed the horse admiringly.

"Walk to town because someone probably will try to steal that good-looking horse of yours," he told Greg. Here you have to watch out for thieves, robbers, and just plain mean people. The saloons are packed at night. Don't go into any alleys. But, as big as you are, I expect you can take care of yourself in a fist fight."

Greg rode out of town to where several caravans were scattered over a large area. He stopped near a man who was harnessing a team of horses and asked, "Who is the wagon master?" The man pointed to a large, heavily whiskered man who was talking to two other men.

"That's him. Rich Slater. He is plenty tough and can be downright mean, but he knows the way. He has trapped in Oregon, Idaho, and Utah."

Greg thanked him and walked up to the three men. He didn't interrupt their conversation, from which he learned that the caravan was about ready to pull out and they were waiting for one more party to arrive.

Slater noticed him and said, "What do you want?"

"Sir, I want to go west and I can drive four horses, shoe them if necessary, and take care of them so they will last."

"The hell you say."

It was then that Greg noticed the steely grey eyes and the straight, thin lips amid the beard. He decided not to yield.

"The hell I said."

"How old are you?" Slater smiled a little. It flashed through Greg's mind that he had better not say eighteen.

"Twenty."

"We are filled up now, but if anything breaks, where will I find you?"

"I'm staying at Mr. Miller's livery stable. Thank you, Mr. Slater." Greg started to walk away.

"Hold on. I want to see if you can drive. Come with me." He stopped an approaching wagon with a team of four horses, which Greg had been watching.

"Amos, I want to see if this greenhorn can drive." The driver tied the reins to the brake and stepped down. After talking firmly and petting each horse in a friendly manner, Greg picked up the right hind foot of the off horse of the rear team. Reaching into his pocket he took out his knife and pried out a small round rock from the frog of the hoof.

"It looked like he was favoring that leg a little," he said to Slater.

"Now let's see if you can drive. Make a tight circle and stop back here."

Greg climbed up onto the seat and untied the reins. After talking to the team, he said, "Get up" and slapped the reins. The team started out as if he had been driving them for a long time. Making the circle was easy and they stopped when he said, "Whoa" and gently but firmly pulled on the lines.

Slater said, "You'll do. Keep in touch."

CHAPTER 3

THE HAINES

Seldon Haines, age thirty-four, was a successful banker and realtor in Kansas City. He hated both, but had followed his father's wishes in spite of his desire to see new places. He had met and married a very beautiful, but almost ignorant, girl from the hill country and she doted on him. Anything he did was all right with her. In spite of being a banker's wife, Rowena was never really accepted by the elite in Kansas City.

Seldon received a letter from his brother, Captain Edward Haines, a very successful ship owner with a lucrative trade between San Francisco and the Orient. It was the answer to both their desires and problems. Edward had purchased a Spanish grant of several thousand acres from the Mexican owner in the Sacramento Valley. Edward's long letter told of the mild climate, oranges, and fruit trees of all kinds. He said the way California was filling up, some of the land could be sold for residential and commercial parcels. The people who really were benefiting from the gold rush were the suppliers of goods and services. Edward wanted them to come to California and suggested that they take passage and send their goods by boat. Seldon thought this would be impossible since Rowena got sick riding on a riverboat, but he was elated about the prospect of going overland to California, escaping from the tiresome routine of his present life. He handed the letter to Rowena.

"Read it carefully. We may move to California."

It took Rowena a long time to read the letter. Seldon was pacing the floor. Rowena looked up at him and said, "I'll go wherever you want to go."

"Rowena, it is going to be nearly a year of a very long and miserable trip."

"I am young and healthy and I am not pregnant. We can start a family after we get there."

"Honey, I don't want to jump into anything on the spur of the moment. We have to think it over. I'll talk to Zeke Hamlin about the problems and details of the trip. I loaned him money to go to California on a wagon train. He fought Indians and trapped, and saved his money. When he got back he became a junk dealer and horse breeder, and is doing well selling horses to the emigrants. If we go, it will take some time to sell our property and my interest in the bank."

Zeke was a good storyteller and Seldon liked to have him tell about his adventures. He got up from his desk to greet Zeke when he entered the bank.

"Mr. Haines, I'm sure glad to see you."

"Zeke, I need your help and I'll pay you for it."

"How can I help you?"

"I am going to California by wagon train. What do you think?"

"I think you and your wife don't know that you are in for one hell of a hard trip for almost a year. It is nearly two thousand miles to California. You have to get started by the first part of April and you might not get started because weather could hold you up. You want to be over the Sierra Nevada Mountains by the last of October. A snow storm could block the pass and you would be snowed in until spring, if anyone was left alive."

"Zeke, a good team should easily be able to make fifteen miles a day."

"Mr. Haines, that is right, but with breakdowns, mud, rain, and Indians, a wagon train is lucky if they average eight to nine. If there was grain and hay at every stop it would be easy. The animals must have time to graze. You start at daybreak. Every so often you stop and let your horses have a breather. About four o'clock you circle the wagons to keep the horses in at night. They have to be allowed to graze until dark and be herded back into the circle because of Indians. Mules, horses, and oxen can't travel or work as long on grass for feed."

Seldon listened intently and jotted down a few notes. Zeke then continued.

"Food is a big problem. You can't buy much and usually not anything after you leave Independence until you get to Fort Laramie. When you get to Utah, the Mormons have irrigated the desert around the Salt Lake Valley and they have plenty to sell at a price. They are friendly people and will try to convert you. If you act interested, you can get better prices."

"Zeke, will you make a list of what we will need? I want you to find a covered wagon."

"Mr. Haines, this will take some doing."

"Remember, I can afford to get the best."

"Getting the mules is easy. I have five three- to four-year-olds that are well broken and I've been plowing with them. Mules are better than horses. They never overeat and can last longer on slim feed and water. The best covered wagons come from Pennsylvania and this late it might be hard to find one."

"I have to dispose of my holdings and that is going to take some time. You go ahead and get me an outfit together and I will pay you fifty dollars for your time and trouble. By the way, get me a good reliable driver for the wagon."

Disposing of the Haines property took longer than expected. Legal problems and financing by the buyers took time. Negotiations dragged through March and into April. Seldon watched the wagon trains leaving, one after another. It was getting late to start. Zeke finally located a new Conestoga wagon, whose owner had abandoned the trip, and loaded it with the supplies that would be needed. His list included horse shoes, nails, farrier tools, jack, axle grease, harness repairs, and horse liniment. Foodstuffs included sacks of flour, rice, beans, cured ham, bacon, canned goods, dried fruit, and a barrel of late-maturing apples. There were three hundred pounds of oats in sacks and barrels of water.

The driver, Sam Tonkins, said he was an experienced teamster. Zeke really didn't like him, but he seemed to be the best of the riffraff that he had contacted. He had handled the four mules very well. When Sam talked to Seldon Haines, he asked for an advance of twenty dollars, a month's salary, to buy clothes and supplies that he would need for the trip. Haines gave him the money. He would drive the outfit from Zeke's farm the next day and they would begin loading. They were to join Rich Slater's caravan, which would be leaving in five days.

Slater had warned Haines that it was almost May and such a late start might mean a layover for the winter in Laramie or in the Salt Lake valley. The valley would be much preferred. The people going to Oregon would be all right, but California was questionable.

Sam didn't show up on the appointed morning. Zeke waited until noon and drove the four-mule team and wagon, with the spare mule and his saddle horse, to town.

Captain Edward had told his brother to travel as light as possible, taking only necessities in bedding and clothing and only family keepsakes that had sentimental value. Seldon had two men waiting to help load. When Rowena wanted to take her piano, Zeke balked.

"Rowena, you are going to see everything under the sun abandoned along the road—chairs, dressers, chests, boxes that were too heavy for the horses to pull. You are going to find deep ruts, mud holes, streams to cross, rocky roads, and mountains."

After tears, Rowena sold the piano to a neighbor.

Sam never showed up. They were to leave in four days. Zeke inquired at the house where Sam had been boarding and learned that he had left town the day before. Haines rode out to the Slater camp.

Slater shook hands and said, "Are you ready to go?"

"I am ready, but my driver has skipped out on me. Can you find me one?"

"It just happens I can find you one. He is young but a good driver. He is also big, big, big! He will be the biggest man in the caravan."

CHAPTER 4

WAGONS WESTWARD

Greg had just finished feeding and grooming Star. He was latching the barn door when Slater rode up.

"Hello, Mr. Slater, do you have good news for me?"

"A driver quit. Mr. Haines needs a driver. You are lucky, it is one of the best outfits in the caravan. If you still want to go, saddle your horse and I'll take you to see Haines."

Seldon was impressed with the big young man with a wide forehead, pleasant face, and intense grey eyes. He offered twenty dollars a month and a fifty dollar bonus at the end of the drive. Greg was happy to accept, thinking it was a lot of money!

It was the second of May. Slater had spent two days checking over each outfit. He eliminated three outfits because their horses or wagons would not stand the long trek, returning their two hundred dollar fee. He had the others hitch up and circle their wagons as they would be doing each night on the trip. He was wearing a pistol when he talked to them that evening. They were told his word was law.

"Folks, you are going to cuss me, hate me, grumble about my orders. In time you will realize that I am only trying to save your lives and get you there. I'll be fair and honest with you. Some of you are going to think I'm downright mean and cruel. You can always talk to me, but you may not like my answers. I've been through this three times. I know what it takes. You don't."

The hobbled mules and horses were taken in from grazing as the skies showed first light. A bugle awakened the caravan. Fires were hurriedly built, some in the open, others in small iron stoves or open grates. Most of the fires were shared by more than one party. At seven o'clock, at the word "Ho" from the wagon master, the caravan started the long journey westward.

They usually stopped about three o'clock in the afternoon, if a suitable campsite and water were available. If water was not available, the stock was watered from two barrels, one on each side of the wagon, which were covered with a canvas and tube to keep water from sloshing out. When they stopped for the night, Greg unharnessed the mules, curried them, washed off the sweat, cleaned their collars, and examined their feet for rocks. Then they were led out to graze and hobbled, with a member of the caravan on horseback to watch them.

There was a tall, slim, heavily bearded young man whose confident manner caused Greg to wonder what his place was. He seemed to be everywhere on his black horse, constantly checking and conferring with Slater. Greg had seen him before, when he drove the team for Slater on the day they met. It turned out Amos Jordan was second in command and at times scouted ahead for trouble, campsites, and water. He was experienced in having lived among the Indians, trapped, and hunted buffalo. Later Greg found out he was also very good at cards.

The road, while dry except for light showers, was not dusty. Deep ruts and occasional mud holes made the horses and mules labor much harder. After twelve days, they reached Independence, Missouri, the last jumping-off place. To Greg, it had been easy. They had made at least twelve miles a day. The caravan camped on the prairie about two miles from town. The wagon master said they would stay there a day to give the animals a rest, and to give the people a chance to make repairs and buy more supplies.

Greg rode Star into Independence. It was a ramshackle town with buildings raised helter-skelter along one street. Loud piano and banjo music came from a saloon. He decided to see what was going on. It was noisy because of the drinking and everyone trying to out-shout the music. As he approached the bar the bartender wiped the spattered counter in front of him.

"What will you have, Sonny?" Greg had noticed a sign, "BEER—FIVE CENTS".

"I'll have a beer." After putting a nickel on the counter, he took a sip. It tasted bitter. He decided to carry it around and take a swallow now and then so nobody would know he wasn't used to drinking beer. The bartender had noted his expression.

"Is that your first drink of beer?"

"Yes, to tell the truth, it is. It doesn't taste all that good."

"Don't stop. After a few more times you will learn to like it."

Greg had played poker for fun with beans, but he had never seen a big poker game. Spectators were allowed to sit on stools away from the felt-covered table with the shaded kerosene light over it. He noticed the large number of bills stacked in front of three of the seven players. Two of them were really dressed, with fancy coats and vests.

"Who are those two?" he asked his neighbor.

"Shh—they will throw you out for talking. They are professional gamblers and the rest are suckers, except maybe the man with the big hat. He seems to be able to hold his own."

Greg suddenly recognized that the man with the big hat was Amos Jordan. He was sitting quietly, smoking a cigar, and watching every move the players made. The game was high-low draw. If no one had a pair of jacks necessary to open, the game reverted to low ball with an ace to a five as the high hand. The game was table stakes. The betting before the draw reached twenty-five dollars to stay. It seemed like a fortune was in the pot. Four of the players stayed. Two of them drew one card each and the last raiser drew two. Amos, who had passed first, stood pat.

Greg whispered to his neighbor, "Why didn't he raise?"

"He has a very low straight and wanted everyone to pass and play low. They all know that. Now, shh."

Amos, in front of the dealer, carefully looked over his cards, and said, "I'll bet twenty-five dollars."

The next man dropped out, but the third man said, "I'll raise you twenty-five."

Greg thought they either had a full house or a flush and he expected Amos to pass and lose all that money.

To his surprise, Amos said, "I'll call and raise the rest of what I have in front of me." He counted out the twenty-five dollars and raised the pot thirty-seven dollars.

Greg pondered his move. He must think they are bluffing because they know he has a small straight and either one or both can beat him, he decided.

The first player looked at his hand and called rather hesitantly as it took almost all of his stack. The next man couldn't wait to get in. As he counted his money, he said, "I wish you suckers had more money." He showed three aces and a pair of eights. The first gambler cursed and threw his cards into the center of the table. As the player with the full house started to rake in the chips, Amos said, quietly, but with authority, "I still have a hand."

"Let's see the small straight."

Amos carefully spread his hand. Four jacks and the three of spades. It was a hand that would happen only one time in thousands. Greg did not know the part it would play in his future.

Amos stacked the bills and folded them in his money belt, then walked over to the bar and said, "Beer for everybody."

Greg was amazed; it would cost Amos over two dollars!"

He decided to leave as tomorrow would be a long day. As he left the saloon, Star nickered from the hitching post across the street. As Greg was untying the halter rope, the opening of the saloon door caught his attention. Amos came out, turning up his collar against the sharp breeze. To relieve himself, he walked back into the shadows between the two buildings. He was fumbling with his pants fly when two men jumped him from out of the shadows and forced him to the ground. Without thinking, Greg's long, running strides took him across the street to help. The two men had Amos down, beating him and trying to get his money belt. Greg grabbed one by the collar and swung a looping right that hit the man behind the ear and collapsed him. Almost instantly, he hit the other man in the kidneys. Amos was up and doing some pounding and the two men were moaning on the ground.

"Amos, should we call the marshal?"

"That wouldn't do any good, but this will." Amos stomped on the hands and fingers of both men. "Now they can eat with their toes. I'll not forget this, Greg. The damned gamblers or bartender set me up. You saved me three hundred fifty dollars." He handed Greg a twenty-dollar bill and it was the beginning of a long friendship.

So far the trip had been relatively easy. There were no serious breakdowns. The days had been mostly warm and sunny with occasional showers. The mules liked Greg, as he talked to them and rubbed their ears during the nightly grooming. They loved the lump of sugar he gave to them at the end of the day. Greg knew mules had to know who's boss. He cracked the whip over them without touching them. Amos congratulated him on his handling of the team.

"A mule is smart and because you treat him kindly, he is going to keep it that way. Every once in a while he will test you out to see who is boss."

Greg named the mules Tom, Dick, Harry, George, and Jenny. Harry was mischievous, would nip gently, and sometimes step on Greg's foot. This was painful and Greg retaliated by standing on Harry's hoof. After a few sessions, the mule caught on. Harry also greeted the first daybreak by braying. The camp didn't need the wake-up bugle. Harry took a definite liking to Greg, who responded by giving him a bit of brown sugar on his oats. People started to tease him about his mule friend.

Greg was concerned that the big, slow-moving oxen were slowing down the progress of the wagon train. When he questioned Amos about it, he answered, "A horse will be long gone and the oxen will still be moving. They are used to grass. As long as they can get a belly full of grass and water, they are content. Notice how they are chewing their cuds while resting. As to pulling the load, they are used to it and accept it as a way of life."

Many of the oxen were nearly six feet tall and weighed close to a ton. Their long, lean legs seemed to move the load slowly and effortlessly.

The members of the caravan had learned a lot about hardships and what it would take to survive on the relatively short trip from Kansas City to Independence. Water, food, and wood were of primary importance. They gathered every piece of wood and dried manure, or buffalo chips, to use as fuel along the route. Amos scouted for campsites with water to replenish their barrels. Fires were shared by groups of three or more. The Haines' small iron bake oven proved to be a godsend. Most of the people fried hard tack in the bacon grease. The women baked bread. Rowena Haines, Sue Miller, and Ruth Johnson took turns preparing the dough during the day and baked it at the afternoon stop. At Kansas City, the Johnson's driver had skipped out.

CHAPTER 5

MOSES

Ernest and Ruth Johnson were a young couple. Ernest had just finished law school and wanted to go west as he thought the opportunities for success would be unlimited there. His wealthy father was financing their trip. Because he had no experience with stock, he needed a driver. A large, well-built black man overheard him inquiring for a driver and mule skinner. He waited patiently until the conversation ended and then approached the man with hat in hand.

"Mister, I heared you say you need a driver for your mules to go to Californie. I know mules and I'z the best driver. I wouldn't expect much pay. Just feed me and pay me a little in cash. 'Course, I'll need clothes."

"What is your name?"

"Moses."

"Put your hat on. From now on you are in free territory. Let's sit down on that bench out of the sun and maybe we can get together. Where are you from?"

"Gawgia, suh."

"How did you get to Kansas City?"

"I had to travel at night and hide by day. A lot of people helped. I stole corn from cribs, chickens, and garden stuff. Bounty hunters pick up any niggers that is walkin' or travellin' alone.

Have to watch out here because they kidnap niggers. A hundred dollars is a lot of money and that or more is what they gits for turnin' in a nigger."

"What plantation were you from?"

"The Farnsworth plantation. There was over seventy-five of us slaves there. I worked in the fields till they put me workin' with mules."

"Why do you want to go to California?"

"I heard they gits big money for fightin' in Californie. I was the nigger that fought other niggers from other plantations to entertain white folk when they had their big parties. Maybe I can make enough money to buy me a small farm."

"You are good at fighting?"

"I was the champeen. Won all my nineteen fights. I don't rush in. I'z a boxer."

Johnson noticed his beautiful build, heavy neck, long arms, wide shoulders, and narrow waist and hips. The nose was slightly flattened and a few small scars were on his face. His pleasant face and his frank, open demeanor appealed to Ernest.

"Moses, you are my driver. Come on and I will buy you some suitable clothes. I'll feed you and pay you ten dollars a month, if that is all right."

When they left the mercantile with Moses dressed in his new outfit, he remarked, "Mister Johnson, I nevah had nothin' like this. I feel like I am somebody."

"Moses, you are somebody and don't you forget it."

That is how Moses became a part of the Haines, Johnson, and Miller group. At first he ate with them but away from them. Soon he became a favorite of all of them because he was so helpful and polite. Rowena remarked to Sue Miller, "He seems always to be there when you need help."

In the evening, when all of the chores were done and the stock was grazing, Moses would run and shadow box. Greg thought that learning to box might be useful. It would also get the kinks out of muscles that were tired from holding reins and sitting for long periods.

"Moses, will you teach me how to box?"

"Mister McKenna, boxin' takes a lot a learnin'. You have to

work at it over and over till it comes natural. Footwork is probably the mostest important. It'll help you keep from gettin' hit. If your feet ain't right, you cain't hit good with power."

Every night they shadow boxed with each other or hit half-hard blows. Moses lightly stuffed a burlap bag with moss and hung it from a tree limb when one was available. Moses was as tall as Greg and had long arms, but Greg had a four-inch reach on him. What surprised Moses was the quickness of Greg's reflexes.

"Mister McKenna, that left of yours is so fast you can dance around, close both your rival's eyes, break his nose, and he can only reach you with punches that has lost most of their power. If you do git hit and hurt, don't git mad and try to git even. Dance and move till your head is clear. Never stop thinkin'. Never pay no mind to people booin' you if you don't mix it up in the kind of sluggin' match they want to see. Remember, you is the one that can git hit."

Driving was often the easy part. Greg started the morning by bringing in his mules and Star while it was still dark. They were unhobbled, watered, and fed a pint of oats, then hitched to the wagon wheels while he ate his breakfast. While the women cleaned up and packed the breakfast tools, the men hitched their teams and spans to the wagons. At rest stops, the animals, harness, and wagons were checked. If it was hot, Greg gave each mule a bucket of water. All of the animals were getting leaner. Seldon learned to drive and helped Greg with the care of the mules, giving Greg a chance to ride Star.

CHAPTER 6

TRAIL DAYS

The panic of 1827 started the migration of a quarter of a million or more people West. The prospect of getting free land by settling in the fertile valleys of the west lured many to their death along the two-thousand-mile route. The ill-equipped, overloaded outfits left a trail of broken wagons and household items. Caravans following used the wood and spare parts. Graves marked with crosses averaged ten to a mile. Cholera, caused by bad drinking water, the swarms of black flies, mosquitoes, the dust, and poor nutrition took their toll.

The caravan had its good days when it was windy after rain. The moisture kept down the dust and the wind blew the flies and gnats away. The droppings of animals in the caravan, buffaloes, and the carcasses of animals, some left in the streams close to campsites, harbored the dreaded cholera. So many caravans had gone through that forage was eaten bare close to camp grounds. Sometimes they camped two or three miles from water in order to have feed for the stock. When wagon master Slater called an evening meeting, he cautioned the people about water.

"Drink only boiled water if possible. Dig a well near the stream. Dig down a foot and throw the dirt at least five feet away from the hole. The top dirt is just as deadly as bad water."

Diarrhea was a constant problem, not only because of polluted water, but also because of spoiled food. Rest stops were not frequent. The women used chamber pots, and the men stood beside the teams on the left side. Sometimes a man could be seen sitting on a chamber pot while trying to drive. A lack of paper and constantly sitting without proper bathing facilities caused serious discomfort. Two elderly women and a young girl died before they reached Laramie.

Amos remarked to Greg, "We are lucky to lose only three. The first time I went to California we lost one out of every five people between Kansas and Laramie."

Flies and mosquitoes drove the horses, mules, and oxen to such frenzy that they sometimes bolted, careening across the prairie until exhausted, leaving a badly damaged and overturned wagon and injured or dead people. Greg followed the advice of Slater and greased his mules' ears and around the eyes, and covered the lower part of their faces with burlap.

The carefully planned and well-equipped wagon train led by Slater was very different from those that had gone in the previous two decades, with inexperienced wagon masters. Even so, daily problems and difficulties occurred.

The Platte River in Nebraska Territory furnished large catfish that Greg caught, using grasshoppers for bait if there was no meat available. The fish seemed to prefer meat that was rank or spoiled. The supplies of canned vegetables, dried fruits, and apples were used sparingly, and often they were spoiled. Because water and feed were an absolute necessity, their route had to follow the river, which meant that the trail wandered back and forth and sometimes actually travelled in an easterly direction before heading west.

The stop at Fort Kearny in Nebraska Territory was a short one. The trading post there had little to offer except the bare necessities such as beans, flour, and salt pork. Some traded tired stock for rested stock that had been traded by earlier emigrants. They had to pay the trader extra money for the transaction. Greg overheard a conversation between Slater and Amos.

"Amos, we have been making good time but our stock is getting worn down some. Can you find a place off the trail that has good feed and water where we can rest the stock and let the people wash and clean up and make repairs?"

"Rich, we may have to go four or five miles. That means we will lose a day coming and going."

"That doesn't matter. It's about five hundred miles to Laramie. If we start fresh we will save time farther on."

In the evening of the second day out of Fort Kearny, Amos asked Greg, "Would you like to ride ahead of the caravan with me tomorrow?"

"I will ask Mr. Haines if it's all right with him."

"I have already done that, son."

They were well on their way when they heard Harry's wake-up bray behind them. Amos maintained a fast pace of alternately walking, trotting, and galloping. After they had travelled an hour and a half, or about eight miles, they saw a small stream that was running almost clear.

Amos said, "That's a good sign. There are no buffalo using it. The damned hide hunters have killed them all off." He pointed to the skulls and bones that littered the area. As they followed the stream, the grass and forage showed fewer signs of being eaten. There were large buffalo wallows that had to be skirted, but the general terrain was almost level. As they approached a sharp bend in the stream that curved to the right and west, Amos held his hand, giving the sign to stop, and then put it over his mouth for "silence." Then he held his nose and pointed. Greg smelled the odor of cattle belching gas as they were chewing their cuds. Tying their reins to scrubby bushes, they climbed over a knoll. There was a large pool of clear water where a spring bubbled up below the hill. Looking downstream, they saw a herd of eight or ten buffalo lying down or standing and switching their tails to ward off flies. The herd was too far away for good shooting.

Greg was excited at the opportunity to shoot a buffalo. Amos had been the only member of the caravan to kill one. He motioned for Greg to move back down the hill, out of sight. When they peered over the top of the ridge, a quarter-mile further downstream, the undisturbed buffalo were slightly over a hundred feet below them, and they could even hear the rumbling of gas in their stomachs.

Amos whispered, "You take those two on your left. Duck down after you shoot to reload. Aim for the head or neck. You can't miss at this range."

Two shots were fired. Two buffalo staggered and crumpled down. Greg, in his haste to reload, tore his cartridge open and it would not enter the breech. Amos had reloaded and downed another cow before the herd spooked and galloped over the hills and out of sight. When Greg started to go to the downed animals, Amos stopped him.

"Reload. That is the first thing you do after you have fired a shot. That may save your life sometime. There is nothing worse than an empty gun in time of trouble."

As they were sliding down toward the dead animals, five Indians walked down the other side of the hill toward them, scowling angrily. Greg was glad that Amos had made him reload.

"Greg, don't point your gun at them. They were stalking the buffalo and we ruined their hunt." He held up his hand, palm forward, and spoke in a native dialect. Then he pointed to the largest buffalo and to them, indicating that it was theirs, and likewise indicated that the other two belonged to himself and Greg. The Indians parlayed among themselves and laughed and nodded. They immediately cut the throat of the large cow so it could bleed. The white hunters followed suit.

"Greg, help me gut them, and be careful not to cut into the guts, as it will make an awful stinking mess."

By the time they had gutted the animals and pulled them out of the way, the Indians, who had been joined by other tribal members, had skinned and cut up the other carcass and rode away with a friendly wave.

"Greg, you ride back and guide the wagon train this way. All you have to do is follow the stream back. Don't worry about the Indians. They're Pawnee and they're friendly. If you hurry, you will be at the stream half an hour before the caravan crosses it."

After giving Star a drink of cool water, he set off at a brisk pace. He was determined not to be late. He kept a sharp eye out for Pawnees, despite what Amos had told him. The papers back East had been full of gruesome accounts of people who had been killed by Indians on the way west. Greg couldn't have known, as Amos did, that the number of people killed by Indians had been greatly exaggerated. When he arrived at the turnoff point where the trail and stream joined, he could see the dust of the wagon train in the distance. The wagon master rode ahead to meet Greg.

"What did you find, McKenna?"

"There is a clear stream and grass that comes up to the stirrups. When I left Amos he was cleaning and skinning the two buffalo cows that we killed. The way is mostly level but it winds around a lot."

"I'll tell everyone there will be fresh buffalo for supper tonight!" Slater said happily.

The caravan made a brief stop to water the stock and pushed on with Greg and Slater leading them. Everyone was eager for a break with a good meal and a more comfortable campsite. Slater directed the placing of the wagons and marked off the areas of the stream where they would water the stock, wash clothing, and bathe, leaving an area at the spring for drinking water. Greg looked for the meat and didn't see any. Amos had put it into the stream to cool, which he later learned was very important, as fresh meat that has never been cooled causes serious digestive problems. The carcasses were cut up and distributed. Soon the air was filled with the smell of frying, roasting, and boiling meat. For the first time in weeks, the stock could graze close to the camp.

Most of the meat was consumed during the two-day stop. The extra was smoked or baked to help preserve it. The emigrants made the most of their time: washing clothes, bathing, repairing equipment, and just resting around the campfires.

At times, Greg wondered if he had made a mistake leaving the comforts of home for an uncertain future. He realized that there was no turning back. It never occurred to him that finding gold was not a certainty. He thought that if other people could find it, he could also.

The Slater party continued their trek, travelling along the south side of the Platte River. Sometimes they could see another caravan travelling along the north side. Slater informed them that those were Mormons on their way to the Salt Lake Valley in Utah. Greg envied them, as they seemed happy and had music and dancing every night. He was missing the company of young people. The quiet, subdued laughter of Seldon and Rowena Haines in the night fed his imagination and he wondered what it would be like to have sex. There were no unmarried girls of his age in the caravan.

Much of the way from Independence was like travelling on an ocean of grass, which billowed and waved with the wind. Sometimes it was so flat that all you could see was grass and the only way you could tell the direction was to look at the sun for your bearing. For days on end it never changed. Generally, they stayed close to Big Sandy Creek and Little Blue River. At Fort Kearny, the trail joined the North Platte River. Finally, near Laramie, the small Mormon caravan crossed the river. The two leaders conferred and agreed that they would travel together as a matter of safety, for they were entering the territory of hostile Sioux and Cheyenne Indians, who picked off stragglers when the opportunity presented itself.

At Fort Laramie they had travelled over five hundred fifty miles in forty days. This was a good pace considering the time they had taken off to rest the stock. Many of the travellers wanted to hurry up and ride longer each day, but Slater would not alter his original plan of trying to keep the stock fresh as possible for the more difficult part of the journey ahead.

The first night at Laramie the Mormons, who called themselves Latter Day Saints, held their usual evening dance. Greg, along with other members of his party, went over to the Mormon camp to listen to their music and watch.

Greg wished he could join the dancers. In Kansas, after the crops were harvested, there was a dance every weekend, and even though he was big, he had learned to be a graceful and popular dancer.

"Would you like to dance with me?" He turned to see a large, young girl with a pleasant face. She wasn't pretty, but rather wholesome looking.

"I sure would, ma'am!" She held out her arm and they were in the midst of a square dance. They never missed a step together. When the music stopped, he thanked her and started to move away.

She grabbed his arm and said, "No, you don't. I found you and you are too good a partner to lose."

Her name was Vera and this was the beginning of their friendship. He liked the glimpse of her large breasts and the swish of her dress and hip. When he tried to get her to walk away from the dance, she refused by telling him that she was being watched, and if they did that, they would not be allowed to dance together again.

It was not until she took her father's place on the first evening watch over the hobbled stock that they really had a chance for conversation. Vera Murdock was the daughter of Aaron, who was going with his two wives and three daughters to join his five sons and a brother in Ogden, Utah. Vera was promised to a forty-year-old man who was prominent in the church, and they would be married in a few months, when she reached sixteen. She was looking forward to being married, as the man was very well-to-do, and his other wives would be like sisters to her. She would live in town and not have to milk cows or do farm work. Her brothers had all married and were settled on farms in the Salt Lake Valley. She explained to him that it was the duty of Mormon women to bring children into the world and they would be rewarded in the hereafter for increasing the number of Saints. It was also the duty of a Mormon woman to serve her husband and add to his comfort.

They were sitting with their backs against a large cottonwood tree on a knoll that overlooked the meadow where the stock were grazing. The moon was full and shining brightly that evening of July second.

"It is cold," she said and leaned against him. His arm went around her and almost instantly they were kissing each other with abandon. He put his hand inside her dress and fondled her breast. She reached over and felt him.

"Greg, you watch so we don't get caught, and I'll give you something to remember me by." She unbuttoned his fly and bent over. The sensation of almost unbearable pleasure didn't last long as she began to kiss again. He had heard older men refer to such sex acts in a derogatory or joking manner. He really didn't think women did such things to men.

"You are really huge."

"How do you know?"

"You are a lot bigger than my brothers."

"You did this with your brothers?"

"My brothers started me doing that and other things when I was twelve years old. Momma caught us and they sent my brothers to Utah. After all, they were nearly twenty years old."

"You liked it?"

"Oh, yes, I liked everything they did. I don't dare let you enter because you might get me pregnant." He was surprised that a girl so young could speak about sex so casually when the minister called it a cardinal sin.

Their closeness caused him to become aroused again and just as he reached for her, he heard a man whistling softly. They got up hurriedly and straightened their clothes. It was Amos looking for him. They were standing a short distance apart when he greeted them.

"Oh, there you are." Greg noticed the slight but knowing smile on his face. Amos tried to put them at ease by remarking how nice a night it was.

"Do you want to go to the fort in the morning, Greg? It seems I need you for a bodyguard. I checked with Haines and it is all right with him." While they were talking, their relief watchman came and they walked back to camp together.

Sleep did not come easily for Greg. He was going over what had happened. It occurred to him that Amos always moved very quietly and he had never heard him whistle before. Undoubtedly, he had seen the whole thing.

CHAPTER 7

AMOS

Amos Jordan was a mystery to most of the people on the wagon train. The women liked him for his quiet and courteous manner. His suggestions were always in a pleasant but firm voice. He seemed to be tireless as he left early in the morning to scout and usually returned just before camping time. He ate with Slater but was often invited to eat with other families. His face was hidden by a heavy beard, which he kept neatly trimmed, quite short. He was tall, slim, and wiry.

After Greg helped him resist the robbers, Amos took an interest in furthering Greg's well-being. When it was Greg's turn to watch the livestock while they grazed in the late afternoon and evening, Amos would often stop by to talk to him about what lay ahead and give him advice.

Wagon-master Slater was talking to Amos about the plans for the next day's travel. When he saw Greg carrying a book as he went to take his turn guarding the horses and mules, he remarked, "That Greg reads every chance he gets, but he doesn't let it interfere with his work. He gets along with people. I've never heard him find fault or criticize. He really respects the rights of other people."

Amos agreed. "He is a very unusual and intelligent young man. He is so full of goodness, willing to help others. When he does something, it is right. He doesn't talk a lot, but he is always thinking. He's a person I like to travel with." Greg was deep in reading when he was startled by a tap on the shoulder. He jumped, throwing the book in the air.

"You'd be dead," Amos admonished. "Never turn your back on the direction that danger is apt to come from. A Sioux or a Cheyenne could slit your throat and take your scalp and that is where you would be found by the relief. Remember this even when you relieve yourself."

Amos picked up the book. "You will find that man has kept repeating himself over thousands of years," he said.

"What do you mean by that?"

"All through history, whenever man became crowded for food, goods, housing, the strong took over the weak, either killing them off or making slaves of them and taking their land."

"Are you talking about Indians, too? The whites seem to think that Indians have no rights."

"The Indians were here first. They have their own culture and customs. We came, killed their buffalo, cut down their forests, settled their land. More of us are coming. They'll fight but they can't win, and many lives will be lost before they are finally subdued."

Greg talked about his hope to find gold in California and to get a small farm.

"You are thinking about eighty acres where you raise corn, wheat, and livestock feed," Amos interjected. "Think in terms of hundreds of acres or even thousands of acres, like the huge ranches in Texas or New Mexico. Cattle are being driven to Montana for sale. The West is going to be settled sooner than you think. They are planning to build a railroad to the coast. The East is getting overcrowded so more and more people will be coming west. There are still millions of acres of desert land that can be filed on and the land is there for the taking."

"If it is desert land, how can you grow anything?"

"Man has been bringing water onto the land for thousands of years. The Etruscans had elaborate irrigation systems. You can build a dam upstream to raise the water level to where it will flow down a ditch to fields that are downstream. You can put in small dikes around the field and flood it. On crops that can't stand flooding, you can make small ditches, called corrugates, to run the water between rows of plants. You could get over twice the yield that would result from rainfall. The Mormons grow a crop for livestock that they call lucerne. It originally came from some place in Asia. Cattle can't graze on it because they swell up so bad with gas and choke to death, but when it is dried, it is more rich in food value than the finest of grass hay. One acre will raise enough lucerne to feed two cows for a year. They have mowing machines that can cut ten acres a day, and derricks that stack it into tall stacks when it is dry. Because there is so little rainfall, it does not spoil."

"If I get a thousand acres, what am I going to do with it? I can't plow it and who am I going to sell my crops to when I am way out in the wilderness?"

"When you find a suitable place, settle on it. You will soon have neighbors. In the beginning, you are going to plow only a small part of it to raise feed for your cattle and horses which will be driven to market. In a few years, the railroad will haul your livestock for you. The government is going to need more and more horses for the Army, and more beef to feed the soldiers."

Greg thought about what Amos said and decided he made a lot of sense. But Amos was still a mystery and Greg wondered how he had become so knowledgeable.

It was apparent from his speech that he was well educated, and he read a lot. Greg saw one of his books—it was about law.

Amos never referred to his own past. This made Greg think that he might be hiding from something. He noticed that Amos received letters at various stops, and would go away from people to sit and read his letters over and over. He also wrote letters that he mailed whenever possible.

CHAPTER 8

THE BOXING MATCH

Fort Laramie was going to celebrate the Fourth of July. The band from the fort would play, a visiting general would give a patriotic speech, and there would be various contests from marksmanship to foot races. Several buffalo had been killed for a grand barbecue. Last, but not least, would be the prize fight between Army champion Swede Gustafson and Butch Wilcox, assistant to the sutler who ran the trading post. This was a long-awaited match and considerable money had been wagered, with soldiers backing Swede heavily. Butch was a huge, muscular man over six feet tall and weighing about two hundred pounds. His very short neck sloped from his head to his shoulders. His small, narrow eyes, small ears, and cruel-looking mouth emphasized the meanness of his character. He was a bully who mistreated smaller men, and the soldiers hated him because he had beaten so many of them. To date, he had never lost a fight and was very boastful. The soldier, Swede, was just as tall but lighter. He too had an undefeated boxing record back East before he had been transferred to Laramie. The fight was to be held on the parade grounds.

Moses was happy to be invited to go to the fort with Amos and Greg. They decided to walk the three miles to give their horses more time to graze. They were surprised to see the large number of teepees and Indians close to the fort.

"Amos, are they apt to steal from us?" asked Greg.

"No. The Army constantly patrols all of the area near the fort, and the Indians know from experience that they will be caught and punished and not allowed to trade, and that is what they are here to do."

When they went through the gate and onto the parade grounds, they saw a crowd watching two men spar in a roped-off square. Moses was all eyes and ears.

"I'z never seen the likes of this, but I heared tell that in England they has rings like this and they fight three minutes and rest one. They has a man in the ring called a referee that sees the fight is accordin' to the rules."

A soldier wearing lieutenant's bars answered, "That is the way this fight is going to be. We are hoping that Swede can beat the hell out of that dirty bastard. I really don't think he has too good a chance. Swede is strong and fast, but Butch has been hit hard in other fights and it doesn't seem to slow him down. He just keeps coming and when he hits, the other man is hurt real bad. Just to be sure there are no brass knuckles, the referee will wrap each fighter's hands with soft cotton cloth and tie cotton gloves over them."

"I sure would like to fight like that!"

The sparring session ended when Butch dropped his sparring partner with a short right. Swede worked out next. He looked good as his punches were very fast and appeared to be damaging, but he was getting hit.

On the way back to the wagon train, Amos asked Moses, "Do you think you could whip Butch?"

"Mister Jordan, I has some thinkin' to do before I answer. He can really take a punch. The only way to beat him is to wear him down. I'z in a lot better shape than he is. He got a bulge in his belly around his belt. He be all right for ten or twelve rounds. If I can last that long, I maybe can beat him. He paws with his left and depends on knockin' 'em out with that most powerful right hand. My arms is longer than his. If I can stay away from his right by circlin' to his left and jabbin' with my left to keep him off center, and stay out of his reach, he's going to get downright flubbed and mad. Then he cain't think good. I'z not goin' to get mad, nohow. The first round I'll keep on hittin' him on the nose, and I can hit hard enuf to break it and make it bleed. Then I'll try to close his left eye so he has to turn his head toward me. His nose is gonna make it hard for him to get his bref. When he is tired, he'll lower his hands and turn his head to see me. Then his chin is there for pastin'. The people's going to boo me and yell for the nigger to fight, but I'z not going to pay no attention to them."

Greg exclaimed, "You know you can beat him!"

Amos added, "At least you have a plan. It's too bad you don't get a chance to fight him. They are charging fifty cents to see the fight and the winner will get fifty dollars and the loser twenty-five."

"Mister Jordan..."

"Stop calling me Mister Jordan. Call me Amos."

"Yassuh, Amos. That is sure a lot of money as I'z never had more than five dollars at one time."

On the morning of the third of July, word came from the fort that Swede Gustafson was in the infirmary with a high fever and diarrhea. Slater heard it first and told Amos. Together they walked out to see Moses who was watching the herd. After telling him about the situation, they asked, "Do you want to fight him, Moses?"

"I sure does. Fifty dollars buys a lot of things!"

"Amos and I will ride into the fort and see if we can arrange it."

The captain at the fort was very pleased when they assured him that Moses had a good chance of beating Butch, and told him of Moses' plan.

"That sounds good to me. We will keep it among ourselves what you just told me. The sutler and the saloon keepers have made a lot of money on Butch in the past. We will play the fight down as your man Moses is just a substitute and we can get real good odds. Are you going to bet on him?"

"We sure are. In fact, we can have Moses act a little slow and awkward as he warms up, but don't have him overdo it. We will have to see Butch to get him to agree to fight Moses."

They found Butch in the saloon, feeling his drinks and bragging about how he would have beaten the Swede.

"Hello, Butch. We have some news for you," the captain began.

"I've had enough bad news. I could have had fifty dollars by knocking out that soldier punk tomorrow."

"Butch, we have somebody that wants the twenty-five dollars real bad. He is a teamster on a wagon train. He is black and not as big as you. We have never seen him fight. He says that he fought several times at plantation celebrations, but for all we know he may be lying and just trying to get the twenty-five dollars. As the manager, I am willing for the fight to go on if it is all right with you."

"I will whip the nigger but a punk like that shouldn't get twenty-five dollars. I will fight if the winner gets sixty-five dollars. He wouldn't know what to do with twenty-five dollars anyway."

After a conference among the captain, Slater and Jordan, they agreed to the terms. After they left the saloon, the captain said, "We got the fish to bite. Now it depends on Moses."

"Don't worry about Moses. He is a very intelligent person. He'll be pleased to hear about the arrangements."

Indeed, Moses was pleased.

"Sixty-five dollars is a lot of money. It will be a start towards havin' my own place in Californie. We has some plannin' to do. It'll be hot when the fight starts. Amos and Mister Slater, will you be my seconds and advisors? And Greg, will you try to keep me cool 'tween rounds by wavin' wet towels to cool 'em and puttin' 'em on my neck and face? We'll need some shade between rounds. If I go early I can get the corner that faces away from the sun. I'll only hit him when he faces the sun and keep away when I'm facin' it. I'z goin' to run a little bit tonight and shadow box a little to loosen up."

The next morning the skies were clear and the sun bright and hot. Ruth Johnson fixed Moses a sumptuous breakfast. Most of the men of the wagon train were going to see their champion fight. All were briefed about doing any bragging or putting out any information about Moses. There was a large procession following the wagon that Slater, Amos, Moses, and Greg rode in. They arrived at half past noon as they had planned. There was a table set up in the shade with the sign, "BETTING". The captain had taken safeguards to protect his soldiers if they bet. The company clerk had prepared envelopes to hold the amounts and names of the bettors. He contended that if the soldiers and the emigrants put up cash, it was only fair that the other party should also put up cash. So far, there had been no betting because Butch's backers were offering only three-to-one odds.

Moses was wearing a pair of dirty overalls and a ragged old white shirt when he climbed into the ring. He grinned at the crowd and started to shadow box slowly. Then he sat down and fanned himself with his frayed straw hat. Finally, odds of five to one were agreed upon. When the supporters of Moses slowed down their betting, the eager opposing bettors raised the odds to seven to one. Another flurry of betting exhausted the supply of cash among Butch's bettors. Greg McKenna placed two dollars at those odds. Amos Jordan held up fifty dollars and waved it in the face of the sutler, badgering him into taking the wager.

Moses climbed out of the ring and sat in the shade until fight time. Still wearing the hat and overalls, he would shadow box slowly, and for only a few seconds, then sit down and talk with his handlers. To them, he did not appear to be the least bit excited and talked in his usual easygoing manner. Under the shade of an umbrella, with an occasional breath of fresh air from a light breeze, he waited for the tardy Butch to make his appearance. When Butch climbed into the ring and sat down to have his wrapping and cotton gloves applied, Moses took off his shirt and stepped out of his overalls. The Butch supporters, who had been yelling obscene remarks at Moses, suddenly became silent as they saw the beautiful, well-muscled body of the colored man. When he got up and began to shadow box with grace and almost lightning-like jabs, they heard cheers for Moses.

The referee was a big, burly Army sergeant. Butch and Moses met in the center of the ring to receive his instructions.

"If there is any biting, gouging, kicking, or hitting below the belt, that fighter will lose all of the prize money. In case of a knockdown, you are to go to a neutral corner and I will start the count."

They touched gloves and backed off. Butch shuffled forward slowly as Moses backed up. He said, "Come on and fight, nigger. I am going to kill you."

"Of course you will try, but you is too fat and ugly to whip anybody." At the end of that remark, he hit Butch on the nose with a fast, hard left jab. Instantly, blood started to flow down Butch's chin. Butch countered with a surprisingly fast right, which missed by inches as Moses danced away to his left. The supporting soldiers cheered Moses. This continued all through the first round. Butch did connect some long rights, but they landed at the end of the swing, as Moses was going away, and had very little power. At the end of the round, Moses had a light sweat which Greg wiped away with the cool, wet towel while Amos held the umbrella.

Amos said, "You are doing great. Don't change your plans."

Moses grinned and nodded. The next six rounds were very much the same. Moses was landing hard lefts to the nose and left eye with an occasional right to the chin. Butch tried rushing him to get him into a corner where he could not escape getting pounded. Some of the spectators were yelling for Moses to get in there and fight and quit dancing around. His backers were encouraging him to keep on doing what he had been doing.

By the tenth round, Butch was beginning to wince when he was hit on his broken, bleeding nose, and he was breathing through the mouth. He was noticeably tiring as his counter punches lacked the speed and power that he had shown at first. Moses started fighting at a furious rate. Near the end of the round he feinted with a left. Butch instinctively threw up his hands to protect his battered face, and was hit with a hard right just above the belt. He gasped and lowered his hands. Moses stepped in for the kill and hit the staggering Butch with unchallenged rights and lefts. It seemed that Butch would go down until he swung a long right that connected squarely on Moses' chin, knocking him down just as the bell rang. There was much consternation as they helped Moses back to his corner. They hurriedly put cold towels on his head and neck. Amos advised him to take deep breaths and to just dance around for the next round until his head cleared up.

Butch clumsily followed him around the ring as he sensed a kill. All he did was tire himself. By the thirteenth round Moses was fully recovered. Butch's left eye was completely closed and his right eye was just a slit. Moses said two words, "This round," and after two minutes of rapid action, he circled to the left. Butch was either surprised or too tired to react. A hard right just below his rib cage on his right side doubled him over. Moses measured the almost helpless man as he stood flatfooted and swung a terrific right to the chin which sent Butch to the floor. He lay there unmoving while the referee counted him out.

Moses was shaking his head as they helped him out of the ring. The captain had an escort of soldiers waiting to protect him from the rush of the mob that followed. It was a good thing, as the Butch's supporters were hostile, swarming toward Moses and the betting table, which was also surrounded by soldiers with bayoneted rifles held at parade rest.

Greg McKenna was one of the last to receive his envelope with fourteen dollars in it. Slater, Haines and Jordan asked if he would like to have a drink at the saloon with them to celebrate. Greg declined, saying that he would mosey along back to the camp. Actually, he wanted to see again the friendly, good-looking young redheaded girl, who stood in the doorway of a shack at the edge of the barracks and invited him to come in and she would show him a good time for a dollar. His companions had kidded him about his interest in her. They warned him about the danger of getting the clap, saying that if he got it he might have the head of his pecker fall off when he took a leak some morning. Haines advised him if he did go to see her, he should be sure to wash it off with soap and water as soon after as he could.

"Benjamin Franklin was supposed to be quite a favorite around women and he advised rinsing it off with brandy. This whiskey will do just as well." Amos handed Greg a small bottle full of yellow liquid. Greg blushed and put it in his pocket.

While he was walking down the road toward the girl's shack, he halfway hoped that she would not be there. The half that hoped she would be there won. She smiled at him when he walked to the door.

"I am glad to see you again. I am lonesome for someone to talk to. Come in and have a cup of coffee." He decided there would be no harm in that, and sat down while she poured two cups of coffee. She asked what had been going on at the fort and was glad to hear that Butch was beaten. He had been rough with her and she locked her doors when she saw him coming. She sat on the divan facing Greg, her ample, pointed breasts almost completely exposed. When she moved her leg the robe she was wearing opened and Greg stared at a mass of curly red pubic hair. His reaction was instantaneous. She closed and bolted the door and led him to the bed. When she had undressed him, she looked at the erect organ and said, "You are really something." After two quick sessions she filled a wash basin and added carbolic acid.

"Use the soap and wash off real good. I am afraid that I may have caught something." Greg was appalled by this and for two weeks after he examined himself every morning, expecting to be red and swollen. This experience stood him in good stead for the rest of his life and saved him from trouble in the California gold camps later on.

CHAPTER 9

THE MORMONS

Rich Slater called a meeting on the evening of July fourth to issue instructions for their departure from Laramie on the sixth.

"Those whose teams have lost weight and are not in the best condition must now lighten their loads. Get rid of every nonessential item. The journey ahead will be through hilly, brushy, and wooded territory. There will be no buffalo chips available and wood must be gathered. The slow stragglers will be left behind and will be the prey of the Sioux and Cheyenne Indians who are hostile because of our invasion of their land."

The Haines did not have to unload anything, and were able to take on additional supplies at the fort.

Vera Murdock and Greg McKenna eyed each other from time to time and could greet each other only with a "Hello" or "How are you?". On a wood-gathering trip, she whispered to him as they passed, "I will meet you at the big tree in the bottom."

"Good. I will keep going this way for a little while and be there in five minutes."

She was gathering wood when he arrived.

"Did anyone see you go this way?" he asked.

"I don't think so. I told Momma that I would gather wood. I had untied my shoelace and was tying it when she went into the wagon."

"Smart girl. I hope you fooled her."

"Greg, Momma is awful smart. She seems to know what I am thinking and what I will do. Let's find a place where no one can see us."

They were looking around when they heard someone coming through the brush. They immediately started to gather wood.

"Oh, there you are. It is good that you found so much wood. I'll help you carry it back."

As they were carrying the wood back, behind her mother's back, Vera mouthed, "I told you so!" From then on Mrs. Murdock never let Vera out of her sight. They could dance together on Sunday, the day that Mormons did not travel. During one of the following Sundays, Vera said, "If you take the Mormon trail at South Pass and go to Utah, we might get together before I get married. I would like to at least once."

The forage at Laramie had been unusually good for that time of year as there had been unseasonable rains all summer. Due to experience and better care, they were averaging fourteen miles a day instead of the twelve they had first averaged. The weather was cooler than usual so they did not suffer from July heat. On August first they reached South Pass, where they would take the Mormon trail to the Salt Lake Valley or the route that went to Fort Hall and followed the Snake River to Oregon. The wagon train split up at Pacific Springs. The Miller, Johnson, and Haines parties were California bound. The Haines especially wanted to stop in Salt Lake for Rowena to see a doctor, as she was three months pregnant and having morning sickness. The larger contingent was going to Oregon and wagon-master Rich Slater would go with them. Amos Jordan volunteered to lead the California group and was immediately accepted.

There were tears as the women hugged and kissed each other and the men shook hands and said good-bye when the groups split. One was going almost straight west and the other south. This took the strain off the forage for the stock. The Jordan caravan planned to take a few days to rest at Salt Lake, so they pressed on harder. They arrived in the valley in mid-August. They had encountered Ute Indians along the way, who were friendly because Brigham Young had established a good relationship with them. The settlers shared food with them in times of short supply.

When the Jordan caravan came down from the hills and saw the green pastures and tall poplar trees, it was like entering another world. There were ditches with running water going out into the fields in small streams. Greg noticed that many of the workers in the fields were carrying shovels. The contrast between the almost bare sagebrush land that was not being irrigated and the lush crops made Greg recall what Amos had said to him.

The train stopped for the noon break by a clear stream. The Haines were inquiring of Vera Murdock's family if they knew of a place where they could stay for a few days.

Aaron Murdock said, "You people have been very friendly to us. We appreciate that. You even attended our church services. You would make good Mormons. Why don't you stay and join us? I am sure you would be welcome." The conversation was interrupted as they watched two horsemen ride up and stop.

One said, "Hello, brothers and sisters. The rider that came in last night said my brother, Aaron Murdock, is with this train."

"He sure is," said Aaron. "Hello, brother Nephi!" The two were joyfully reunited after several years apart. Aaron introduced the Haines group, saying, "These are nice people and they need a place to rest for a few days before going to California."

"They can stay at my place. We have plenty of room and feed."

Seldon Haines said, "That is very generous of you. Of course, we will pay for everything."

"That will be fine. I am sure my neighbors would be glad to take in the rest of the train, as we can all use the cash."

They were amazed at the size of some of the farms. Ruth Johnson remarked, "They have conquered the wilderness and done it in such a short time." As they passed through the streets of Salt Lake City, she remarked how wide they were, and wondered if Brigham Young had made them that wide on purpose to take care of the increased traffic that they could expect in the next hundred years.

Nephi replied, "He made them wide because he was such a terrible driver that he needed that much room to be able to turn around." Of course, he laughed as he said it.

To the Haines, Johnsons, Millers, Greg, and Amos, the

Murdock ranch was a heavenly oasis after the long, tiring trek from Kansas City. They camped in a luxurious pasture of green grass and blooming white clover. Poplar trees gave them shade and some privacy. The stream of water was cold and clear. They enjoyed the plentiful green vegetables from the large Murdock garden, after months of canned and dried food.

It was only a few miles into Salt Lake City. The Haines rented a team and surrey and spent several trips sight-seeing. Amos rode his horse into town and spent most of the time reading and taking notes at the library.

After dinner the group discussed the things they had seen and learned. Ruth Johnson remarked, "They are the most kindly and helpful people. Of course, they really try hard to get you to join the church. Amos, what is the Lion House? You know a lot about Salt Lake City."

"Ruth, it's that big building and the smaller ones surrounded by that high fence. The building houses the twenty-some wives of Brigham Young and his children. They have their own store and school."

"Who pays for all that?"

"Probably it comes out of the tithing. You have seen the tithing stations."

"Amos, would you call that a harem?"

"I can't say as I don't know what a harem is like."

Greg said, "I'm sure it isn't a harem because it doesn't have any dancing girls, and all harems have dancing girls."

Seldon Haines added, "He is said to mark on the doors of the wives he plans to visit that night."

Rowena said, "That isn't at all nice."

"Honey, you will think it awful that they say the women erase the marks on the doors of others and put marks on their own."

"Women are not like that."

Ruth Johnson said, "Oh, yes, they are! If I were one of twenty-seven wives, I might want to change a few marks from time to time." This brought on a laugh and Rowena blushed.

During one of the evening discussions, Seldon Haines said, "Brigham Young has to be listed as one of the great organizers of all time because of the way that everything has been laid out. The wide streets are easily found by their orderly numbers. In a few years they have irrigated the valley, established water systems, sewage, banks, and schools. They have a saw mill and no more log cabins with dirt floors. He recruited converts from all over the world with the special trades they needed."

"Not all over the world," Amos said. "He recruited in the States and England, Switzerland, and the Scandinavian countries. How many coloreds have you seen?"

"Only Moses."

"According to the Seeing Eye and the Book of Mormon, coloreds are the descendants of Cain and can never be elders in the church, although teenagers can be."

"You have to admire them for the way they look after each other," Greg said. "Most of the new converts come here with nothing but their clothes. The neighbors either find a job for them or land to settle, and help them build a house, put in crops, and furnish food until they can produce their own. They worship Brigham Young, and it seems they should, but what I can't understand is that nobody questions his decisions and rulings. There are always troublemakers, but here there are no dissenters or gripes."

Amos replied, "I can answer that. Up until last year he had an enforcer named Porter Rockwell. It is hearsay that troublemakers or dissenters left or disappeared. Some were sent to outlying areas to colonize. Rockwell never did any physical labor and answered only to Brigham Young. People dreaded seeing him and conformed."

"Is Rockwell still in Salt Lake?" Greg asked.

"No. He is dead."

"What happened?"

"It depends on whose story you believe. Brigham Young said that Rockwell got in an altercation with a renegade blacksmith named John Breckenridge and 'was sorely wounded thereof.' Breckenridge was a convert from England. He left a diary which states that he became displeased with the church after the Mountain Meadow massacre, in which the avenging angels killed all the non-Mormon adults and older children. He wanted to get married, but all the desirable girls were claimed by an elder with multiple wives as soon as they reached sixteen. He told Young that he was going to leave. Porter Rockwell sneaked up to the window of the blacksmith shop and shot at Breckenridge, hitting him in the back, but the double strap of his buffalo hide apron stopped the bullet. Breckenridge caught Rockwell and threw him through the wall of the blacksmith shop."

Amos made daily rounds of the other wagon train families, who were scattered throughout the valley, to check on their progress in getting their equipment ready for the next lap of the journey. Greg reshod the mules and Star, tightened braces and tires on the wagon, and greased the axles. When Murdock asked him to help irrigate, offering to reduce the price for the Haines' stay, Greg gladly agreed. He was beginning to envision a large irrigated ranch that would support a big herd of cattle. Murdock worked with him for a few days to show him how, then left him to irrigate a large field of wheat, which would take at least a week. He changed the water morning and night, moving across the field. This last watering was important, as the heads were in the milk and filling out.

Until this time he had only brief encounters with Vera and always in the presence of somebody else. It was nearly a mile from the house and one of the Murdock girls brought a big jug of water and lunch to the workers. He hoped that Vera would come when he was working alone. As the sun reached its zenith, a rider approached, and joyfully he recognized her. She tied the reins to a fence post and carried the jug and lunch to him, setting it on the ground.

"You can eat after I am gone. I have to hurry back." They walked into the tall grain and trampled a small space.

"You lie down. I don't want to stain my dress. I'll do the work." Vera wet his penis with her mouth and slowly and gingerly sat down on it.

"Does it hurt?"

"Some, but it's wonderful." It was only a few moments until he said, "Get off quick—I'm coming!" Instead, she grabbed his hips and pumped furiously. After they were through, he asked, "Why didn't you get off?"

"Greg, it just felt too good."

"Did your brothers ever stop?"

"Nope, they really squirted me full."

"Why didn't you get pregnant?"

"I guess it's because they both had mumps. They haven't had any kids since they got married either."

"What if you get pregnant?"

"It won't matter. I am getting married in two weeks, and a Mormon woman's duty is to bring more Saints into the world."

CHAPTER 10

TO RAFT RIVER

A mountain man, Claude Jones, was the guide for the fourteen other wagons that joined the Jordan caravan in Salt Lake. Claude had trapped in Montana, Idaho, and Wyoming with the Jedidiah Smith expedition of 1826, and had made three trips to California. He was intelligent and observant and had the ability to tell the travellers what they would encounter each day. He liked to talk, and Greg pumped him to tell of his experiences.

Claude asked, "Son, what are you going to do in California?"

"I want to find enough gold to buy and stock a big ranch with cattle and horses."

"What do you mean by big?"

"Like 'big' in Texas. Not hundreds of acres but a thousand or more. From what I've seen of the irrigation in Utah, there must be some places in the West that have water and good soil that will be settled soon."

"Well, there's a lot of real good land in Washington territory and Idaho that could be irrigated. The Injuns are gonna be bothersome, but not for long. The whites are gonna drive them out. There's a place in Idaho, in the Pahsimeroi Valley, close to the headwaters of the Salmon River. The Injuns call it *E-dah-how* or 'light on the mountains'. We wintered there and trapped and fished our fill. There is a pretty stream that's got salmon—big silver fish with red meat running through it. Actually, it is a large meadow about a mile wide and three miles long, before the timber closes in, and then it opens into a broad valley. The winters are mild as the surrounding hills catch most of the snow. The grass is as high as a horse's belly, and it is full of a plant that has big yellow blooms which livestock like to eat. The Injuns call it 'bitterroot'. You can bet someone will file on it in the next twenty years or sooner by the way people are leavin' the East. You know you can file on three hundred twenty acres a person, or six hundred forty for a man and wife."

Amos entered the conversation with, "It will probably take that long before we find enough gold to finance it."

"Amos, what do you mean by 'we'?" Greg asked.

"Greg, don't you know we are going to be partners? Did you think I was going to let a juvenile go gold hunting by himself?" Greg reached over and they shook hands.

Greg asked, "Claude, did you look for gold in California?"

"I sure did, and I was really a greenhorn. It takes a lot of knowin' to find gold. If I was doin' it over, I'd hire out and work for someone who has a good claim. You'll save a lot of time and money if you know what to have for an outfit. They's some good books on gold minin' but I don't read too well. Havin' water is the most important part of gold minin' next to havin' gold. And you can't find gold on the highest hills."

"Did you find gold?"

"Yes, lots of it, but gettin' it out was somethin' else. You had to dig down through gravel about six feet to bedrock where most of the gold had settled. Then you had to carry the dirt down to water or carry water to it for pannin'. If you had a runnin' stream, you could hit it rich and run it down along a sluice box. We had to dig it out and pan. We could make five dollars a day if we worked hard for twelve hours. Food and supplies were too damned high, and the minin' camps are pretty rough places to stay, so I quit it and went back to guidin' caravans. But you two young'uns could do it. I'm near forty and too old to look in places that are new. Be the first to file near water so you have first use. The Rocky Mountains go all the way from up in Canada to Mexico. California isn't the only place where there is gold."

Amos and Greg were listening attentively, so Claude continued. "You won't find gold up in the mountains. It's worked its way down to the foothills. It's has been washed by water in the creeks and rivers and has settled in the still pools below rapids. I am too old or lazy to look for the very fine gold that is probably in the sand along Snake River. There has to be a passel of gold somewhere up the streams that run into the Snake. It is going to take a lot of shoe leather and walkin' unless you're lucky. I find most luck comes from hard work."

"How about riding horses instead of all that walking?" Greg asked.

"Looking after horses and findin' feed is right bothersome. You need a pack horse and you carry a pack. If I had my druthers, I would have a mule, as they have more sense than horses."

This started Greg thinking about Harry. He was dreading the thought of parting with his affectionate and loyal friend. Maybe he could trade Star for the mule.

In nine days they had travelled over one hundred fifty miles and were camped on a branch of the Raft River near Steeple Rocks in Idaho. A short distance from their camping circle were holes several feet deep and mounds of dirt with patches of rust on them. At the meeting that night, Amos explained why the holes were so close to the stream: "There was no record as to what really happened in the 1830s to a wagon train that was attacked at this site because there were no coherent survivors. The only information was from the Indians and they gave out very little. It was a large caravan, so well-equipped and powerful that some of the members shot at Indians for no reason. The Utes, Bannocks, and Shoshonis banded together and sent out a war party to follow the caravan to find a place for ambush. When the caravan parked wagons in a circle about one hundred yards from a stream, the Indians blocked them from water. Exhausted by starvation and thirst, the members of the wagon train were overrun and killed. The wagons were ransacked, looted, and burned. Brigham Young had teamsters haul the iron scrap from the wagons to Salt Lake."

Ruth Johnson asked, "Did anyone escape?"

"It is reported a thirteen-year-old girl hid in the bushes and followed the river down to the Snake River, where a wagon train picked her up. She was too shocked and never was able to be coherent about what happened."

"Weren't the people missed?"

"If your relatives do hear from you out here, how will they get in touch with you?"

"What about Indian trouble from here on?"

"We are too far south of the Blackfeet, so all we might expect to encounter are small groups of hunters from small bands, and they will be friendly if we are. I doubt that we will see very many Indians. In the spring they migrate from winter quarters in Nevada to the Sawtooth valleys in Idaho to dig camas lily roots for winter. They dry fish and eat rockchucks. They also hunt deer and make jerky or pemmican."

Claude warned the group by saying, "Never take anything for granted about Indians. They are natural thieves. It's a way of life with them, so we'll be watchin' all the time."

They were headed south on the head waters of Salmon Creek where feed and water were plentiful. It had been cloudy and cool, and with easy travelling they had made twenty miles by mid-afternoon.

Amos returned from scouting ahead and said, "There is a good camp ground about a mile ahead with plenty of feed and juniper trees for firewood. There is a small band of Indians camped there. They have women and children so they won't cause any trouble. Just be careful of small things that they can steal and hide. We will stay there two days to give the stock a rest, catch up on the washing, and check wagons and harnesses."

It was a good stop. They camped about a mile from the three skin lodges of the Indians, who rode up shortly after they were settled. The leader stopped and gave the peace sign with upraised arm, palm open and forward. Amos rode to meet them, also giving the peace sign. They wanted to trade dried salmon that they had caught near the upper Salmon Falls of the Snake River for powder and lead. Both Amos and Claude could converse in Sioux and Cheyenne and, along with signs, they could communicate. They traded for enough smoked salmon for one day's meal. The Indian women had moccasins and leather jackets to trade to the caravan women for pots, pans, and knives. On the advice of

Claude, they did not let the Indians see into the wagons. In all, it was a friendly meeting and bartering.

Antelope were very plentiful but they kept their distance and bounded away in long, graceful leaps when approached. The Indians wanted fresh meat but could not get within bow and arrow or musket range of the animals. The chief asked the white men to join them in a hunting party, and they agreed. Amos, Claude, and Greg rode out the next day with six Indian men and two young squaws. They spotted a large herd about two miles away. The chief stopped and dismounted, indicating that the white men do the same. He squatted, smoothed out the dirt, and with a twig drew out his plan. His band would take a long detour and surround the antelope, spreading out in a U-shape. Greg, Amos, and Claude were to hide their horses and get behind tall sagebrush above a draw in the hill that opened into a wide valley. He drew a line to indicate the route that the antelope would follow. The white men would be responsible for the shooting. The Indians rode off.

Greg said, "I hope he knows that the antelope will run by here."

Amos nodded. "Don't worry, Greg, he knows they will. Just worry about your shooting. The antelope can run twice as fast as a horse. That means you will have to lead them by about six feet at a hundred yards. Some say they have seven times our vision, so keep very still and don't rise up to shoot until they are opposite you, as they will be looking ahead."

Claude chipped in, "They are strange critters, as they follow the leader. If we can down the leader, they may mill around and we can make a good kill. Greg, you will stay here and try to kill off the leader first." He moved about fifty feet down the draw and said, "This is a good place for Amos. I'll move another fifty feet farther down. Keep looking through the bushes."

It was a long wait. Greg began to wonder if the antelope had broken through the Indians' circle. He cast a glance at Amos, who put his finger to his lips and pointed. Greg could see the antelope nearly a mile away, heading for the draw. He was standing with his legs apart, resting the stock of his long-barreled Sharps, watching the approaching herd, when he heard a slight scraping sound. Without moving, he looked down to see a thick, four-foot rattlesnake slowly moving between his feet. He shifted his weight slightly to the left and stomped the snake with his heel just behind the head. He watched it struggle and slowly die, as he had broken its back and squashed it flat. He took some deep breaths and tried to calm himself so that he could shoot accurately. Peeping through the brush, he could see the antelope moving leisurely toward the draw. The leader would stop and look back toward the Indians a mile behind and then move on.

When the lead antelope crossed in front of him, Greg drew a bead on him and felled the antelope behind the leader with a shot in the neck. When the shooting was over, Amos said, "I aimed at the second antelope and shot the fourth. They are supposed to be able to go a mile a minute."

When it was all over, there were five animals down. The Indians took the two largest antelope, leaving three smaller ones for the caravan. Greg asked Claude, "Why did you give the two largest antelope to the Indians?"

"Son, an old antelope is so strong-smelling, even after it is cooked, a dog might carry it out and bury it. But, it will taste good to the Indians."

The fresh meat was a welcome change in the diet of the caravaners. After the evening meal, Amos instructed them, "Be sure to fill your water barrels and have all your pots and pans full of water. The trail will be mostly level with a few hills, but no water. It has turned off hot and the stock will need all the available water. No bathing, washing, and use as little as you can for dishwashing."

After leaving the Raft River they travelled from the Humboldt River to the Truckee River in Nevada with dry stretches and ponds of poisonous water containing carcasses of animals that had bolted to ease their thirst. The ponds contained arsenic, a white mineral contained in the soil in some areas of Arizona, Nevada, and Utah. Water-soluble, it leached into streams, settling in strong concentration in ponds.

Amos had the caravan stop for two days on the Truckee before beginning the steep climb to Donner Summit, about twenty miles away. At the camp meeting he told them how long it would take to reach the summit because the oxen, mules, and horses would have to stop to rest about every hundred yards. They could travel only as fast as the slowest team. He arranged the travel lineup so that the slowest teams were last. Greg and his mules were to lead, followed by the other two parties of his group.

Amos told them to get sacks of the newly harvested oats and to chop the new feed, lucerne, into burlap sacks. He said that he hoped for rains, which usually occurred around the first week of September.

They were in luck as it started to rain the last week in August and continued to rain for five days. When the rain stopped, the trail, with its elevation of five thousand feet, dried out quickly. Water and feed were no problem and Amos would not have to scout far ahead to find camping places.

They were ready to move the day after the rain stopped. Amos told them what to expect on the trail ahead.

"Going up will be the easy part of the trip. All you have to do is place a chock of wood behind the rear wheels when resting," Amos said. "It is hell when going down. You have to keep the wagons from running over the oxen because the grade is too steep for them to hold the wagons. Check your brake shoes and get stout poles to drive into the ground for leverage. In places we may have to chain the wheels to slide."

It was a nightmare, as in many places the rocky road was barely wide enough for a wagon and there were many wrecked wagons hundreds of feet below. Moses was tireless in helping on every occasion that called for his powerful strength. Water was no problem. There were level spots for camping, but most of them had no feed for the stock. The thirty miles up and down the pass took seven days. When they reached the end of the steep grade, the weather was warm and balmy as they neared Sacramento. Feed was abundant. They could see people panning for gold in the streams alongside the road. There was considerable traffic on the road.

Seldon Haines remarked to his wife, "I have never seen such a mixture of people as are in these camps. Most of the women are camp followers of every race or age. A lot of them have no teeth and are filthy. I heard that large numbers of women from brothels in Mexico, South America, and France have come to California to practice their trade."

"Seldon, while you have been looking at the women, I've been looking at the men," said Rowena. "Some of them are young, dirty, wild and lawless, drinking, gambling, whoring creatures. It is no wonder Amos has guards patrolling the camp at night. I'll be glad when we get to Sacramento."

Two days later they reached the outskirts of Sacramento. There were tears and handshakes as the three families split up. Amos, whose contract was up, planned to go with Greg and the Haines to the acreage Captain Edward Haines had purchased. Moses was in tears as he said good-bye.

"Greg, it's a short ride to Sacramento. I have an itchy feeling I would like to get rid of. Do you want to go?"

"Amos, I'm all for it."

"I think we should take only twenty dollars with us. You never know what will happen."

Wearing their good clothes, they left at daybreak the next morning. The well-rested horses were anxious to travel and they made good time, arriving in town in the late afternoon. After getting their beards trimmed and a haircut, they went to a saloon in an imposing building and ordered a drink. The bar and fixtures showed taste and class. Greg noticed that Amos was looking at a table where six men were playing poker.

"Amos, why don't you try your luck for an hour?"

"I'd like to. Fellows, is this game filled up?"

"Stranger, you're welcome. Table stakes are high-low and jack or better to open."

When Amos bought fifty dollars worth of chips, Greg smiled. Amos thinks he has to look out for me, he thought, remembering his twenty dollar limit. Amos won a small pot the first hand. In about an hour he was a little over one hundred dollars ahead. Pushing back his chair, he said, "Cash me in. I have an appointment with a lady. I may be back later."

After they left the saloon, he handed Greg fifty dollars, saying, "We're partners." A short way down the street, they entered another saloon and ordered a drink. The friendly bartender asked if they were new in town and told them the Oxford Hotel was a clean, reasonable place to stay. They answered they were already registered there. A short time later, Amos noticed the bartender talking to the piano player, who put on his coat and left. In a little while he was back playing, and a few minutes later two good-looking women entered and sat down at a table near them.

"Greg, don't look at them, but I have a feeling they are going to try to set us up. Under no circumstances drink anything unless I tell you to. Now, look at them and smile."

Both the girls smiled back. Greg said, "Would you like to join us for a drink?" They moved to the men's table.

"I am Amos Jordan and this is my friend, Greg McKenna."

"Glad t'meecha. I'm Marge and she is Mabel." They questioned Greg and Amos about their situation and past.

"Where are you staying?"

"The Oxford Hotel."

"We are new in town and we're staying there, too. We have a couple bottles of liquor in our room. Why don't we go there and have a party?"

Greg said, "That would be great."

Mabel said, "Why don't we go to the hotel now. What is your room number?"

"Twenty-nine."

"We will see you fellas in a few minutes."

As they left the saloon, Greg said, "We sure lucked out!"

"Lucked out, hell. There are two kinds of luck—good and bad. This is a set-up. We could wind up doped, broke, on a ship to China as seamen. They are trying to shanghai us and they will get paid about twenty dollars each for doing it."

Greg and Amos had been in their room only a few minutes when there was a knock on the door. The girls were wearing robes and carrying glasses and two bottles of Old Crow, one of which was less than half full. Marge set four glasses on the dresser and emptied the partially filled bottle into two of them, which she handed to Greg and Amos. Then she opened the new bottle and poured about the same volume into the remaining glasses.

Mabel said, "Marge, I have to go pee."

"I'll go with you. We will be back in a few minutes. Go ahead with your drinks, boys."

After they left, Amos took Greg's glass and exchanged their drinks with the ones the girls poured for themselves. Winking at Greg, he said, "Don't drink until they come back."

When they returned, the girls were surprised that they had not taken a drink. Greg was now in the spirit of things and said, "We waited for you. Let's go bottoms up on this one and enjoy the next. We are dry. Marge, you give the signal and the first one empty gets this five dollar gold piece." It worked. They gulped their drinks down.

Amos said, "It's a tie. You each get five dollars."

Marge's eyes crossed. She said, "You bastard!" and collapsed on the bed. Mabel just keeled over quietly.

"They must have really loaded those drinks. Amos, what do we do now?"

"I suggest that we examine the goods that have been thrust upon us. But let's have another drink to celebrate. A drunk woman isn't all that good, but they beat nothing at all," said Amos. "They seem to be clean and free from disease, but we'll wash good and use whiskey after."

Amos downed a drink and pulled off Marge's robe, while Greg began undressing Mabel.

Amos watched as Greg was ready to enter Mabel. "Boy, she is going to be sore and think she was mounted by a horse."

They gathered the women's clothes, found the key to the women's room and left, locking the women in their room.

"We'll just leave them there all night and we'll sleep in their room," Amos said. "I want to find out who set us up and why, and for their clothes they will tell us or we will summon the sheriff."

They woke up as usual at daylight, and after a trip to the washroom, they went down the carpeted hall and unlocked their door. The women were lying on their backs, mouths open and snoring.

Amos said, "They look really raunchy this morning."

After repeated applications of cold washrags to their faces, the women woke up, very indignant. Amos squelched their complaints with, "You tried to set us up, and we can go get the sheriff. You won't get your clothes until you come clean."

"We don't know for sure."

"We are going to have breakfast. You will be locked in and you can refresh your memory before we come back."

Marge vented a stream of profanity and said, "We will talk."

They revealed that they were to receive ten dollars each and whatever they could find in Amos and Greg's pockets, which they would split with the bartender who arranged the deal. Sailors were deserting the ships for the gold fields and it was a common practice to shanghai men. Greg and Amos would have been on a ship this morning on their way to China. Greg was impressed at the skill of Amos's questioning to insure the women were telling the truth.

Mabel remarked, "Are you a lawyer or something?"

As they were packing their gear, Greg said, "I would like to do something to get even but I don't know what."

"I feel the same way. We can get breakfast and ride our horses back to the camp, or we can get even and have some fun."

"What do you suggest?"

"I'm hungry. Let's saddle up our horses and tie them to the hitching rack in the back of the saloon while we get breakfast. Then we will hide across the street and hope the bartender is the one that opens the saloon this morning. I know what to do with him. He is going to be suspicious, but we will be friendly and put him at his ease. You grab his right shoulder. I'll grab his left with my left and grab a handful of that bristly black hair and bang his head down on the bar a few times to quiet him."

"Amos, that is a good plan. Then let's take cue sticks and wreck the joint and leave town."

They watched the bartender unlock the saloon at nine o'clock. A few minutes later they walked across the almost deserted street and entered the bar. The bartender looked at them distrustfully, but they greeted him with a cheerful, "Hello. Can you pour us a drink? We sure had one hell of a fun night with those girls you set us up with. They were really something. We really owe you!"

The apprehensive bartender was so relieved that he said, "I'll give you a drink on the house and I'll have one with you." He poured three generous drinks. As he leaned forward he found himself restrained at the shoulders and his bushy hair held by a large hand which yanked his head back.

"What's the big idea? I ain't done nothin'," he gasped.

"You are a dirty, no-good louse. You tried to get us shanghaied," Amos said, and slammed his face down on the counter.

The bartender screamed but was knocked unconscious by two more smashes. Greg and Amos closed the curtains, locked the door, and with two pool cues they quickly broke the mirrors and bottles of liquor, smashed chairs over the bar, and wrecked everything possible. As Amos walked by the moaning bartender, he gave him a hard kick between his legs.

"That will give him something to remember us by."

They went out the back door to their horses, laughing at their escapade.

"Amos, you certainly know your way around. I would have been on my way to China and seasick. Seems like you are always saving me from trouble."

"Greg, think back. We are a team, and a good one. We watch out for each other."

CHAPTER 11

THE HAINES RANCH

It took most of a day to travel to the Haines ranch, and they were glad to get there. Mexican ranch hands took over the care of the mules and horses and unloading the wagon, carrying their belongings into a large, thick-walled adobe hacienda with tastefully furnished rooms. Edward Haines told his brother and friends to stay as long as they needed to get their feet on the ground and decide when and where they would go. Rowena welcomed the rest as she thought about the weeks ahead, before the baby was due. Seldon Haines gave Greg and Amos each a bonus of fifty dollars for their work. Greg did not want to part with his mule friend, Harry, so he offered to buy him. Seldon thought a bit and laughed.

"Harry would raise hell if you left him and keep everybody awake. I'll give him to you. I'll make out a bill of sale."

They cleaned up for the evening meal. The main dish was fried chicken, which they had not eaten for nearly a year, tortillas, beans, and fruit.

Edward said, "I prefer biscuits with chicken gravy. I have repeatedly told the cook, but the next time she forgets and I get tortillas again. I have had a hell of a time with that cook and too much pepper. I guess it is a carry-over of hundreds of years to hide the taste of spoiled food. Someone said the pepper makes the poor Mexican stomach feel full." He gave a short blessing and they started to eat, but stopped when the pretty Mexican maid brought in a short, heavy-set man.

"Hello, Shorty. Draw up a chair; you are just in time. We'll eat and talk later. Folks, this is my partner in the gold mine, Emerson Gill. He doesn't mind being called Shorty."

Shorty was slightly over five feet tall, with a pug nose, twinkling blue eyes, and red hair. He walked with a limp.

After dinner the men gathered in the spacious living room where the heat from a fireplace broke the slight evening chill. Shorty had come to the ranch for a two-week supply of goods and replacement of mining tools. He gave Edward Haines his share of nearly three ounces of gold. He complained that the two men who had been working for them at the mine were robbing them blind.

"They are supposed to be shoveling the muck into the sluice box. The claim is unusual because occasionally there are large nuggets, sometimes as large as a pea or bean. When they pick off the large gravel from the shovel, they palm the nuggets and very few get into the sluice box. A friend of mine dropped by yesterday and said they got drunk in Sacramento and showed off the large nuggets. I am going to fire them when they return."

Edward Haines said, "You are in luck. Greg and Amos are looking for work and you will have two absolutely honest men working together. I'll vouch for them."

Shorty was delighted. He said, "You're hired. Ten dollars a day and grub."

"We accept," said Amos. "We will work only ten hours a day, though. We don't want to be old young men, but you will be satisfied."

"That will be all right with me." They shook hands.

They learned that the Spanish land grant was in leagues from a certain land mark, and so many leagues to another, and back to the ranch. Captain Haines had it properly surveyed and recorded, and installed monuments that established the boundaries.

"Is there gold on your property?" asked Seldon.

"Yes, thank goodness, there is some in a small area on a tributary to the American River. Shorty rents it from me. He works the gold mine and gives me twenty percent. You'll be able to learn a lot about mining working for him. I also have some good books on gold mining by geologists and engineers, which you are welcome to read."

The partners decided to rest a few days, enjoying the good food, especially the fresh vegetables, oranges, and figs. They lost no time in getting the books on mining and studied them outdoors in the shade of the large oak trees. They read that rock, principally granite, was igneous or had been heated and melted together, and in cooling formed cracks. Water, carrying minute dissolved minerals, filled these cracks over long periods of time. Under intense heat these cracks became molten. After eons of time the granite was exposed due to weather and even earthquakes. The deterioration process continued and water washed and made gravel. Gold, being much heavier, sank down through the sieve-like gravel to bedrock.

They found out that panning consisted of a large iron pan with deep slanting sides. The operation of the pan was based on one of the qualities of gold—its unusual weight. A given volume of gold far outweighed the equivalent volume of all kinds of rock and earth. This caused streams to drop their precious freight. The pan was filled with gravel and water, which was kneaded into a mixture, sorting out the large stones. The pan was then immersed in water, held tilted with one side higher than the other, and rotated. This created a revolving current of water which carried away the lighter material. Then you picked out the remaining pebbles, leaving the gold in flakes, dust and irregularly shaped nuggets. It was hard work and unless it was a very rich claim, very few made more than wages.

The sluice box was usually twelve feet long, eighteen to twenty-four inches wide, and at least twenty-four inches deep. It had slats or riffles to catch the heavier gold and it simulated nature and acted like a sieve. They also found out that through long periods of time streams changed their courses and the gravel gold-bearing deposits could be a long way from the stream, in all sizes and shapes.

Greg and Amos thought it would be only a few miles to the claim, but found that it was located on another Spanish grant that Edward Haines had purchased, nearly thirty miles away. As they packed the mule and horses, Shorty said, "We will need to take a ranch hand with us to bring back the mule and horses. There is only enough feed for one horse at the mine."

The trail to the claim was a rough, rocky, crooked path with cutbacks. They were glad to see the little cabin at the claim. They enjoyed the evening meal of fresh beef and vegetables that Shorty prepared. Amos was sitting at the table facing the open door and looking down the trail. He straightened up, took another look, and said, "We are going to have company!"

Shorty reached under the bed and brought out a double-barreled shotgun with nipples capped. Amos said, "I'll handle the gun. You do the talking. I'll take care of them if it is necessary."

Amos and Greg stood out of sight beside the door. The riders dismounted and were grinning as they walked toward Shorty, who was blocking the door.

One said, "Stand back, Shorty. We are just in time for supper."

"You two are fired. Get the hell off my claim."

The larger ruffian pulled out a pistol and said, "The hell you say. We are taking over and we'll let you leave when we are damned good and ready."

Amos touched Shorty on the back and he moved to the side.

"Yes, the hell you say," Amos said. "Drop that gun, or you'll have a hole in your chest."

The man's eyes bugged out and he quickly dropped the gun.

"We was only foolin'."

Greg stepped out and picked up the gun. Winking at Amos, he said, "Hell has been said a lot in the last few minutes and I'll say it again. You two take shovels and dig a hole six feet long, four feet deep and four feet wide." Amos fired a shotgun blast at their feet. They both jumped to get the shovels and started to dig. Gleefully, Shorty said, "We might as well enjoy their work as we oversee the diggin'. I'll get us drinks and a snack and we can have a picnic while we watch."

When the hole was deep enough, Greg said, "You can quit and lie down in the hole." The two men began to beg for their lives.

Amos said, "Greg, you forgot to search them. It would be a shame to bury some money!" A search of their money belts produced a surprising nine hundred dollars. Shorty was furious.

"I knew they were stealing, but I had no idea how much." He walked to the tall thief and swung an overhand right that smashed his nose.

Greg said, "Let's get them in the hole and bury them."

"No," Amos answered. "That would be taking a man's life. We'll let them get the hell out of here." Without looking back the two jumped on their horses and took off down the trail.

Shorty handed Greg and Amos each one hundred twenty dollars. "This is for the two week's wages I paid them. Edward Haines gets one-fifth, which is one hundred fifty-six dollars, and that leaves me seven hundred twenty-four dollars."

After shaking hands, they finished another drink.

Shorty told them the deposit of gold was not typical. Large nuggets were unusual, and the small stream did not deposit the gold. It had probably been deposited thousands of years earlier, leaving a pear-shaped deposit of gravel covered with about two feet of soil. The small, ever-flowing spring tumbled down the rocks and levelled out and flowed quietly to a crack in the rocks on its way to the Sacramento River. A flume was placed at the spring's emergence from the rocks to carry the water to the sluice box. He was a good teacher and they learned about regulating the speed of water and adjusting the sluice box, in addition to his knowledge of where gold deposits could be found.

They had been working about a month when Shorty gave them each a fifty dollar bonus in addition to the two hundred fifty dollars in wages they had earned. He asked them to deposit his share in the Wells Fargo Bank at Sacramento. Amos and Greg also deposited their money in a savings account that drew five percent interest.

They began making fortnightly trips into Sacramento, with the exception of two excursions to San Francisco, where they were amazed at the busy seaport. They attended the plush theaters. Greg was awed by the splendor of the pretentious mansions on "Snob Hill". Whenever a ship docked, there would be a long line of people from all walks of life carrying their belongings. The partners were watching the passengers disembark from a large ship.

Amos said, "Would you look at those?" He pointed to a group of very well-dressed, attractive young women. "They could name their own price in a mining camp, but they will stay in San Francisco and service the rich who have made the big strike."

"I can't understand what they are chattering about."

"I can't either, but I know it is French."

"Amos, they look like they would be safe."

"They look that way, but don't take any chances. Use the old Ben Franklin recipe."

In Sacramento, they often attended church on Sunday morning because Greg liked to sing. Amos remarked, "It makes you feel good and clean after sinning the night before. The minister had the same old theme of hellfire and damnation about sex and sin."

"Fat chance it is going to change the natural sex habits of people, except a few old maids that only have water rights!" Amos remarked. "Greg, I have an idea. We are going to tell Shorty we have learned enough and are going to start out on our own."

"Amos, we have never had it so good. We can't afford to quit."

"We can always change our minds. Just leave it to me. Do you realize that Shorty deposited over fifty-five hundred dollars after giving Haines his twenty percent and paying us a thousand dollars each? I know we never had it so good, but I think we can make a better deal."

Amos had mailed a couple of letters and had received a fat thick one. There was also a letter to Shorty in the uncertain handwriting of a child. He waved it and said, "It is from my ten-year-old son."

After dinner they were sitting on the porch, smoking and watching the spectacular sunset with its tinted gold cumulus clouds.

Amos spoke. "Shorty, you are not going to like what I have to say. We have been thinking that we have learned enough to go out on our own. We are going to leave in two weeks, so you can find someone to take our place."

Shorty got red in the face and exploded as he said, "You can't quit! You've never had it so good. You haven't one chance in a thousand of finding a claim that pays more than you are getting."

"We really appreciate the way you have treated us, but our minds are kinda made up."

The small man sat quietly, looking at them as he sucked on his empty pipe. Finally, he broke the silence and said, "Just what will it take to get you to stay here?"

Greg said, "Amos, I think we should consider an offer. We like Shorty and we like this place."

"Greg, if you feel that way, I'll go along with you," said Shorty. "In three years this place will be worked out. I'll buy a small ranch and send for my motherless boys who are living with an aunt. Let me do some figuring and I'll make you damned high binders an offer you can't refuse because any other help will rob me blind again."

Shorty found a stub of a pencil and started to write figures on the back of a paper sack. Finally, he said, "Against my better judgment, I'll give you forty percent. This is a stupid final offer, but this claim is unbelievably rich. You have to stay until it is cleaned out and if the gold peters out some and you are working for less than wages, I'll hold you to your bargain."

The surprised partners looked at each other.

"That's a generous, tempting offer. What do you think, Amos?"

"It's too tempting to turn down. I'll make out two copies of a legal, binding contract for us to sign. There is enough gold for everyone. I doubt if there are many diggings as rich as this one. However, on one bar of the Marias River the miners committee allowed only one hundred square feet per claim because it was so rich in gold. Since we are partners, we will share forty percent of the expenses." This brought a smile to Shorty's face.

The next day the partners really pitched in. At noon Shorty said, "Those riffles are really looking good and we are getting some good big nuggets."

Greg was picking the larger pieces of gravel off his shovel. He stopped, stared, and said, "Amos."

"Pick it up, Greg. It might be brass."

Greg picked up the flat but rounded piece that was over half an inch across and yelled, "Shorty, catch this."

Shorty looked up and caught it with one hand. He was speechless for a moment, then gave a loud yell. They all gathered around and passed the three-ounce gold nugget back and forth.

But, Shorty was right about the deposit varying. Sometimes they made less than one thousand dollars each for the month. Then they would hit a rich stretch near the bedrock and make up to two thousand dollars each for the month. In the evenings they read. Amos was still reading law books and making notes. Occasionally he read classics, which Greg also read. Sometimes they played pitch for quarters, keeping a running score and never settling up. Shorty was an excellent checker player, but in time they all played equally well.

It finally occurred to Greg that Amos had been systematically subjecting him to an educational program from the books that he got for them to read. Because of their scarcity, they were usually read two or three times. Then Amos would have a discussion, getting Greg to give his thinking on the subject. Sometimes they disagreed and friendly arguments were carried on. History, especially ancient history, fascinated Greg. When asked what he thought about the comparison between people of ancient times and the present, his reply to Amos was, "We may have more convenient things to make our lives easier, but man still has to be controlled or he is completely lawless, cruel, and even inhumane. Actually, relatively few people, maybe ten percent, keep the rest of the population in line."

"Greg, when we get to the mining camps, you will find you are right. There will be almost no law, with the strongest and meanest prevailing," Shorty said.

"Amos, at this rate we will have almost enough to start that ranch Claude Jones told us about in the Salmon River country."

"How much do you think it will take?"

"After you settle on a ranch it takes quite a while for it to start to pay off. I guess forty or fifty thousand if we are going to run a thousand acres or more, with at least two hundred cows and forty brood mares for raising colts to send to the Army."

The next two years and nine months passed quickly as they were always busy.

CHAPTER 12

ON THEIR OWN

It was mid-May and the Emerson Gill claim had been cleared of the last bit of gold. Both Greg McKenna and Amos Jordan were reluctant to leave the lucrative diggings. They gathered and packed their belongings and the tools and equipment given to them by Shorty, which included a gold pan, carpenter tools, cooking utensils, and some bedding that they could use when they set out to prospect on their own. Each had over twenty thousand dollars deposited in savings drawing five percent interest at the Wells Fargo Bank in Sacramento.

As they were packing, Greg remarked, "Compared to ninety-nine percent of the miners, we are very lucky."

"Luck plays a very important part in one's life. Now we need only one more good strike and you can get your cattle ranch, get married, and raise a family. But it may take several years before we can find it."

"We will find it, Amos. I feel in my bones that we will." Little did they know that Amos' prediction as to time was so true.

They were welcomed back at the Haines ranch. Edward needed Amos' help with contracts, checking land grants and registering titles of the seven thousand acres in the Spanish grant. Greg trimmed and shod horse hooves, supervised fencing, and helped lay out irrigation systems. After a week, the partners decided to spend a few days in San Francisco. After riding their horses to Sacramento, they boarded a crowded, double-sided paddle-wheeler that could operate in only a few feet of water, and headed down the Sacramento River to San Francisco Bay.

They were dressed in good, well-fitting clothes. Their hair was cut and beards trimmed. The two big men stood out in an impressive manner from the motley crowd.

As they approached the dock, they noticed the large number of anchored, empty ships in the bay. The crews had deserted, responding to the lure of the gold fields.

"We'll have to be very careful about getting shanghaied. Each of those deserted ships has a captain desperate for a crew and he'll use any means to get one. We'll stay together and keep our money in our money belts. Your big fist and quickness are a match for any man, and I have an equalizer, a double-barreled thirty-five-caliber derringer, in my right boot. We will never have more than two drinks at one time and only in the best saloons with a reputation for respectability. We want to have a safe, pleasant, relaxing time. What would you like to do?"

"Amos, there are so many things to see and do. I'd like to go to church, see a good play, spend some time in the library, do a little shopping, and a lot of looking."

"I guess you're too bashful to mention some good-looking girls. We can do all those things. We'd better buy two pairs of comfortable boots for walking. We are going to need them for getting around the city as well as the long, hard trip ahead. We'll spend some time in the library looking at maps of California, Nevada, Oregon, and Idaho. Each night, we will plan the next day's activities. We don't have to go at it, as Claude said, 'like hell fightin' a bear.'"

They enjoyed their six-day stay in San Francisco and were glad to leave for Sacramento, where they purchased a waterproof tent, a tiny tin stove, two backpacks, and a supply of beans, rice, dried fruit, and other staples to be picked up when they left the Haines ranch.

After packing Harry with the bed rolls and putting the slickers on the horses, they set out for Placerville on the South Fork of the American River. It was a booming, shabby mining town that had everything at very inflated prices. Miners who had hit it rich, because there was very little to buy, squandered their money on liquor and women, and were easy victims for professional gamblers. The miners were mostly young, footloose, and often uneducated riffraff. They were first of a polyglot of people seeking instant riches. Among them were those who had mortgaged their properties, sold their businesses, and left their families to seek gold and become rich. Women were scarce and the prostitutes were all ages, some minus teeth, some actually old hags, and most of them diseased. The death rate was high from disease, malnutrition, and lack of suitable shelter. Robbery and murder were almost daily occurrences.

People from all walks of life rushed to each new strike. Prostitutes from France, South America, and all over the world gathered at the larger strikes. Gamblers flocked in to shear the inept miners.

Amos remarked, "When people hit it rich there isn't much to buy, so they poop it off on the mattress or sitting in a chair at the tables."

Greg mentioned the deplorable condition of the prostitutes and added, "If Harry was a jenny, we would be able to go ranching in a year."

Amos chuckled, "You're right. Let's get the hell out of here."

"That suits me just fine. You were right about the boots. The horses are too much trouble to find feed and care for."

They put the word out that they had two saddle horses for sale, and soon sold them for five hundred dollars each to two lucky miners.

For the following six years, they tramped the rough, rocky, and often steep hills and mountains prospecting and mining along streams in the four hundred thousand square miles of the Sierra Nevadas. They did find some gold, but not enough to make much over expenses. They had added little more than three thousand dollars to their bank accounts.

Flooding from fall rains had stopped activity at their latest claim at Weaverville. It had not been a good claim as after one hard day they had averaged only about two and a half ounces of gold, worth twenty-six dollars and seven cents at the San Francisco mint. They were eating supper near the small stove and Harry was under a pine tree with a waterproof blanket. The silent meal reflected their discouragement.

Amos said, "What do you think?"

"I actually think, damn it, that we are getting nowhere and we and Harry are not getting any younger," Greg answered. "Let's try one more time and if we don't hit it, we settle on a ranch in Idaho. Now just where to try once more? I've been thinking about Claude Jones saying there is fine gold anywhere in the sands on Snake River. We could go up Snake River and check some streams on our way. That would kill two birds with one stone."

"What are we going to do about Harry?"

"Harry is going with us, even if I have to walk the whole way. He's the only other friend I've got."

"The easiest way would be to take a boat to Portland, then go to Walla Walla." They packed Harry with their belongings and walked with him to Sacramento.

Thousands of people were going to Portland, the gateway to the mountain ranges of the Northwest where strike after strike of gold had been found. For nearly two weeks they checked the shipping and the waterfront without finding a captain who would take Harry at any price. One morning they were having breakfast in a dingy restaurant near the wharf. Greg commented on the red-striped tablecloth with its scars from many meals.

"From the looks of this place we would be lucky not to get the crud. We should have eaten uptown." He was right, as the eggs were old and runny, the fried potatoes greasy, and the bacon was just slabs of fat.

Amos started to reply, but put his finger to his lips and pointed to two men at a nearby table. He had heard the words "cattle" and "Portland." They listened to the two men talking about taking a shipment of cattle and horses to Portland. They introduced themselves and the men were friendly. Due to the large influx of people to Portland, meat and horses were in short supply. The two men, Arnie and Ralph, had signed on to feed the stock and help clean up after them. The ship would leave Sacramento in a couple of days. After obtaining the name of the boat, the captain, and the company, Amos and Greg hurried to the dock to arrange for their passage as well as Harry's.

Fortunately, unprecedented calm weather prevailed for the four-day trip. It had been extremely uncomfortable on the crowded ship, which reeked of horse manure and urine. When they landed in Portland, Greg picked up a handful of dirt and said, "This feels downright wonderful!" Harry shook himself after taking a few steps, then wrinkled his nose and cavorted a little to show his relief.

Amos said, "We stink to high heaven of horse shit and piss. We need a bath and our clothes washed. Harry also needs a bath and curry."

Portland was the supply center for the Northwest, with the bulk of supplies going to Walla Walla in the Washington Territory, where they were freighted by wagon to Idaho, Oregon, and Montana mining camps and settlements. Amos and Greg, both experienced drivers, easily obtained work driving six-horse freight wagons over the very muddy, and at times almost impassable, roads to Walla Walla and back.

CHAPTER 13

NORA

Some people thought that Nora Jones was beautiful; everyone considered her very attractive. Her blue-eyed mother was of Swedish descent. Her father, Aaron, was a large, rather handsome man with blue eyes to match his blond hair. He and a partner, John Hagen, owned a small brewery which had started with two vats and gradually increased as the St. Louis population multiplied. The family was not rich but was considered well-to-do. The first twelve years of Nora's life were happy years for her and her brother. Then things changed.

Jones and Hagen had never drawn up a legal contract between them. Unknown to Jones, his partner was speculating in land and had bought a large tract, expecting it to go up in price. There was a land boom and fortunes were being made as a result of the rapidly increasing number of businesses and houses being built. The total price for the block of land was twenty-five thousand dollars. Hagen had paid ten thousand dollars down and had mortgaged the brewery for the balance of fifteen thousand due in two years. Interest was at eight percent, which was high for the time. He did not tell his partner about this transaction because he was sure that he would make a big profit, and was equally sure that Jones would not consent to the mortgage.

Almost immediately after he had completed the transaction, the economy had worsened. The panic of 1844 was at its worst by

June. The note came due July First. Hagen tried to sell the property for fifteen thousand dollars to protect the firm, but there were no takers and banks were closing or in serious financial trouble.

Aaron Jones went into shock when he learned that his lifelong friend and partner hanged himself on June twenty-fifth. He knew that his partner had been depressed and morose for a long time, but had been rebuffed when he tried to find out the cause. On July first, the sheriff, accompanied by two well-dressed men, showed him the mortgage and gave him thirty days to pay or vacate the prosperous brewery. He could not comprehend what was happening to him and his family.

No money was available and he was evicted. He took to drink, then started abusing his wife and children. Returning home drunk and late one night, he crawled in bed with Nora, slapped her when she started to scream, then raped her. She had been a steady churchgoer. Her life was shattered, with a feeling of guilt, remorse, and fear. Nora's mother had jobs doing housework and whenever her father found her alone, he would slap her into submission and attack her again. She tried to wash away the unclean feelings she had but it didn't help. She decided to run away, but feared that she would not get very far without being caught and brought back. Finally, she was able to hide away ten dollars from the small amount she made doing housework. Most of her money went to help out with food, and her father took away from her anything he knew she had. She hoped to slip away while both her parents were out and get aboard a steamboat going down river. She carefully packed a small suitcase with her few belongings. Now all she needed was the right time.

She woke at four o'clock one morning. Her mother was babysitting overnight. She checked the house, and she was alone. Her father was probably passed out in some alley. Now was her chance. As she started back to her room, her father stumbled in the door.

"Hello, darlin'. I'm glad you're up. I've been needing you. Are you going to be a good girl and let me have it nice so I won't have to hit you?"

"Where do you want to do it?"

"On the rug." He turned his back and started to unbutton his pants. She grabbed a poker from the fireplace. The long swing of her strong arms must have had a lot of force as she heard a distinct crack when it hit diagonally across the side of his head, behind the ear. There was blood coming from his nose as he fell. In a panic, she dressed hurriedly, poked her money down her bodice, and grabbed her suitcase. She forced herself to walk, not run, to the levee. All was quiet on the big stern-wheeler docked there. Tiptoeing around the ship to find a place to hide, she saw a closet. She went in and closed the door. She sat on the floor and waited, trying to sleep, but the morning's events were going around in her mind in a confusing kaleidoscope. Now she was a murderess. With relief, she felt the vibration of the boat beginning to move.

When a large, dark-skinned cook opened the closet, she saw Nora lying on the floor.

"Y'all is a stowaway. Where do you think you're goin'?"

"I want to go to New Orleans."

"Chile, you can get there but y'all is goin' to have to work mighty hard on the way."

Hard work was scrubbing dishes, pots, pans, floors, and tables, among other things. Big Flora, as the cook was called, eased up a little when she saw how hard the girl was trying to please her. Nora was given a cot and blanket.

The elegance of the fixtures in the dining salon, with its sparkling crystal and china, combined with the dress of the diners. For Nora, it was like seeing another world in which she could never live. She watched in awe throughout the voyage.

In New Orleans, Madam LeClerc was sitting in her immaculate carriage watching the passengers emerge from the Mississippi Belle. The coachman in his red coat and high hat was holding the reins of the shiny, well-groomed, matched pair of black horses. The madam was looking for recruits for her elite, fancy house. At first she took only a passing glance at the poorly dressed, strawberry blond-haired girl that walked down the gangplank toward her. Her eyes went back to the girl because of the gracefulness of her walk and the way she carried her body. The coachman helped Madam LeClerc out of the carriage and she greeted the somewhat bewildered girl, who had stopped and was looking around as if trying to decide what to do.

"Are you lost? Can I help you?"

"I'm not lost, ma'am. I need work and a place to stay. I've very little money and I don't know where to go."

"What is your name?"

"Nora Jones, ma'am." By now the madam had assessed the natural beauty of the girl.

"Perhaps I can help you. You can stay with me for a few days until you get settled." Jess, the coachman, put Nora's suitcase under the rear compartment and helped them both into the carriage, then drove them up Riverton Street to the higher ground above the river. He stopped and helped them down before a pretentious-looking mansion with a neatly clipped lawn and magnolias in bloom. A butler appeared to carry the madam's packages and Nora's suitcase into the building. The living room was tastefully furnished. Nora noticed several beautiful, well-dressed young women sitting around the dining table.

The madam said, "You are tired. I'll show you to your room and after you wash up we'll have lunch and talk."

Nora tried not to show that she was hungry and greedy, but the lunch of fried chicken, sandwiches, and salad was so good that she cleaned up everything.

Madam LeClerc observed, "You must really have been hungry. Why don't you take a nap now, and after you wake up the maid will bring in a tub for you to take a bath and change clothes. You will meet the girls and have dinner with those who do not have engagements tonight. Those who do will have dinner with their guests in their rooms. You probably are aware that we are in the business of entertaining gentlemen. We have only the highest class customers. If you would like to stay and work here, you would be welcome to do so."

Later that evening, Nora and two trainees were seated at the dining table across from the very pretty, well-groomed young women. What impressed Nora most was their conversation. They were talking about what they had read in the newspapers. There was laughter and the trainees were made to feel welcome. For women to read newspapers and discuss them struck Nora as being rather odd. Finally, it dawned on her that they were acting on orders and this was part of the training. She had read very little in newspapers as they had never taken one at home.

"How old are you, Nora?"

"Almost sixteen."

"I think you will like it here if you decide to stay."

After dinner, Nora made up her mind and told the madam that she would like to stay.

"If you work hard and study, I am sure you will be very successful. You have the looks and figure, along with your pleasing personality, to become a favorite among the men. But I think you should change your name. Is there a name that you would like to use?"

"I think 'Marianne' is pretty."

"Fine. After you have had your walk and breakfast in the morning, we will have you fitted for clothes."

"I don't have very much money, only ten dollars."

"You will pay for it monthly out of your wages."

The next morning they again rode in the carriage to the dressmaker's shop. They were greeted effusively by the owner.

"Marianne needs two complete outfits from the skin out. You know what kind of dresses I like. Since it is nearly fall, she will need dresses that complement the season."

"I have just received two bolts of cloth, one emerald green and one deep amber. They will accent the hair and her eyes." She left the room to get the fabric. Marianne noticed that the front door was closed and locked, apparently to prevent other customers from entering the shop.

The dressmaker returned with the bolts of cloth, unrolled a length and held them in front of Marianne while Madam stood back and evaluated. She had them interchanged several times. Finally, she said, "Your taste is very good. The fabrics are excellent. We will take one of each."

In the curtained booth Marianne tried on lingerie. The dressmaker appeared with a corset.

Madame LeClerc said, "She doesn't need a corset with her figure. Most women have to wear a corset to get that shape. Men don't like corsets, they want to feel what is underneath."

"She might put on weight."

"She is sixteen and has most of her growth. She will eat sensibly and be active. She should be able to keep that figure for years. It's up to her."

Marianne was almost ready to drop from exhaustion while the seamstress measured and pinned. Finally, she brought out shoes for Marianne to try.

"These are the largest size I have."

"That is not important. Men never look at feet on a woman. They are interested in things higher up." Luckily, the shoes were big enough.

Madam was a martinet when it came to exercise. No matter how busy they had been the night before, the girls had to take their mile-long walk after their morning cup of coffee. Then, they had breakfast, and classes began after a short morning break, lasting until lunch. After lunch, classes resumed. Sometimes Madam LeClerc conducted the classes, other times the more experienced women gave the lectures. They were reminded that they were actresses. They must act like ladies at all times, and keep themselves informed on current events in order to carry on intelligent conversation with their clients. They must be polite, entertaining, vivacious, and complimentary.

"Men come here to relax, forget their problems, and have their egos boosted. Most of them are married, in their late thirties to seventies. You will often hear information that is very confidential, and you are never to repeat it to anyone. When they leave, they want to feel satisfied, relaxed, and pleased with their sexual prowess. You have to pretend that they have given you pleasure, even though you have found them distasteful."

Instruction in bedroom technique, with demonstration by the older women, followed. Then each trainee had to do her graduate demonstration. Marianne was very nervous until she remembered that she was an actress. She had always liked play acting. Madam was pleased with her performance and complimented Marianne for the progress she was making.

Her first real customer was a forty-year-old man named Clarence, who was president of one of the leading banks in New Orleans. He told her that he had been a bank clerk in his father-in-law's bank. The banker offered to promote him if he would marry his daughter. She was a thirty-year-old spinster, plain, big, awkward, and badly spoiled. She had never had a suitor, and when the personable bank clerk started to call and take her to dinner and shows, she really worked at trying to please him. He was weighing the idea of stopping the courtship when her father suffered a slight heart attack. Cecelia was his only heir, as her mother had died a few years before. If he married her he would become president of the bank. The temptation was too great and he proposed. There was no hesitation on her part in saying yes. She grabbed him and smothered him with kisses. He thought it would not be so bad if she responded like that in the bedroom. During the two-week honeymoon, he had a rude awakening. She was frigid. She was a whiner, finding fault with everything. She was pregnant in a month and nauseated every morning. Shortly after their daughter, Amy, was born, Cecelia's father had a stroke and died.

Clarence worked long hours to escape the carping company of his wife, and the bank prospered. In the business world, he was highly respected and was invited to join a prestigious club. He was playing in the weekly poker game and remarked that his wife was out of town for a month and he could stay later than usual. One of his friends said, "You really should take the opportunity to kick up your heels. Let us fix you up for the time of your life. You need to get your ashes hauled. We will get you the green card for Madam LeClerc's. Those girls will give you a new outlook on life."

At the next poker session they gave him his card and told him to be at Madam's at six o'clock Saturday night for dinner and entertainment.

He was hesitant and uncertain when he rang the doorbell. Madam's cordial greeting put him at ease. She took him to Marianne's room and introduced him. Marianne smiled and greeted him warmly. He said, "This is the first time I have done anything like this."

"It is the first time for me, so we are even. Let me pour you a drink before dinner. Do you like bourbon?" The drink relaxed him and she was able to get him to talk freely.

He was active in bed. Keeping in mind that she was only acting, Marianne was not bothered by what she was doing. He left discretely through the back entrance, feeling well-pleased with himself, and looking forward to the appointment that he had made for the following Saturday evening.

CHAPTER 14

LAWRENCE

Twenty-year-old Lawrence Breckenridge slowly paced the deck of the steamboat. He was thinking about how to greet his father and what to say to him. He knew that he could never fool him. The large, profitable rice plantation had no appeal for him. He was opposed to slavery. There was no way he could cover up his expulsion from Yale, where he had been studying finance because his father had insisted on it. It would be a relief to end the long journey from New Haven to St. Louis by train and then steamboat to New Orleans. Thinking of the two thousand dollars poker winnings he kept in the money belt under his shirt gave him satisfaction. He had found that he could hold his own against the immaculately dressed river boat gamblers.

He was surprised when he stepped off the gangplank and a soft, familiar voice said, "This way, Mistah Lawrence. You is a sight for sore eyes."

"Jeremy, it is surely good to see you. I've missed you. How did you know I was coming?"

"I didn't know. It's jest the mastah had me meeting the boats for a week."

His mother greeted him at home with a hug and tears.

"Lawrence, do you realize that you have been gone for nearly a year? You are filthy. Take a bath and get ready for dinner. Your father is very upset and cannot understand why you have been expelled from college."

When his father returned from the field, they shook hands and he was greeted warmly. The conversation at the dinner table was light, mostly about his journey. They laughed about how he had almost missed the train when he had gotten off to get something to eat. He was able to grasp the handrail on the last car and pull himself aboard, much to the delight of the passengers.

After dinner, his father motioned him into the study. There was little resemblance between them. He was two inches taller than his father's five feet ten inches, and slightly lighter in build.

"Lawrence, you have always been a good son, never in any serious trouble like some young men get into from gambling and drinking. You have never been challenged to a duel by a jealous husband. We have been proud of you."

"Father, they kicked me out because I broke the rules. I ran a gambling game in my room. The only excuse I have, and it is not a good one, is that I was bored with my classes and wanted to get started in the business world."

"What do you want to do? You have never shown any interest in the plantation."

"I would like to be in a brokerage firm."

"That can be arranged. Brannan and Forbes are both good friends of mine. I am sure that they will give you a try."

Lawrence had a talent for forecasting what certain stocks would do, and soon he established rapport with his clients about buying and selling in the futures market. He worked hard and studied the newspapers. Personal contacts with other people in the stock market became his most accurate sources of information. Because his position as a stockbroker was one of respectability he became a member of one of the most elite clubs in New Orleans. He was also a member of the very prestigious Masons. Periodically, he would take a trip by steamboat to St. Louis and back. His quiet and unobtrusive manner enabled him to get businessmen and planters to discuss their crops and businesses. Also, he could play poker with the passengers, often winning large amounts without hurting friendships or being accused of being a card shark, which he was. Many a river boat gambler found himself taking a heavy loss while playing with a seemingly happy-go-lucky, naive young man. His grandfather had done an excellent job tutoring him in card playing while he was growing up.

Four years after he returned home, he owned a moderate-sized, well-kept home in a respectable neighborhood, with a cook and housekeeper, Claudia, who really looked after him in the bossy manner that he liked. Jeb, the coachman, looked after the grounds and drove the team of bays. He had a sizeable amount deposited in banks and well secured mortgages. As a very eligible bachelor, he was sought after by the debutantes and their anxious mothers. He considered the balls a waste of time and only attended when family obligations required his presence. For feminine company, he preferred older widows, who were in abundance.

Lawrence Breckenridge was troubled when he discussed the state of the government with friends from Atlanta. Emotions were mixed. He argued that there was no way the South would be successful leaving the Union, as it lacked industry and depended on agricultural products for its prosperity.

When asked if he was loyal to the South, his reply was, "First, I am a Southerner, but I am also loyal to the United States of America. How can the South finance such a war? It won't be over in a few weeks or months."

"It's supposed to be a secret, but the plans to print the South's own currency are already underway," his friends countered.

He learned that groups of men were meeting, drilling, and calling themselves "Companies".

Someone said, "Those hotheads from South Carolina will probably start it and get everybody involved." It occurred to Lawrence that he would be expected to fight for the South. The brokerage business would come to a complete stop as there would be no communication with New York.

CHAPTER 15

OROFINO

Walla Walla, founded by the missionary Marcus Whitman, was a central supply point for a very large area covering southeast Washington, northeast Oregon, and much of western and southern Idaho. Missionaries Henry and Eliza Spalding established a school near the Clearwater River in 1836, where Eliza taught the Indians English and religion. The Nez Perce Indians were friendly, gentle people, a contented tribe with rich grassland for stock and plentiful game. The Snake and Clearwater Rivers were teeming with salmon and sturgeon which they caught and smoked. They closely guarded their much sought-after spotted-rumped Appaloosa war horses. In 1847, after they had suffered a measles epidemic brought on by an infected emigrant, they had killed both Dr. Whitman and his wife, along with fourteen other whites at the mission near Walla Walla. It was the custom of the Nez Perce to kill the medicine man if he could not cure the sick.

It was the winter of 1859–60 when Amos and Greg began to get jobs as area freight wagon drivers from Portland to Walla Walla, Washington. The route was long and rough and it took a rugged man with a strong constitution to handle the job. They would take the job only if both could go at the same time and travel together. After two round trips that consumed almost two months, they decided to spend the rest of the winter in Lewiston,

Idaho, because it had almost no rainfall or snow. Its elevation of around six hundred feet and the shelter of the Snake River canyon made it a nice place to winter.

Amos and Greg got room and board at a farm close to Lewiston. The area was being settled by farmers who even had some fruit trees producing in the mild climate. After purchasing two Appaloosa geldings, they hunted deer and elk, which they sold, and they scouted the area and waited for spring to open the passes.

They were hunting along the Clearwater River a few miles above where it enters the Snake. They had just finished dressing out a large, fat, dry doe and were standing by a gravel bar at the edge of the stream, washing the blood from their hands.

Greg said, "Amos," and pointed at the sand in his hand.

Amos said, "Gold!"

"It is so fine, it had to come from a considerable distance upstream. Let's go up and find it. We'll have to hurry because when spring comes there will be miners all over the place."

Hunting was a good cover. As their trips lengthened, they started to camp out overnight, returning with game and to renew their supplies. As they worked upstream, the flashes of gold became more frequent, but were not really numerous. About forty miles from Lewiston, the canyon widened and a short stream came out of the canyon wall into a flat meadow and entered the Clearwater three hundred feet below. When they came up to the stream, they stopped and nodded at each other in perfect understanding.

"Amos, this is almost a duplicate of the Emerson Gill diggings."

"It sure looks like it. The question is, is there anything under that dirt?"

"Probably there is gravel about four feet down in the creek. I'll get the shovel, you get the pan ready."

Greg dug down deep to get a shovel full of dirt and gravel. After picking out the large pieces of rock, he dumped the dirt and coarse sand into the pan. Amos expertly tilted the pan into the water and started the circular motion that caused the sand to be washed away by the swirl. In a short time, he held the pan out for

Greg to see. There was still sand left, sprinkled with bright flakes and some small irregular nuggets about an eighth of an inch across. They took pannings at intervals in the two hundred fifty foot long stream with the same results. This stream entered a larger stream which ran to the Clearwater River half a mile below. After checking gravel in the larger stream, which showed similar promise, they decided to file a claim on the original find. They would not be crowded, and by putting a dam where the water came out of the canyon wall, they could file on the forty-inch stream and not have to worry about water disputes with neighbors.

The partners talked long into the night. Greg remarked, "We want to be well set up and present when the hordes arrive. From the looks of the numerous gulches and streams in the area, it will be a big strike."

"Right. There will be a town of good size here in a few weeks. We want people to come because they will bring supplies and shelter we can use. Also, we won't have to rustle our grub, we'll have mail deliveries and the Wells Fargo stage will keep us in touch with the rest of the world. We can do a lot about determining what kind of camp or town this place is going to be."

"You are always looking ahead and figuring things out. How can we do that?"

"Easy. We can organize the committee ahead of time. Right now we have to get supplies to last at least a month and we have to do it quietly."

In a week they had made their trips for supplies that they stored in a cut-bank lean-to. Apparently, their activity had aroused no suspicion.

"There is plenty of cedar that we can easily split to make a sluice box," Greg observed.

"There will be a sawmill here in a month. We can shovel off the dirt, build a dam, and dig the ditch to our sluice box. We can start work on a log cabin which we will furnish and line with lumber after we get the sawmill. Then we will build the sluice box."

Spring was unusually late, and the miners wintering in Lewiston had not ventured out. The two men had packed Harry, and Greg decided to go for their diggings. Amos wanted to stay to organize a committee. He said, "There is a fellow named George Grimes in Orofino who seems to be an honest man and a leader, and there are a dozen or so experienced California miners who could form a respectable committee to control things until town officials can be established."

He met with Grimes and told him that if he would cooperate and keep confidential what was told him, Amos would let Grimes in on a very promising gold find.

"Mr. Grimes, we need to have the miners' committee set up before the gold rush starts. You swear into secrecy nine reliable men, and they, Greg McKenna, and I will make twelve."

"Jordan, that's a good idea. Where is the find?"

"The members will have to be sworn to secrecy. In fact, they will not be told until they are packed, saddled, and well on the way to the find. They will be travelling about sixty miles."

"I know you and McKenna have a right good reputation, but I need a little more convincin'."

Amos pulled a buckskin poke from his pocket. Grimes opened it and gently poured some of the contents into the palm of his hand. When he saw the size of the nuggets, he said, "I believe you got a deal. What is the formation?"

"That is puzzling me. There is no igneous rock or granite formation in the area that has gold in it. It had to be transported by a glacier, maybe all the way from Canada. It probably will be rich while it lasts—maybe not more than two to five years."

The plan worked out perfectly. The Grimes party arrived at the site and filed claims on May 1, 1861. They put out their notices of filing on each side, covering the length of the stream, its outlet, and part of the hill above. Everything was done according to California filing laws.

In three weeks there was a town, saloons, blacksmith shop, stores, lawyers, camp followers, and gamblers. The committee kept things under control and was quick to banish wrongdoers.

Amos was sitting in a high stakes poker game that was always in session on Saturday night. Greg sat out as they never played in the same game to avoid getting accused of playing partners. Arnie Youngstrom was a new arrival in the camp. In two weeks, the immaculately dressed gambler in his fancy coat and vest had really cleaned up and appeared to be extremely lucky. Amos was slightly ahead and was sitting out the hand. Youngstrom was betting heavily before the draw with two miners. After the draw, the betting continued until both of the miners had all of their chips in the pot, which was now over two thousand dollars. Youngstrom, the dealer, started to rake in the pot with a winning hand of a full house—three aces and two eights.

Amos put his hands on the chips and said, "Just a minute."

"Take your hands off my chips. I won the pot fair and square."

"Let the pot stay until we count cards."

"Stranger, you are accusing me of cheating." He stood up and reached for his gun. Greg, having moved over behind him, landed a big-fisted right behind his ear, knocking him down. The derringer went flying out of his hand. Greg put his foot on the gun and pointed to the ace and king that had fallen out of Youngstrom's sleeve.

There were six of the committee present and they held court. The crowd wanted to hang him, but the committee prevented that. They stripped him of his clothes down to his underwear, shoes, and socks. His money belt was distributed back to the other five players. However, at Greg's suggestion, they reserved one thousand dollars to build a schoolhouse for families with children. The gambler was given thirty minutes to leave town or be tarred and feathered.

"Amos," Greg asked, "what made you think he was crooked?"

"There were several things. He won the big pots on his deal. You just can't be that lucky that often. And he was one of the smoothest dealers I have ever seen. I learned about card sharks when I was in college."

Greg knew that Amos seemed well-educated, but he had never mentioned college before. He knew someday Amos would tell him his story, but not until he was good and ready.

CHAPTER 16

LEAVING FOR FORT BOISE

The years 1860 and 1861 passed quickly. The returns from the claim were profitable but not really great. It was late in May and they had just deposited four thousand dollars each in the Wells Fargo Bank. They had mined considerably more than that, but prices were very high. Bacon sold for five dollars a pound, flour sometimes fifty dollars a sack, due to the boom. Because they were only a half-mile from town, they often ate at the Sisters Cafe, owned by two middle-aged sisters who were plump, as Greg called them, and buxom by Amos' language. Although they were nearly twice as old as Amos and Greg, they became their favorites. Their friendship with Audrey and Judy developed rapidly. Both parties knew that it would be only friendship and could end at any time.

Amos summarized, "Both parties are fortunate. They are free from disease and lonely at times, just as we are."

After a Saturday night with Audrey, Amos was sitting at a table at the cafe waiting for his breakfast to be served. Greg walked in and sat down beside him. Judy squealed when she saw him, walked over and gave him a big kiss in front of the customers.

"What would you like for breakfast? How about ham and eggs and hot cakes?"

"That would be great." After the women returned to the kitchen, Greg asked, "Did you have a good night?"

"Very satisfying."

"Amos, they are going to miss us and we'll miss them. They are so willing and handy. Of course, we have paid about triple for meals, but it has been worth it. What would you think about selling the claim? I think we can get two thousand dollars for it. There is still gold left in it but it would take a lot of time to get it out. I'd like to get the hell out of here and go to Boise Valley."

Amos reached over to shake his hand and said, "Good deal. When do we leave?"

Three days later, after spending two nights with the sisters, who gave them a tearful farewell, they left riding the two Appaloosa geldings they had purchased from the Nez Perce Indians. Harry, who matched Amos' six feet in height, seemed to get into the spirit of things with his long, effortless strides. It was early in June so they decided they would not need a tent, a tarp would be sufficient, and no mining tools. But they relented and took the pan to mix bread in.

The weather was ideal for travelling and they were making about twenty-five miles a day. The winding back-and-forth descent of the two thousand feet at Whitebird Hill, which followed game and Indian trails, was tiring. They found a suitable camping spot at the mouth of a small stream, Whitebird Creek, that emptied into the Salmon River. They circled the area as a precaution against being robbed. They took a big drink of whiskey before going to bed. Harry and the Appaloosa geldings were hobbled in a corner of the two streams, and they made their beds between. Anyone trying to steal the animals would have to go past them.

Amos awoke about five o'clock and could see no horses. He yelled at Greg.

"What's the matter?"

"We are afoot. Someone has stolen the horses, but didn't touch anything else." While looking for signs and tracks, Greg found a cut hobble.

"Indians did it. These horses were raised by Indians and felt comfortable with them. They just led the horses across the stream. I guess they think Appaloosas are theirs anyhow, and nobody else should have them. Lord only knows where they are now."

Amos was furious. "Damn it to hell. Seems like something

always goes wrong, no matter how careful we are. Well, we have done a lot of walking before and we can do it again. It will be about ten days to Fort Boise."

"At least we have Harry and our gear. He is such a smart mule. Sometimes I think he is smarter than we are."

"Greg, you are right about that."

CHAPTER 17

MARIANNE

Lawrence Breckenridge was walking along Bourbon Street in New Orleans on his way to the bank when he noticed a lady in a summery yellow dress walking ahead of him. He became aware of how gracefully she walked, with a smooth but not exaggerated swinging of her hips. He could see the sun shining on her beautiful hair, and thought that a person with such a graceful walk and pretty hair must have a face to match, and he wanted to see it. He followed her into a stationery store. When she had made her purchase and turned to leave, they were face to face. He was surprised when she acknowledged the tip of his hat with a radiant smile. To make his entry into the shop look legitimate, he purchased some writing paper. During a lull in the afternoon he found himself thinking about the girl, wondering who she was and whether they would meet again.

Meanwhile, Marianne said to her close friend, "Jenny, I saw the most interesting man this afternoon."

"Honey, he is probably married, has kids, and a mistress."

"Anyway, I wish I could see him again."

"Marianne, you can dream and it won't cost you anything."

What neither of them knew was that they lived on opposite sides of the large municipal park. Both were early risers. Marianne liked to get her daily mile walk early in the morning.

Larry, as most of his friends called him, also enjoyed a daily walk in the park. Marianne and Lawrence passed each other on a Sunday morning. Each turned and looked back. They waved at each other and trotted on.

"Jenny, I got to see him again; he is gorgeous! It would be wonderful to have a man like that all your own and have a home and children."

"Marianne, you are dreaming again."

At the weekly Saturday night poker game, Larry was asked, "I haven't seen you with Jennifer lately. Have you split?"

"She met a widower on her last trip and married him. I am temporarily unattached. But I saw a beautiful girl recently and I'm going to try to find her."

"I have an appointment at Madam LeClerc's Wednesday evening for dinner and whatever. Why don't you join me?"

"Sounds like a good idea. But I don't have a green card."

"I'll take care of that."

"All right. I'll pick up the check." Larry was feeling a little guilty about winning a sizeable sum from his friend.

"We should be there at six o'clock. Take a bath just before you go or Madam will make you take one there."

Larry had had a few experiences in brothels while attending Yale. He was surprised at the elegance of furnishings and the courtesy that he received. Madam LeClerc seemed to be impressed with him. She said, "You are a new customer and I have someone special for you. Follow me and I will introduce you to her."

Larry was speechless at the introduction and late in saying, "It is my pleasure to meet you." I have found her, he thought, in a brothel. He looked at her and couldn't help smiling when she said, "You!" Her smile was radiant as she took his hand in a firm, warm fashion.

"Would you like a drink, Mr. Breckenridge?"

"Yes. Bourbon would be fine."

She poured one for herself, too. Usually she sipped on a small glass of wine.

He said, "We have seen each other before and I have wanted to meet you."

During dinner they talked about each other's past and what

they liked. He was surprised at how intelligent she was, and how he could be talking to a prostitute as if she were a well-bred lady. She had a hard time remembering that she was supposed to be acting, and felt that for the first time she would enjoy having a man in bed with her. He may never come back, she thought, but I will give him a night that he will never forget. She was enveloped with desire. He was experiencing the same. He awakened first in the morning and looked at the beautiful person snuggled up against him, and knew for the first time he was in love. What should he you do about it?

She woke up smiling and gave him a hug and kiss. He said, "Good morning, darling."

"You are the most wonderful man. I know it is not ladylike to ask, but will I see you again?"

"You surely will. Next Wednesday night, if you are available."

"I will be available." Almost instantly, they were making love again, each trying to please the other.

She and Jenny took their morning walk together. She could hardly wait to tell Jenny that she had met her dream man last night and he was unbelievably wonderful, and he was going to see her again next Wednesday. Jenny felt great sorrow for the heartache and disappointment that Marianne would be sure to experience.

Marianne discovered, early in her years at Madame LeClerc's, that she had a talent for music. In a short time she was able to play by ear almost any tune that she had heard. She often entertained by playing the piano and singing in her deep contralto voice. That morning she really made the parlor ring with joyous playing and song. She kept it up much longer than usual. It did not go unnoticed by the madam.

Her preparation for Wednesday evening started with trotting the whole mile because it put such nice color in her cheeks. She took a nap after lunch before beginning the most careful preparation for the evening. She finished her grooming half an hour before the appointed time. It seemed that it took forever for the thirty minutes to pass. She stood listening, and after hearing the chimes at the door and Madam saying, "Hello, Mr. Breckenridge," she sat down on the sofa. She tried not to hurry as she answered the door.

"I am glad to see you again, Marianne."

"I'm glad that you called again." She walked toward him, holding out her hand. To her surprise and delight, the handshake turned into her being held tightly by two strong arms and then kissed.

When they finally parted, he gasped, "I think we both should have a drink."

They ended up sitting side by side, holding hands. She was aware that her love for him could only be temporary, and his infatuation for her was probably only passion and in no way could be a lasting relationship. For any man who was well accepted by society to keep company with a prostitute would be quite impossible.

Their lovemaking was even more intense than the first meeting. They had difficulty parting in the morning. Larry said, "I have to go to St. Louis on business, and will be gone for about three weeks. I will contact you the minute I get back. We can't go on like this. By that time I will have some plans for us in regard to the future."

During the three weeks that Larry was gone, Marianne went over and over his words, wondering what they meant. She confided in Jenny.

"He can't marry you and live here. Society would not accept you. Usually a man puts his mistress up in a nice house and supports her until he gets tired of her or finds a younger woman, but he never marries her."

"What if we moved to another part of the country?"

"Marianne, you are just dreaming. He isn't going to do that and leave everything behind just because he finds you special in bed. Honey, you just can't win."

"It doesn't hurt to dream of what might be. It's up to Larry. Whatever he wants me to do, I will do it just to be near him."

Larry had been busy at St. Louis during the three-week stay. A brokerage firm had agreed to hire him on a commission basis, with an option based on his performance during the next year. He made a down payment on a house in the fashionable part of the city.

Marianne didn't have to wait long before finding out if Larry was serious.

Lawrence and Marianne Breckinridge were married quietly by a justice of the peace at the courthouse in St. Louis. They were a very happy couple and both became active in civic affairs in the rapidly growing city.

Larry was constantly surprised at how well-read and intelligent his bride was. Marianne hoped she would never awaken from the beautiful dream.

They were furious and terribly disappointed when he sent a draft to transfer his account from the bank in New Orleans. The bank sent the money by ship to England and from there back to St. Louis as it was the only way mail could get around the Union blockade during the war between the states. All twelve thousand dollars was in Confederate money and worthless in the North. After paying for the house, Marianne had nearly three thousand dollars of her savings, which brought their total cash to about five thousand dollars. Marianne was a month pregnant and both were thrilled at the prospect of having a child.

Larry had to register for the draft, but it appeared that he would not have to go for at least a year. Two months later, due to heavy losses by the Union army, his draft number was stepped up to where he would have to report to the U.S. Army in a month to six weeks. When the notice came, they discussed it. She did not want him to go, and he did not want to fight against his brother and other relatives in the South. They decided to go to San Francisco.

They planned to go by train to the end of the rail line that was pushing west, take the stage from there to Portland, and take a steamer to San Francisco. The difficulty was that federal officers were at the depot to check the identification of all rail passengers because of the large number of men leaving for the West to avoid the draft.

Marianne boarded the train at St. Louis with two suitcases and a small trunk full of necessities. She stashed part of their money in a special corset. Larry took the rest in his money belt and rode thirty miles on horseback to the next town and boarded the train there. When he arrived at the next town, he stabled his horse and went to a restaurant for supper. He noticed two men in uniform sitting at a nearby table. According to their conversation, they were pleased that they had not caught any draft evaders because they would have had to take them to St. Louis where they would have immediately been inducted into the Army. The next day Larry rode another thirty miles to a place where there was a water tank and coal chute for the locomotives. There were no Union soldiers around. He hoped the train would stop for either water or coal.

A quarter of a mile away was a white farm house and a red barn. It entered his mind that he might get something to eat and get rid of his horse.

The farmer and his wife were glad to have company, as the area was sparsely settled. They told him the five o'clock passenger train always stopped for water and coal. He said, "I would like to leave my horse and I will pay for his keep. You can use him, and if I am not back within a month, you may have him and the saddle."

The train approached so fast that he was afraid it was not going to stop, but the engineer put on the squeaky brakes and the cars noisily bumped into each other. The conductor had left the door open and the steps down to the vestibule on one of the cars. A group of men got out to smoke and stretch their legs. Larry joined them, unnoticed, and entered the car when they did. The conductor took his cash and punched his ticket. Twelve hours later Marianne met him at the depot in Independence.

"I was so worried about you. I have been meeting every train for three days. I was so afraid the federals got you, or something else bad happened."

"I was worried about you, too. It is wonderful to be together again." The railroad was pushing westward and they were only a hundred miles from the end of construction.

"Larry, I checked, and they are not only checking the trains, but the stages as well."

They bought two tickets for Salt Lake, seven hundred miles away, and two cushions to sit on. Independence was a meal and rest stop, where teams were changed for fresh horses. Larry found the stage driver and offered him twenty dollars if he would pick him up two miles down the road. The driver winked and they shook hands. Larry started walking briskly toward the west. An hour later the stage stopped and he climbed aboard and sat by Marianne, She kissed him in front of strangers, and handed him a cushion.

"You are going to need it," she said.

When they arrived in Salt Lake and were unpacked in a boarding house, Marianne rested in bed. "We will have to stay here a few days," she said. "I have been bleeding for the last two days. We need to get a doctor."

"Honey, you were so brave on that long stage ride. I'll go and find a doctor at once."

After examining her, the doctor was not optimistic. He told her to stay in bed, but in all probability she would miscarry, and she did. Infection set in, but Larry nursed her back to health. The doctor said it was doubtful she could have children ever.

Larry had been hearing about gold strikes in the Boise Basin in Idaho, and decided that money could be made there. He said, "What do you think about going to Idaho before we go to California?"

"I will be happy to go anywhere you want to go." As soon as Marianne felt strong enough, they boarded the stage for Fort Boise.

CHAPTER 18

ROBBERY

Late in July of 1862, Greg and Amos were in the Salmon River canyon in Idaho. The three thousand dollars they had taken from their Orofino placer claim was stored in one hundred dollar bills in their money belts.

During the years they had been prospecting, they had never hit it big. They decided this would be the last year they would prospect. If they didn't find much, they would file on land that could be irrigated somewhere in the Pahsimeroi or Lemhi Valleys which Claude Jones had described to them.

They remembered Claude's words: "When we went over the Lowman Pass and down into the basin of the Boise River, we were met by a mounted band of Bannock Indians and they actually drove us down near Boise and across Snake River. When I was fillin' a canteen from a small clear creek, I picked up a handful of sand and gravel and there were several small flakes of gold in it."

They had heard of the rich strike at Fabulous Florence, but knew from past experience that going there would be chasing a rainbow. They were carrying packs of about forty pounds each. The rest of their equipment was loaded on the ever-faithful Harry. The stop that evening was in a grove of larch and fir trees, with a small stream of water that entered the Salmon River a few hundred feet to the west. Their camp was well hidden from the trail.

They had been walking at least twenty miles a day for seven days.

"Amos, let's stay here a day. Harry needs rest and the feed is really good."

"Harry isn't the only one that needs rest. We'll wash our clothes and clean up, then rest tomorrow."

Before going to bed that night, they encircled the area, each heading in a different direction and meeting. As they walked back to camp, they talked about how well-travelled the trail was, and of the danger of being held up and robbed.

Greg said, "Maybe we should have let the Wells Fargo stage take most of our stake to the bank. I have a feeling something is going to happen."

They gave Harry a good rubdown and fed him a lump of brown sugar on a biscuit. They moved their gear from the open space to thick foliage. When they bedded down, they were apart but within calling. The murmur of the small stream and the sound of rapids in the river lulled them to sleep.

As usual, they awakened at sunup. After a leisurely breakfast, they lingered over a second cup of coffee.

"I'm glad Harry quit letting out his horrible braying each morning. Why he stopped that when we left the other mules, I'll never know."

"Amos, I know how that mule thinks. He did it to show the other mules who was the he-man."

They spent a very relaxing day. They found another clearing deeper in the trees and moved Harry there for a fresh supply of feed. They were so comfortable, their guard dropped. About six o'clock they were enjoying a meal of fool hens that they had been able to knock out of a tree with rocks. By throwing at the bottom bird in the tree, it didn't flush the ones above.

A voice said, "Put your hands up." Another voice behind them said, "Stand up." They obeyed. Two robbers took their bootlaces and tied their hands behind them and their feet together. They searched them and found their money belts. The short, heavy-set robber had a scar from his ear to his mouth.

"Boys, look what we found. We'll have a time in Portland and Frisco," said Scarface. The two backpacks were near the fire, and apparently the robbers thought that was the extent of their possessions.

Amos winked at Greg and said, "You boys have made a really good haul. When we took it off the other fellows we thought the same as you. How would you like a drink of whiskey? If you take what we've got and leave us tied, someone will find us in a day or two. If you agree to that, I'll tell you where the whiskey is."

The tall, narrow-faced robber with small eyes said, "We'll find the whiskey ourselves and do as we damn well please. It probably is in the creek to cool." They looked in the creek and gave up.

Amos addressed the taller man, who seemed to be the leader.

"I am sure you are a man of your word, and when you give it, you will keep it." The partners were planning to have a nightcap before they retired, and had put the whiskey bottle under a cut bank out of sight.

"Feller, you are right," said the lead robber. "We Higgins always keeps our word, and we'll leave you tied up if you tell us where the whiskey is. But if you don't have any, your carcasses will be floating in Snake River in a few days."

Greg directed him to the bank of the creek and told him to reach back under the bank. When he brought out the gallon jug, he said gleefully, "It's plumb full!" They each took a long drink and finished off the grouse and biscuits. They left with the pistols and rifles, as well as the slabs of bacon and a small sack of flour. They decided not to take the boots because they were "too damned big." Amos had told them that he and Greg walked thirty miles that day and were pooped out.

After the robbers left, Amos said, "They are not going to get away with this. Sit up and turn your back to me. Maybe I can untie your laces. It won't be easy."

They had double knotted the tough rawhide laces and it seemed that he could make no progress. After an hour, he said, "Rest on your side a bit. My hands are cramping and I have almost no feeling in them. I have long eyeteeth and I'm going to try to gnaw them in two."

Sure enough, in half an hour Amos had weakened the rawhide enough that he was able to break it. Hurriedly Greg untied his feet and then untied Amos. It took a while to get the kinks out of their arms and legs. They still had Harry and his pack, but no gun or knife.

Greg asked, "What do we do now?"

"We go after them and get our money back. Thank goodness we are rested and fresh. It is three hours until dark and they don't dare travel at night as it's the dark of the moon. Their horses will be tired. About fifteen miles is all they will travel. They will also be drunk as skunks. Actually, they have only two hours start on us. If we alternately walk, trot, and run, we can go about as fast as they do."

"Amos, I'll bet you're right. We can put on our moccasins to move quietly and get a couple of big sticks for clubs."

It was a cool evening and the trail downhill was easy to follow. During a short rest stop, Greg said, "If I were them, I would camp at the spring we saw coming down the hill about twelve miles ahead."

It was dark after they had been travelling about two hours. Often they stopped and sniffed for smoke. Each had found a stout stick. They carefully checked out each likely place to camp in the canyon. Fortunately, the wide spots were few and far between. They actually heard voices and singing. The drunken robbers were celebrating. They carefully slipped close to the camp. They could see the robbers sitting at the fire, which reflected on the nearly empty whiskey jug.

Scarface said, "I think we should have cut their throats and got rid of them."

"Naw, we've come fifteen miles and they were all pooped out," said the tall leader. "They couldn't get loose. We'll keep watch. I'll take the first turn. Let's kill the jug and get some sleep and get the hell out of here." Scarface rolled up in his blanket and was soon snoring. His partner staggered around a bit, then sat with his back to a tree, facing the fire, while he finished off the jug of whiskey. His gun was in his lap with his hands holding it. Cautioning Greg for silence, Amos crept toward him as he dozed. He did not dare grab the gun, so he hit the robber over the head with his heavy club, and he slumped over with only a slight grunt. Amos took his rifle and they stepped over and took the rifles that were beside the sleeping Scarface. When he awoke to stare at the cocked rifles pointed at him, he swore drunkenly. He was ordered to lie face down and was securely trussed. Greg and Amos found their money belts.

"Mine is heavier," Greg said. In addition to getting their own money back, they had an extra eleven hundred dollars.

"This is the best claim we have found for a while!"

They put each man against a small tree and tied their hands behind and around the tree, with legs tied out in front of them. Scarface did a lot of swearing, but the other was quiet because he was still groggy. Amos and Greg gathered up the guns and knives, took the bedding, and went a quarter of a mile into the woods, where they went to sleep, covered by the robbers' blankets.

They arose at daybreak and slipped back to the camp. Their prisoners were cramped and in pain, begging to be cut loose and making many promises. They cut them loose and let them drink one at a time.

Amos told them, "You can walk down the road and carry what you want of your outfit. Because you didn't kill us, we are letting you live. We will leave your blankets and knives, but you will be on foot."

When they were out of sight, Greg and Amos mounted their horses and took off at a fast pace down the trail toward Fort Boise. Two hours later, they were back at their own camp and packing Harry. They travelled thirty more miles that day. That night they camped just over a long hill and could see a lake in the basin below them. They took no chance of being surprised. They ate facing each other and bedded down in a thick patch of small blue spruce trees. Four days later, they were in Fort Boise.

CHAPTER 19

BOISE BASIN

Fort Boise was a rapidly growing town with the influx of settlers bound for Oregon, plus people who settled on the rich farm land west of Boise, and last but not least, miners who flocked in on their way to Nevada and Idaho finds.

Greg McKenna and Amos Jordan found a livery stable for Harry and their horses. They tipped the stable hand a dollar and promised him more if he took especially good care of Harry. They took their depleted packs with them and registered at the Palace Hotel, where they cleaned up and changed clothes. Just before going to bed, they decided that it would be a good idea to carry the "stealables" from Harry's pack to the hotel. As they approached the barn, they noticed several horses in the corral showed sweat and cinch marks, indicating they had been ridden a long way. The stable hand had left. They heard footsteps approaching the barn. Amos motioned Greg to be quiet.

The two men never looked into the barn, but forked more hay to the horses in the corral.

One said, "I think we should have shot the hell out of the hyenas."

"There were too many of them and it is going to be a huge strike. If we can get one hundred men from Lewiston, we can drive them out of the basin. We'd better keep our mouths shut about finding gold."

After the men left, Greg and Amos slipped out and went back to the hotel. In their room, they discussed what they had heard.

Amos said, "I'll bet they were in Boise basin. Maybe we can find out from the stable hand in the morning." They had breakfast before they went to check on Harry. The horses were gone from the corral. The stable hand said, "They left at daybreak as if they were in one hell of a hurry."

"Do you know where they rode in from last night?"

"I sure do. My brother was fishing up the Boise River and they came riding downstream."

Out of earshot of the groom, Amos told Greg, "If we go up river there are Indians and they are hostile. I heard our friend Grimes from Orofino got killed up the river here. They are not sure whether Indians did it or one of his own party. We could lose our hair."

"We both can speak or use sign language. Amos, what about taking some gifts and trading with them so that they get the best of the boot? It has worked before for us. If worse comes to worst, we have the fifteen-shot rifles that we paid almost five hundred dollars for. Finally, we have a chance to be first for once, and pick out claims that have plenty of water all year."

"Greg, you are right about everything. Those Indians will want tobacco, salt, powder, and lead. We will have small amounts in sacks to make them think that is all we have. Maybe we can get a buffalo robe and some moccasins. We will buy an old cap and ball rifle for trading."

After they finished shopping, they went to the barber shop for haircuts, beard trimming, and a bath. At dawn the next morning they took the century-old trail up the Boise River. Twelve hours later, they camped by the river. They could see a large basin with breaks and ridges running toward the river. Checking the area, they saw no sign of Indians but took the precaution of camping in thick woods.

They talked about what they would do tomorrow.

"Amos, If we can find a stream big enough and we can file on where it starts, we will have it made."

They were about a mile into the basin, and were checking a large stream that entered the river from the southeast, when seven

Indians on horseback appeared from around the bend. Trees had hidden their approach.

"Let me handle this, Greg. Don't point your gun, but hold it so you can use it quickly."

The two parties faced each other about a hundred yards apart. Amos held up his hand in the peace sign, as did Greg. The Indians did not respond. They also kept their weapons ready.

"Greg, we'll ride up halfway and give the peace sign and hold the sack of chewing tobacco to show them what we have in it."

When they gave the peace sign again, the Indians moved closer. They gave each a plug of tobacco. Greg showed them only two were left, and gave one to Amos and put one in his pocket. Amos addressed them in Blackfoot language, which was similar to Bannock.

"We are friends of the brave Bannock, and would like to trade for two buffalo robes."

"No buffalo robes. Good elk and deer robes for powder, lead, and guns."

After much haggling, they ended up with two large well-tanned elk robes that had been softened by chewing. The Indians felt that they got the best of the deal since they had the cap-and-ball rifle, a quart of black powder, a hundred-fifty-caliber shot, twenty fish hooks, and some line. They seemed pleased and acted as if they wanted to get back to their camp and show their bargains.

"I think we made them happy. They seemed to want to get away before we changed our minds," said Greg.

"I was going to suggest that we pan this riffle," Amos responded. "But maybe we should let them think that we are just passing through."

A half-mile further up the creek, Greg, who was leading Harry, pointed and said, "Would you look at that!" There was a spring coming out of the rock wall and flowing at right angles to enter the larger creek. Amos rode up beside him.

"There is enough water, at least fifty inches, to run an eighteen-inch sluice box. Wouldn't it be something if there was gold in between it and the creek?"

"I don't want to get my hopes too high. We've been through this more than a few times before," answered Greg.

"If we stake our claims to take in where the spring comes out, we can file on the rocks behind it for a mineral claim, as well as filing on the whole stream of water."

"We found flakes of gold in the river last night, and if this doesn't pay off, we know there is gold somewhere here," said Amos. "We'll have a whole month to find it before those men get back from Lewiston."

"Well, what are we waiting for? Let's make camp in the woods next to the spring." They unpacked Harry and hobbled him to graze in the tall, thick grass and willow leaves of the little meadow. Amos took the gold pan and Greg took the shovel. Greg paced the distance from the spring to the creek.

"If we file two claims, our last stake will take us just across the creek." He took a large shovelful of sand from the bottom of a riffle in the spring near where it entered the creek. He picked the rocks off until nothing was left but fine gravel and sand, then dumped it into the gold pan. As the fine black sand was washed by Amos' expert panning, they were amazed at the amount of fine gold flakes that appeared.

"That's at least five dollars worth of gold!" Greg cried gleefully.

"We're nowhere near bedrock. Let's dig down to bedrock about ten feet from the spring. It must be pretty rich down there."

They didn't stop for lunch and dug a hole big enough to stand in and shovel two feet through the top layer of dirt and three feet into the gravel. They took turns digging and panning. As they went into the gravel the number of flakes and irregular specks of gold were larger and more numerous. They grinned as each showed the other the results of each new panning. They had not yet reached bedrock, when Amos worked his shovel deep into the bottom of the hole and there was more black sand than usual. When he carefully filled Greg's pan he pointed out the flecks of gold that were showing. They both watched the panning. When it was finished, the bottom of the pan was almost covered in places with flecks of gold and shot-sized nuggets. They hugged each other and danced about, shouting "We've made it!"

"We don't have to look anymore. This is good enough," Amos said.

After digging more holes, they found that almost all of their proposed filing had gravel under the topsoil. They peeled small lodgepole pines for stakes and attached their filing notices to them. They would have to go to Fort Boise to file their claims and get provisions for a long stay, as they would have to stay close to the claim and guard it. The supplies and tools were hidden under some fallen trees. Taking turns leading Harry, they made the trip to Fort Boise in ten hours.

The supplies they needed included boards, nails, hammer, saw, and heavy wire screen to keep the heavy gravel out of the sluice box. In order to pack the lumber on the mule, it could not be over six feet long and had to be hung on each side to balance.

"It looks like we'll have to stay the winter at the camp," said Amos. "We'll need rubber boots and warm clothing. We can build a fireplace in a dugout. Better have some pots and a long-handled skillet. And we'd better get a wheel and axle for making a wheelbarrow."

When they purchased their food supplies and figured up how much all that would weigh, they came to the conclusion that even if they each carried fifty pounds and Harry two hundred, there would still be two hundred pounds of goods left.

"We need another mule."

"Greg, we'll have to cut grass and willows for Harry over the winter, and another mule or horse would eat too much. Maybe we could butcher a horse after it gets cold enough to keep the meat. We ate a lot of horse meat in California."

"We've forgotten some things. We need a hand sickle to cut grass. And we need some paper. I am tired of using leaves and grass when I go. Let's talk to the owner of the livery stable about a pack horse."

When they approached the livery barn, the owner was currying a mule.

"That is a fine mule," Amos said.

"Yeah, and she is one smart mule. What do you fellers need?"

Greg explained the situation.

"You say you are going thirty miles to your camp and trap? I have a better proposition than buying a pack horse. But it will cost you twenty dollars. You can take Maude with you. When you are through with her, feed her and turn her loose. She'll be back here looking over the corral fence in less than twelve hours."

They gave him a twenty dollar gold piece and the next morning they packed the mules and took off at daybreak. Twelve hours later, dog tired, they arrived at the diggings. After unpacking the mules they hobbled Harry and turned Maude loose. They ate a cold supper and crawled into their blankets, dressed except for their boots. In the morning Maude was gone.

The two adjoining placer claims took up an area three hundred by two hundred feet. The hard rock or mineral claim would extend to the top of the hill, ridge or mountain. They were eager to start mining but first they had to get their camp established and the sluice box built. They dug into the hillside for three walls of their dugout; posts and logs covered the front. The roof was made of dirt over branches. They had a window covered with canvas and made a door and hung it on leather hinges made from an old boot top. Inside at the back they built a fireplace and chimney of clay and rock. Their furnishings were two three-foot lengths of log for chairs and a larger one of cedar for a table.

By working from sunup to sundown, the partners had accomplished a surprising number of necessary projects. Early in September, the dugout was complete. The twelve-foot sluice box was in place at the bottom of the claims. Water could be diverted to it and turned on and off by a head gate.

Nights were getting chilly. The small sheet metal stove actually gave off more heat than the fireplace.

Amos said, "It's going to get mighty cold in here in the winter. We'll need to pile up a lot of wood." Another job.

Greg said, "The Bannocks are scattered in small bands, but we will have to spend time each day checking for Indians so we can still keep our hair."

"I hope you are right. Let's get a good breakfast and spend the rest of the day sluicing and see what we can get. We've only scraped the gravel."

The area they had cleared of dirt was about ten by ten feet. The two feet of soil had been washed away into the creek. Five feet of gravel had been carted off by wheelbarrow and piled where it could be shoveled into the sluice box. This gave them a place to put their tailings. Because there was some gold, even in the top of the gravel, by mixing it with the richer bottom gravel it would still pay off. The flow of water and angle of the sluice box had been adjusted, and they started shoveling in the gravel. They picked out the larger gravel by hand before shoveling it onto the screen, which let gravel larger than three-eighths of an inch roll down into the tailings. Often they would stop, clear off the screen, and look at the cleats or baffles where the heavier gold settled.

"Amos, I can't stand it any longer. Let's see what we've got."

They unbuttoned the screen and for the first time they could see the results of their labor. Using a pancake turner and a whisk broom, they scooped the gold and a few bits of black sand into the gold pan.

"Amos, how much gold do we have?"

"After we get the sand washed off, I'd guess one to one and a half ounces. That is thirty-five dollars to forty dollars. We've never seen anything like this before, even in some of the richest California strikes. You'll be rich and can get the ranch you've always wanted."

"I was beginning to think we'd never make it. This is from the lower end of our claim, and while it's richer, our test holes show that all of our claim will pay off. Let's see if we can make two hundred dollars today."

They were exhausted when they emptied the sluice box at six o'clock and both agreed they had made the two hundred dollars and maybe a little more. They decided to take the next day, Sunday, off and rest up.

In spite of being tired, they awakened as usual at daybreak. After breakfast and cleaning up the dugout, they decided to read. Greg had the Bible and Amos had a law book.

Later, Amos checked his watch and got up. "It's nearly four o'clock and the deer will be feeding. I am going to see if we can have deer liver for supper. I'll check for Indians down below."

Greg expected Amos back before six o'clock. It was now seven, and the red sun was touching the skyline on the hills. He had heard no shooting. Taking his rifle, he started out to look for Amos. He was looking down the trail when he heard the clink of a pebble rolling down the hill behind. Startled, he pivoted with gun ready, and there was Amos grinning at him.

"Man, you scared hell out of me. How come no deer?"

"Greg, we have a problem. In fact, we may be in big trouble. I was about to shoot a young buck when nine Indians rode up and camped about a mile and a half down the creek. They have no women and it looks like they're hunting trouble. They had quite a powwow and were roasting a small deer. One left the camp and headed this way. I was lucky and followed him without being seen. He stayed in the edge of the timber across the creek, a rifle shot away from you. He made a half-circle around our camp and even got a good look at Harry."

"Do you think they are going to try to take us? Shall we run or fight?"

"They won't attack until dawn. Indians don't like to fight at night because if they get killed their spirits can't see the way to the happy hunting grounds. We have the edge because we know what they are planning to do. We have fifteen shots in our rifles and we can reload in a hurry. We'll clean and oil our rifles and have our cartridges in belts. We'll sleep in the trees, on each side of the meadow, and when they ride up and start to dismount, we will start shooting as fast as we can. Shoot low at both horses and Indians. We don't want to kill any Indians, but we'll kill a couple of horses. They hate to lose their horses. I believe that if we shoot alternately and move a little between shots, we can make them think there's a whole bunch of white men. They probably will run, hopefully back toward the Yellowstone and Snake Rivers. They lost a lot of men in a 1854 battle and that broke the tribe up into small bands."

They made their beds in the timber above the dugout. They were restless and both were awake at three o'clock. They slipped back to the dugout and ate a cold breakfast of meat and corn bread. It was still dark when they assumed their positions on each side of the meadow, where the Indians would be bunched up as they dismounted and left their horses for the final sneak.

Wearing headbands with foliage stuck in them to match the bushes, Greg and Amos crouched behind the bushes. When a doe and two fawns came bounding up the stream, they thought the Indians would be right behind, and they were correct. They heard the occasional sound of a hoof hitting a rock. The Indians rode into the opening and stopped to dismount. At that moment, Harry let loose his ungodly braying, punctuated by loud farting as he took a deep breath between brays. The partners shot and downed two horses. The next shots hit two Bannocks low in the legs. They went down and got up limping. The rapid fire from different locations caused the Indians to pick up their wounded and ride double to get out of the ambush. When they were out of sight and sound, Greg and Amos patted each other and roared with laughter.

"I am going to give Harry an extra bit of oats. That is one damn smart mule. They probably had never heard a mule bray like that before and he helped scare the hell out of them."

"I hope it will scare them clean out of the valley for good. Maybe they will think there is a devil or an evil spirit in here. Let's sneak along behind them and see what they do."

The Indians stopped at their camp, gathered gear, bound up the wounded men's legs, and strung out single file going east up the Boise River toward Lowman Pass.

After the Indian attack, life on the claim settled into a routine of daily panning. As autumn approached, Greg realized Harry's feed for the winter was a problem. They had put off cutting the tall grass and the abundant supply of nutritious yellow-flowered plants that animals seemed to like. They had been too busy sluicing out gold. When the first frost came in mid-September, they realized their mistake and spent two weeks working hard, taking turns with the sickle, cutting everything that would nourish Harry and storing it in a pole-fenced area. In October, they thought they had enough to last him for the winter.

"Amos, this is the most beautiful time of the year. I like the warm, lazy days and the big red harvest moon."

"We are having so much fun and success with this claim that I have a feeling it can't last," Amos responded. "I'm afraid we are going to have company right soon."

Sure enough, only two days later, two heavily-bearded men appeared as they were about to clean their sluice box. Greg and Amos were holding their rifles as they faced the approaching men, who rode up, leaving their guns in the scabbards.

"We are with the fifty-four men from Lewiston. We are looking for claims to file on." Greg and Amos were glad that they would have company. They felt that in sixty days the area would have stores, saloons, and sawmills, and would grow into a city overnight. The newcomers asked about the size of their claims and where the boundaries were.

Amos said, "We filed using the California law for size. We sampled the gravel below here and it looked good. This is the first place we tried and it is good." They were pleased with the sincerity and friendliness of the newcomers, who thanked them.

Jack Hasen, the small, round-faced man, said to his partner, Slim Wiseman, "Let's take a look-see." An hour later they were back and said, "This looks plenty good enough. According to your claim notice, you have filed up on the spring. If we can use it below your sluice box it will save us a lot of diggin'."

Amos said, "We'll talk it over and let you know." They went out of earshot.

"Amos, I think they'd be good neighbors. We could let them use the water, but they can't charge anybody who wants to use it below them. We as owners can turn it back into the creek at any time."

Upon hearing their decision, Slim Wiseman said, "That's mighty thoughtful of you and you'll never regret it. I'll see if I can get Russ White and Fat Summers to file below us. They would be great neighbors and we can all help and protect each other."

It turned out that the three sets of partners got along exceptionally well and in Amos' words, "They are not riffraff. You can count on them."

In two weeks the word had spread, and the whole stream had been filed on, from its source to its entry into the Boise River. People were finding and filing on more claims every day.

CHAPTER 20

WONG AND CHING LEE

On their first trip to the new mining town, named Bannock, in November, they found it teeming with people trying to get established, housed, in business, or employed. They did not dare leave their place unguarded as they had a large supply of gold cached in their dugout. Greg took Harry to bring out what meager supplies he could find in Bannock. Everything was very high. A fifty-pound sack of flour cost fifty dollars, and two pounds lard, ten dollars. As he was leaving town, he saw two tall Chinese who were walking along with their round hats and swaying queues, or pigtails. As they drew near him, he held up his hand and said, "Hello, friends." To his surprise the Chinamen both laughed and said, "Lo, flend."

Greg had a sudden idea. "Do you want work? I can put you to work for five dollars a day, ten hours." They conversed rapidly in Chinese.

"We want job. Good wolk—no steal. Need food."

Greg shook hands with one of them and said, "Follow me."

Amos saw them coming and he had things pretty well figured out. Greg introduced Wong and Ching Lee and said they were hungry. Amos started the fire in the stove and put on a kettle of water. He put a generous portion of bacon in a skillet and dumped rice into boiling water. While they were eating, Amos said, "They can stay with us in the dugout, but it will be crowded. We sure need a cabin."

Ching Lee said, "We build good cabin—chop chop."

Amos said, "Chop chop means right quick."

With a pencil and a piece of paper sack they drew a plan for an eighteen-by-twelve-foot log cabin. It would have two bunks, a stove, cupboard, shelves for books, and a table and pegs for clothes. When they showed the plan to the Chinese, they said, "Can do."

"What tools do you need?"

"Saw, axe, hammer, adze. Plenty logs," they said, pointing to the large stand of lodgepole pines that grew fifty feet tall with almost no variation in size for the first twenty feet.

It was a revelation to Greg and Amos how quickly and easily these workmen could trim and smooth off the sides of the logs to make them fit together perfectly. Within a month they had a snug log cabin with two windows with four nine-by-twelve-inch panes. That was the largest glass that could be freighted from Portland.

There was now a rough, winding, but passable road of many steep grades that wound back and forth as it followed the old Indian and game trails. Although it was a relatively mild winter, there were days when they couldn't operate the sluice box due to freezing. Ching Lee and Wong were kept busy shoveling off dirt and carting it by wheelbarrow to the edges of the claim. Saloons in Bannock now had safes where they could deposit their gold pokes.

Amos noticed a slim, attractive Chinese girl named Chung Lee. He heard that she had been betrayed by her fiance, who paid her passage from China and then sold her to Hip Sing, a venerable head of one of the many tongs. She was doing laundry and housework to buy her freedom from him. When Amos brought her to the cabin to clean up and wash clothes, Greg kidded him.

"I'll bet you have ideas about her that have nothing to do with dishes or washing clothes."

"I confess that I have ideas. There are no suitable women available and she is very beautiful."

The winter of 1862–63 quickly faded into an early spring. The mountain passes were open in May.

Amos could see that Greg was "antsy" as he called it, so after considerable thought, he said, "Greg, I think you should go to the Lemhi Valley and stake out land for your ranch. I talked with a former Mormon missionary who worked in the valley in 1855 when Brigham Young decided to form a State of Zion, which would take in the territories of Utah, Idaho, Arizona, and part of Montana. The government heard about it and placed a fort in Salt Lake. That was the end of Brigham's dream. Incidentally, the Lemhi was named after King Lemhi in the Book of Mormon. In 1855, the Mormon missionaries and settlers arrived and built Fort Lemhi. It was the policy to send out Mormons to settle new areas and also to get the malcontents and troublemakers out of Utah. You may be in luck as they abandoned the settlers because of money problems and Indian troubles in 1858. Many of them left the area, but a few stayed. Wong, Ching Lee, and I can take care of the mining end, so you and Harry take a month to find out about a ranch."

Greg gave his partner a big hug.

CHAPTER 21

BANNOCK—NOW IDAHO CITY

In a month Bannock was turning from an upstart town into a city as people from all walks of life poured in. Miners, gamblers, shop and store owners, a sawmill, and the usual large following of camp women were part of the growing community. Saloons, boarding houses, and stores were built. There was now a wagon road to Boise, which at times was crowded with people and supplies. Goods and freight came in from Salt Lake and Walla Walla. Late that fall, Doc W. B. Noble laid out the streets of Bannock, which later was to become Idaho City. The first settlers were mostly from California. They were veteran miners, expert and skilled in the best methods of rocking and sluicing. They established a miners' court to handle disputes over claims and water rights. To his surprise, Greg McKenna was elected to the seven-man board headed by Doc Noble, chairman, and W. Graham, vice-chairman. A handsome young man from New Orleans was appointed as claims recorder and mapper for the area. The job would be a lucrative one, but would require considerable skill and knowledge, in addition to absolute honesty, to properly administer and record claims.

Before Greg left to find his ranch, he and Amos were on their way to town to deposit a five-pound canvas bag of gold—the result of one month of labor—and to have their claims properly recorded. Being one of the original filings, they were allowed to keep their oversized filings, which late-comers with smaller claims called "Hog'em Claims". After having their pokes weighed, recorded, and placed in the Bannock saloon safe, they went to the recorder's office. The handsome young man behind the counter held out his hand and said, "I am Lawrence Breckenridge." Turning to a beautiful lady who was sorting papers at a desk, "This is my wife, Marianne. We are glad to meet you. How can I help you?"

"We would like to record our claims properly." Amos handed over the copy of their filing claims. Breckenridge looked them over and in a few minutes said, "I am pleased with the proper way you have filed your claims. A lawyer couldn't do it any better." Amos smiled and said, "Thank you."

The Breckenridges were fast accumulating money. He received a dollar a month from all working claims, and they numbered over one thousand. There were always several all-night poker games, but he limited his playing to one or two nights a week to keep from being labeled a gambler. Newly rich miners with too much to drink were easy picking. Marianne volunteered to work two days a week at the new hospital and she spent considerable time with the women's relief organization. On Saturday nights she sang at the Golden Nugget saloon, where she was a favorite attraction. Songs like "Blue Tail Fly", "Shenandoah", "Battle Hymn of the Republic", "Dixie", "Sweet Betsy from Pike", and "Home Sweet Home" in her sweet contralto voice were a hit with the miners. She liked to get them to sing along with her. "Sweet Betsy from Pike" was one of her favorites and when she came to the place where Brigham stomped like a steer, she put her fingers by her head to imitate horns and stomped. The miners, singing along, did the same.

The Breckenridges and Amos and Greg became good friends. Marianne's beauty and wit captivated both of them. Greg said, "I'd like to find a wife like that."

Amos said, "Fat chance of finding one here."

The Mason's Lodge was founded in 1864 with Masons from Portland conducting the initiation ceremonies. Amos was instrumental in getting Greg to join.

"I've observed that Masons are usually very good and influential people and seem to be very loyal and supportive of each other. You have to ask a Mason for instructions on how to join. If your application is accepted, I understand you have to learn the ritual, secret signs, and be initiated. From what I have learned, it takes a lot of memorizing and you keep your oath of secrecy for life."

They approached Lawrence Breckenridge, saying they would like to join. He was enthusiastic.

"You will enjoy being a Mason. One gets a lot of satisfaction from helping his fellow man." Lawrence coached them in the memory work and they were quickly accepted. Greg was surprised at the ease with which Amos was able to memorize the rituals. Once again, he felt that Amos was hiding something of his past.

CHAPTER 22

TO THE LEMHI

Greg left his old and new friends behind and rode his new Appaloosa mare, with Harry following, into the Lemhi Valley some fifteen miles above where the Lemhi River entered the Salmon River. Across to the east and toward the Bitterroot Mountains was a valley with a large stream that joined the river. This cul-de-sac was over two miles long and over a mile wide. His first impression was "I have found it!" When he crossed the shallow Lemhi and rode a mile up the valley he was looking at yellow blossoms of the nutritious bitterroot plant and the abundance of tall bunch grass and other grasses. When he rode around a small hill, there was a good-sized log cabin with smoke coming out of the chimney. As he got nearer to the house, he saw about forty acres that had been plowed and planted to hay and grain, with ditches laid out for irrigating. He said to Harry, "Damn it, this place is ideal, but it has been taken."

When he rode up to the house, he noticed a short, heavy-set man working in a well-kept garden. Two young boys also were hoeing. As he neared the rancher, he was greeted with a friendly "Hello."

"I am Greg McKenna and I'm glad to meet you."

"I am Angus Latham. We are glad to see you. Company is

scarce except for Indians. My wife, Martha, will be glad to hear the latest news. Would you like to stay for a few days? We can put you up easily."

"Thank you. I'd be grateful." Greg knew by his accent that he was British.

The Lathams were glad to have company. Over dinner they talked freely about themselves. They were among the first Mormon settlers in Utah. They became disenchanted with some of the church practices, such as polygamy, and the sudden wealth that the high officials attained. This made them prime candidates to colonize new areas for the spread of the religion. When the church abandoned the colony in 1858, the Lathams were one of the three families that stayed. They hoped that people would come and settle the valley. The church was still sending meager supplies to the remaining families, hoping to establish another church community, but their last neighbors were now planning to move out.

Angus Latham said they were thinking about leaving, too.

"It is just too lonesome here. We will be the only ones left. But we hate to leave as we have forty acres under irrigation out of the three hundred sixty we filed on. In a short time Darrell, now thirteen, and Donald, eleven, will be able to take a man's place. I know that people will move in eventually. We could expand the cultivated land and raise cattle. But, we have waited it out about as long as we can."

"Would you consider selling for one thousand dollars cash?"

After some thought, Angus said, "That offer is mighty tempting. What do you think, Martha?"

"Angus, I am your wife and will abide by whatever you decide."

"If I buy your ranch, I plan to stock it with cattle and horses that will have to be driven over from Boise. I will need someone to look after them until I settle here permanently. In addition, I will pay thirty dollars a month and bring in such supplies as I can by pack train."

"Mr. McKenna, it's getting late. Martha and I will talk it over and sleep on it. We'll let you know in the morning. It's mighty invitin'."

In the morning, Greg was treated to canned peaches, fresh eggs and ham, all from the Latham's supplies. After the blessing, Latham said, "We are a'mind to accept your offer."

Martha said, "When you bring supplies, please bring a bride. It would be so nice to have another woman for company."

"Martha, I'm trying, but the right kind of women are very scarce. Angus, what about the land below you?"

"The three hundred sixty acres adjoining my place is abandoned and you can file on it. I will help you place the notices. The two adjoining three hundred sixty-acre places are for sale as those people are moving out." Greg was delighted.

"I will give you five hundred dollars now and when I return I'll pay you the additional five hundred dollars and your monthly wages."

Greg quickly filed on the three hundred sixty acres, and bought seven hundred twenty acres more, making a total of fourteen hundred forty acres, mostly rich bottom land or land suitable for pasture.

Greg asked, "Didn't the Indians bother you?"

Angus laughed and replied, "They love Martha. She was a nurse and doctor's assistant in England and to them she is 'medicine woman'. Because there was no doctor for the new colony, the church gave her medical tools and medicines. In fact, through some mistake she was given two shipments."

The Lathams had been in the valley a few weeks when the Indians camped to catch and dry salmon. The chief's young squaw broke a tooth and her jaw swelled up. The chief brought her to the Latham's camp. With sign language, Martha made her understand that it had to be pulled. The tooth had split and was easily extracted with forceps that had been supplied to Martha. The year-old boy the squaw was carrying kept scratching his head. Martha examined him and found lice. With soap and a pan of warm water, she washed his head, then applied a lard and sulphur mix to his scalp. She gave the mother a pint of the salve and a bar of soap. There was an epidemic of pinkeye in the tribe, and Martha had an ointment that cured it quickly. The next week the Indians brought them a dressed, two-pronged buck deer.

On the morning Greg was preparing to leave, a large herd of cattle were driven in and were grazing on the unfenced grassland next to Latham's fenced forty acres.

"Whose cattle are they?" Greg asked.

"They are Mounce cattle. He says he has grazing rights and we don't have it fenced. There isn't a meaner, more ruthless person in the territory. He drives the cattle from Lost River through a narrow gorge at the head of the creek."

Greg smiled at first, then his face hardened and he said, "I'll take care of that."

When Greg returned to Idaho City from the Latham ranch, he was greeted by his partner. He noticed that the cabin was downright messy, with a pile of dirty clothes. Amos explained that Chung Lee had to leave.

"Amos, I'm downright curious. Did you ever get next to her?"

Amos laughed. "You'll get a kick out of this. I asked her to sleep with me for fifty dollars a night. Her reply was, 'I no fuckee you. Only fuckee husband. You marry me, plenty fuckee you.' When I asked if she fuckee Hip Sing, she said, 'Hip Sing no can fuckee' and curled her finger over. There was a big poker game and a young miner won her from old Hip Sing. He married her and they are moving to settle somewhere near your ranch. They could be your neighbors."

CHAPTER 23

IDAHO CITY 1864

In 1864 Bannock, by then known as Idaho City, had almost everything. The weekly paper published a survey of the businesses. It listed twenty dry goods and clothing stores, three grocery stores, nine bakeries, five cigar stands, three stove shops, twenty-five law offices, a livery stable, twenty-four carpenter shops, ten Chinese warehouses, six barber shops, and over forty saloons.

Greg remarked, "Forty saloons are a lot of saloons." Amos replied, "Most of the men are single and only use their cabin or tent to sleep in. The saloon is warm, they have company, can get food, drink, gamble, or get a woman in bed."

Most of the saloons had women for hire. There were several small towns located only a few miles from Idaho City, including Centerville, Pioneerville, and Quartzburg, with populations of less than one hundred.

All were a part of Boise County, which was established when President Lincoln signed the bill creating the Idaho Territory. With government came taxes.

"Amos, what are we going to do about income tax?" Greg asked. "The three percent wasn't bad. But now that the Union is in trouble and needs money, they have added five percent, making the tax eight percent. That is too high."

Amos considered the matter. "We want the Union to win the war and we should be willing to pay a reasonable amount. We have been paying on the basis of the gold we deposit in the bank. We can cut down on the amount we deposit and put the rest in bank vaults and the safes in the saloon. I think we should sell out this spring and get with the ranching."

Travelling troupes of entertainers went from one mining camp to another as the miners were starved for entertainment. Greg and Amos decided to see the French troupe. They really laughed at the dancers and their jokes but most of all their effect on the audience. They danced gracefully, vigorously kicking high to expose their thighs and small colored strip of their panties. When they finished their numbers, they turned their backs and bowed over, flipping up their skirts and shaking their exposed buttocks. This brought on pandemonium of noise and a shower of coins, mostly silver dollars and an occasional five-dollar gold piece. They turned their backs as they bent down to pick up the coins and wriggled their rear ends, which brought another shower of coins.

After the show, the two soon-to-be ranchers went to a restaurant. They were about to leave when the waitress, upset and in tears, approached them, saying, "Lawrence Breckenridge is dead. They found him in an alley with his head bashed in. They said he won almost two thousand in a poker game, but there was no money on him."

Greg and Amos looked at each other, aghast. Greg said, "We've got to go to Marianne and see if we can help and comfort her."

"Yes. What a shame. They were so much in love. There's not much we can do, but she will need the support of friends."

Marianne tearfully hugged them both, saying, "I'm so glad you came." At first she was silent, but then began to talk about the wonderful times they had shared. Amos offered to make the funeral arrangements. Greg said, "I'll stay here with her until you come back."

After Amos left, Marianne poured out her heart. "I'm going to get out of this hell-hole. I had thought about what I would do if I ever lost Larry. I have capital, and I am going to start an exclusive fancy house in Boise." At Greg's look of astonishment, she continued, "Larry found me in a brothel in New Orleans. A very fancy one. Actually, it is the only business I know."

CHAPTER 24

THE BIG POKER GAME

Greg, under the tutelage of Amos, had become a very good poker player. Both were successful when they occasionally played on Saturday nights when the weather was too miserable to work. One such night, Greg decided to go to the Palace, which was a combination saloon and gambling place, have a couple drinks, and watch the poker game and the show until he felt more relaxed. Six men were sitting down at the high stakes table. Two appeared to be professional gamblers. They wore the "gambler's uniform" of white shirt, black tie, black coat. The other four were wealthy owners of mining property.

"Why don't you join us, McKenna?" one of the gamblers asked.

"What are the stakes?"

"You have to have two thousand dollars to buy-in. Of course, you can buy more if you want."

"That is too rich for my blood."

"So you are afraid you might lose."

"You might say that."

The house issued poker chips that were paid for by gold, in most cases on deposit in the saloon safe. No one carried much money on account of robberies. Since no one trusted anyone, the house had dealers that dealt and managed the games. Greg watched the men play a few hands, then walked over to the cashier's cage and signed for twenty-five hundred dollars.

The game was five card high-low, which meant you had to have a pair of jacks or better to open or the game became lowball with an ace, deuce, trey, four, and five as the best lowball hand. During the first two hours, Greg played conservatively and was ahead nearly two thousand dollars. Some players had bought in more than once. Several stacks of one-hundred-dollar chips were in front of the gamblers along with some one-thousand-dollar chips. Table stakes and the ante for each hand was twenty-five dollars before the cards were dealt.

Greg carefully shielded his cards with his big hands. When he looked at the corner of each, he could see that they were all hearts. He kept his composure as he spread the cards to get a better look. He had a hand that happens once in several hundred thousand deals, a wheel in hearts or an ace to a five spot. This would be a winning hand in lowball and there was only one chance in a million or so of two straight flushes in the same deal. Greg was sitting on the dealer's left and was first bidder. He passed because no other player might have jacks or better to open. The next player opened with a bet of one hundred dollars. Two players passed and threw their hands to the dealer. The others all raised in turn. Greg, after looking at his cards and hesitating, called without raising. The other players knew he had a pat low hand. They all drew cards, then began to raise. Greg thought they had all filled their hands. When the last of the players to the right of the dealer bet two thousand dollars, it took almost all of Greg's chips to cover it. One other player called the bet. The big bettor said, "Read 'em and weep!" and gleefully showed four nines and reached for the pot.

Greg said, "Sorry, but you lose," and showed his straight flush. There was over seven thousand dollars in the pot.

Back at the cabin, Amos said, "Everyone knows you are leaving and that you have been depositing your money in Boise. Even the Idaho City sheriff is suspected of being crooked. You can bet that somebody is going to rob you. I am going to ride with you to Boise. From now on, every move you make will be watched."

"Amos, you will never know how lucky I feel to have a friend and partner like you. I'd like to leave day after tomorrow."

"You can't hide the withdrawal of your money from the Palace safe. They'll be watching and waiting. We will do that tomorrow. I'll take the fifteen-shot rifle and pistol and you take the double-barrel loaded with buckshot. I sure hope nothing is going to happen."

Nothing did. At Amos' suggestion, they put the horses out to pasture as if nothing were going to happen and brought them in at four o'clock in the morning when they loaded the gold in their saddle bags. The money in large bills was packed in the money belts worn next to their skin. As they rode through Idaho City, Greg remarked, "No one seems to be watching."

"They probably are already in place along the trail to Boise. There are three spots the robbers have been using. The best place for an ambush is where the road is only wide enough for a wagon and a huge boulder makes the road take a sharp turn around it. If I was planning a holdup, that's where I'd be."

The first ten miles everything seemed tranquil. The sun was bright and warm, flowers covered the hillsides, birds chirped.

"Greg, everything is too beautiful and quiet. I don't like what I think is going to happen. The dirty crooks will not only try to hold us up, they'll want to kill us on sight. Robbers and thieves are usually not too smart, though, so maybe we can handle it."

When they approached the first place where the road narrowed, they stopped and rode a short way into the timber. Amos walked up the hill until he could see the back of the rocky formation that narrowed the road, telling Greg not to worry if he took half an hour, as he wanted to look it over carefully with field glasses. When he returned, he was greeted with, "Man, I was getting jittery. It seemed like hours."

"It's all clear."

When they neared the next possible ambush spot, they stopped to let the horses drink at a spring. Amos surveyed the rocky outcrop with glasses.

"It seems to be all clear."

"How can you tell?"

"A magpie is sitting on top of the rock and another one on the road to the side. Magpies are spooky. I learned from a mountain man to see everything and the reason for it. There is only one more likely ambush, but it's the best one and many people have been relieved of their pokes there. What would you do if you were a robber?"

Greg thought awhile, then said, "There might be three of them. I would put two behind the rock and the other, best shot, on the ridge behind for a backup."

"You probably are right. If we can keep them from getting suspicious, I'll climb the hill behind the backup and take him out without their knowing it. It is near lunch time. We'll stop at the spring, which is about six hundred yards short of the rocks, go into the timber, and build a fire. They will think we're cooking lunch. You stay with the horses and build a fire, adding some green wood to make a smoke. I'll put on moccasins and take the shotgun. Nobody is fool enough to make a move with a shotgun aimed at him, because they make such a big hole."

The partners rode down the rutted road at a brisk walk with very little conversation. They never relaxed their scrutiny of the terrain on the left. The river on the right was so close to the road that it offered little cover for a hiding place.

Amos said, "I hope we are taking all these precautions for nothing."

When the big boulder came in sight, they were about a mile away. Amos warned Greg, "Act natural, as if we hadn't a care in the world." The road curved, and they were out of sight of the boulder for a short time. Amos said, "Give me the glasses and I will slip up on the hill to where I can see it." He was gone only a short time. In a low voice, he said, "We're in for trouble. When I looked at the boulder the damned fool had his black hat on and raised his head to peek. I stood in the shade to avoid a reflection off the glasses. I looked up at a vantage point about two hundred feet above the hat and saw a flash of light reflecting from a rifle barrel. That's the backup sniper. There is a ridge of brush behind him that will allow me to sneak up on him. You get the fire ready, but wait fifteen minutes before lighting it. Don't get anxious, it will take me about an hour to get up there behind him. If you hear a shot, walk out to where you can see the boulder."

As Greg gathered wood, he kept looking at his watch. The minutes crawled by. After fifteen, he lit the fire. There was very little wind, and the smoke went straight up. He spent the next forty-five minutes worrying about what might happen to Amos and what he should do if it did. Should he try to shoot it out with the robbers or go back to Idaho City for help? Then he heard the big boom of a shotgun. When he broke out into the open, he saw Amos standing on top of the boulder, waving his hat. He mounted his horse, and leading Amos' horse by the reins, galloped to the boulder. Amos climbed down with a big grin on his face.

"Come see what we've got behind the boulder!" They laughed and patted each other on the back.

Greg said, "That was the longest hour of my life."

"It took a long time because I had to crawl nearly two hundred yards. There was no cover until I reached the ridge of brush. He had a bottle and was taking nips. I was able to put the barrel into his back and said, 'If you make a sound or move, I'll blow a hole in you. Put your hands above your head.' He was scared spitless. I hit him a good clip with his rifle barrel and he was out cold. I tied his feet and hands together behind his back and stuffed his bandana into his mouth and tied it tight. I didn't give a damn if he choked. I've got the other two trussed up the same way. If you'll help me bring the rats down, we'll decide what to do with them."

"Amos, they aren't going anywhere. I'm hungry. Let's eat lunch first."

"Good idea." They made coffee and ate cold venison sandwiches. They discussed what to do with the prisoners. Amos said, "Right now, I think three bullets in the head would be the answer."

"If we kill them and don't let the law take its course, we are as bad as they are."

"Greg, you are so right. But if we take them into Boise and turn them over to the sheriff, there will have to be a trial and they will be turned loose for lack of evidence. They can say they were on the way to Idaho City and stopped to take a rest. Any halfway good lawyer could get them acquitted."

Greg said, "Let's get their horses and check their packs."

The packs yielded only food and ammunition. Untying the feet of the robbers one by one, they searched and found over five thousand dollars in gold coins and bills in their money belts. When the last robber stood up, they looked at each other in astonishment. There was a long scar from the left corner of his mouth to his ear. He was one of the three that had robbed them on the Salmon River three years before.

Amos said, "If we keep the money, we are thieves. We can give it to the miner's board and have them turn it over to charity, to help the down and out."

They unsaddled the thieves' horses and drove them at a gallop a mile down the road. One of the horses must have thought he was going home and continued to trot with the others following. The guns, gun belts, and boots they threw into the rapidly flowing Boise River. They untied one robber at a time and sent him down the road with a warning that if they showed up in Idaho City they would hang.

"Amos, did the one you caught on the hill look familiar?"

"Come to think of it, I'll bet he is one of the sheriff's new deputies."

They quickly returned to the road and reached Boise without any other problems.

The Union was hard-pressed for money and issued bonds. Because of the pinch on finances and the uncertainty of the war, early bond buyers were trying to unload. Amos was convinced that the Union would stand, and they bought many bonds at nearly half their printed value. The bonds were to earn five percent interest and in a few years would be worth their full value plus interest. The miners were skeptical of greenbacks and sold them at a reduced price for gold. The partners exchanged their loose gold for currency. They were relieved when they finished their deposits and arrangements with the bank president, who was very pleased to have nearly twenty thousand dollars deposited in his bank.

Greg had an agent in Boise who purchased cattle for him. He had been informed that the agent had twenty-two head of heifers and young cows purchased from the settlers moving to Oregon. He and Amos walked briskly in the cool morning air to the livery stable to get their horses to ride out to the pasture where the cattle were kept. When they entered the stable, a tall man with a tan complexion was currying Greg's horse. Greg said, "Looks like you took good care of him."

"Señor, he is ready to ride." When the man stood up, he showed his handsome classical Spanish features.

"Your English is very good. Are you Mexican?"

"I am Castilian," the man said proudly. "We Ortegas have kept the blood pure for over two hundred years. My parents had us study English at the University of Mexico in Mexico City. My name is Raul Ortega."

"How do you happen to be in Boise?"

"I was on a cattle drive from Texas to Montana. It's a long story."

It occurred to Greg that if he hired an experienced cattle driver to help him drive his cattle to the ranch, a problem that had been worrying him would be solved. The cattle had been led behind wagons, and were not used to being driven.

"Raul, why did you leave Mexico?"

"There's a price on my head. The Ortegas were very prominent in Mexico. My father had voiced strong opposition to the corrupt government in Mexico City. Domingo, whose ranch bordered ours, was a loyal supporter of the government and because of his support, any lawless act that he wanted to make would be overlooked.

"One night when my cousin Rosita and I were camped with two vaqueros about fifteen miles from the hacienda, our guards must have fallen asleep. The Domingos and their vaqueros slipped in and killed my mother and father. Our surprised people were either killed or driven off, but one escaped to warn us. I gave Rosita all the money I had and told her to ride to El Paso, where lawyer Ed Brannon, a longtime friend of my family, would make her welcome. I had to avenge my father.

"The night was dark. I rode within a half-mile of the hacienda and tied up my horse. On foot I carefully scouted the area ahead to see if they had guards. There were none. I could hear the noise of celebration long before I could see the hacienda. I slipped off my boots and left them at a corner of the corral. I crept up to the corner of the house and waited until, having drunk themselves into a stupor, they were passed out and quiet. It was easy to slip into the house as drunk men were snoring all over.

Domingo was in my parent's bedroom, flat on his back, with a fat-bottomed woman beside him. I had my pistol ready to shoot, but I wanted to use my knife. I put my hand over his mouth. He struggled and opened his eyes. I whispered, 'You are a dirty dog and you are going to die like one.' I loved his look of terror as I plunged the knife up to the hilt into his heart. The woman turned over and muttered but did not wake up. I was able to escape unnoticed. Two days later I was in El Paso.

"Rosita had no place to go, so we were married by a priest. Already there was a ten thousand dollar reward for me, dead or alive. A friend arranged for me to hire on as cowboy for a cattle drive to Montana. They hired Rosita to cook. We stopped here in Boise to rest our horses and I got this job at the livery stable."

When he mentioned Rosita was a cook, Greg knew both of them could be of help to him. He would need a cook and housekeeper for the big house he planned to build, and he certainly needed a cattle driver immediately. He suggested this to Raul.

The owner of the livery stable came in and yelled, "How come you are not working?"

"I'm not working for you anymore."

"You are interrupting our conversation," Greg said. The man took a look at Greg's size and went away, muttering.

Greg told Raul about his ranch on the Pahsimeroi and offered them a job with generous pay. Rosita would be cook and Raul would be ranch foreman in charge of the cattle. They had been talking for four hours, and it was near lunchtime.

"We'll take you and Rosita to lunch and discuss it."

Rosita was delighted. She said, "Señor, we'll try six months and if it works out, then we stay."

In the afternoon, they all rode with the agent out to the pasture to see the cattle. Greg was especially pleased with a young shorthorn bull.

The agent said, "That bull cost three hundred dollars." He whistled at the price, but then said, "He's worth it. Shorthorns have thick hair and can stand cold weather. They produce high-quality beef. Raul, how are we going to get these cattle to the ranch?"

"It will be easy. See that cow who moves other cows out of the way, and they all seem to be afraid of her? That is the boss cow, head honcho. Rosita can lead her on a rope and the others will all follow. You and I will ride in the rear and herd the rest. Rosita must ride slowly as she is three months along."

Amos left them at Idaho City to return to the claims and they proceeded without incident to the ranch. Forage was plentiful and the cattle grazed around the camps, filled up quickly, and bedded down for the night early.

When they arrived at the ranch, the Lathams were delighted to have the Ortegas live with them until another house could be built. Greg said, "We have an enormous amount of work to do. We need to fence the property and build a house for me and Amos and one for Raul and Rosita. I hear that Salmon has a sawmill now where we can get lumber, but we will have to haul it down. I am going to see what I can get in the way of carpenters. I'll leave Raul to look after the cattle while they graze. We'll have to plow up more of the bottomland to raise lucerne and cut and stack it for feeding the cattle through the winter. If we plant grain, we can feed the cattle and sell them for a premium price."

After a good night's rest, he headed out for the return trip to the mining claims with Harry. Wong and Ching Lee were very glad to see him.

Wong said, "Much tubble."

"What kind of trouble?"

"Much talk, no likee Chinee men. Meeting of white men union. Want dlive out Chinee. No likee. Velly bad, McKenna. Chinee beaten and killed."

Greg and Amos attended the miners' meeting in the Union Hall. The vote was almost unanimous that the Chinese had to move out of Idaho City in five days or they would kill the ones who remained. The plea of the mine owners that they would be in serious trouble if this was carried out fell on deaf ears.

As they were walking back to their cabin, Amos said, "That really raises all hell."

"Yes, it does. But it is the answer to my labor problem."

They asked Wong to contact the head of his tong and bring him to them. He was a distinguished, elderly gentleman. They asked him to share tea with them.

Greg said, "Honorable Wong Ho, we have work for twelve

big, strong men for three months. We will pay them four dollars a day and furnish rice, corn meal, and beans. They will have to have a tent to live in. The men will work ten hours a day, six days a week. At least four of them must be carpenters who can build a house according to plans. At least four must be able to drive horses and use an axe and saw. You will receive the same wage and act as boss foreman, as some of them cannot speak or understand English. There are many large fish in the stream that they can catch and eat. We have much land. We need houses, fences, and long ditches for irrigation. Can you do this?"

"You honest man. Can do."

"We have a long walk to go. Pay will start day after tomorrow." They bowed, shook hands, and Wong Ho left.

Amos had rounded up eight heavy work horses for a pack train, and the following day they purchased supplies. When the Chinese assembled, they loaded the pack horses with rice, beans, dried fruit, tools, nails, wire, and a large tent. Harry carried his usual four fifty-pound sacks of flour. They also had carefully crated panes of glass for the houses.

Amos had remarked, "Harry is sure a smart mule."

"What has he done now to show he is so smart?" Greg asked.

"He always insists on being in the lead. He hates the dust."

It was a beautiful, clear late April morning and the dew sparkled like diamonds on the grass. Early flowers, yellow crocuses, and blue flags filled the wet spots along the trail. Greg was riding his Appaloosa with Harry behind. The old Indian trail was easy to follow, but the work horses were soft from an idle winter and had to be rested frequently as they climbed steadily uphill to the Lowman Pass. The Chinese walked steadily in a line, a few paces from each other.

They arrived at the ranch shortly after noon, three days later. Angus Latham greeted them enthusiastically. "We are sure glad to see you. We're getting mighty short on supplies. I never saw so many Chinese. What are you going to do with them?"

"They are going to build fences, ditches, and houses. I talked to the engineer in Idaho City, and he had me buy a transit and learn how to use it. We will survey the fence lines and the water system. Will you help me?"

"Sure. There's a whole passel of Mounce's cattle feedin' on the lower end of the ranch. We sure need fences."

The Chinese busily set up their tent and unloaded the pack horses, setting up housekeeping and storing supplies in Latham's barn. They gathered rocks and made a fireplace for cooking their food.

During the following days, while Greg and Latham surveyed and marked the fence lines and the main irrigation canal, the Chinese, under the supervision of Wong Ho, cut lodgepole pine in thirty-foot lengths from a dense stand in a flat on the east side. Because of the density of the trees, they were tall and slim, tapering from twelve to ten inches in diameter. They also cut large cedar trees to split into six-foot lengths for fence posts. Angus Latham noted the cedar wouldn't rot and would last for years.

The land sloped gently to the north. Greg was glad of the experience he had gained from irrigating in Utah. The work he had done with ditches and flumes while mining also was helpful. The large tributary of the Pahsimeroi River came down from the hills, entered the ranch on the northwest corner, angled to the north, and became almost a straight line. The survey showed they could run the irrigation canal almost straight down the west boundary. It could meander back and forth so that there would be no more than a two-inch fall per hundred feet to prevent washing. Angus put in a substantial rock and log dam to divert the water.

The Chinese were well satisfied with their surroundings. Large salmon crowded in the stream to spawn in the gravel beds. The Chinese caught and ate them, not minding that they were dying. In the shallow water of small ponds they dug cattails and ate the roots, as well as the seed heads when they were immature. On Sundays they washed clothes, sat and smoked their pipes, and gambled. The sweet smell of the pipes, Greg knew, was opium. He discussed it with Amos.

"It doesn't seem to bother them like it does white people. They have used it for thousands of years, and they are tolerant of it."

CHAPTER 25

SELLING THE CLAIMS

Greg McKenna was satisfied that the Chinese laborers would get the ranch ready to stock with cattle and he was looking forward to a long, pleasant, and profitable partnership with Amos. Angus proved to be invaluable, supervising while Greg made his frequent trips for supplies.

On the second trip back, he found a different Amos. He was clean-shaven and Greg was amazed at how young he looked. He can't be more than seven years older than me, he thought. Amos seemed to be extraordinarily lighthearted and talkative, in contrast to the very precise individual who wasted few words.

"It's really a relief to get rid of those miserable whiskers. Let's have dinner tonight at the Palace Cafe. I have a lot to tell you that will shock and surprise you. And we have a lot to talk about. Get us a table in the back upstairs where we can have some privacy. I have some business to attend to and will meet you there at seven o'clock."

Greg was sitting at the table when Amos walked in, looking very handsome.

"Let's eat some steaks first and then we'll talk."

Greg told him about events at the ranch. When the waiter had cleared the table and brought in a bottle of bourbon, Amos poured generous drinks.

"Have a big one. We are going to need it. Greg, I have always enjoyed your company and will continue to love you like a brother, but after we sell the claims and settle up, we will no longer be partners. I have only about a two thousand dollar interest in the ranch and I do not want to be a rancher now. As you may have guessed by the books I read, I am a lawyer, and I am planning to practice law in Boise. My real name is Leonard Wilson."

"Amos—Leonard, why did you change your name?"

"I was sentenced to hang for a murder I didn't commit in Boston. My brothers and cousins arranged a jail break by doping the jailer. They had fast horses stationed at intervals of about twenty miles and I was able to get well away before it was discovered. I had plenty of money, and by staying away from large towns I reached St. Louis in two months. When I picked up my mail at the St. Louis post office, there was a wanted picture of me. Fortunately, I had grown a heavy beard and was not recognized. I wanted to go West where there would be less chance of getting caught.

"I arrived in Kansas City as trappers were bringing in their furs to sell and get supplies. I met Zeke Casper. He was a mountain man and trapper. He was being beaten up by two men who were trying to rob him of his furs. I helped him leave them moaning on the ground."

Greg nodded, still astonished at the new side of Amos he was seeing.

"Zeke had lost his partner by drowning and asked me to go along with him. I told him my name was Amos Jordan. I spent the winter trapping with him and he taught me much about survival in the wilderness.

When we came out in the spring, caravans were forming to go West. I hired on as scout. The trip where we met was my third.

There was a girl. She was only sixteen years old and I was twenty. We were in love. She wanted to get married, but I said she would have to wait until she was at least eighteen. She said, 'I will wait forever.' We have corresponded over the years. When the war started, she married an officer who died in the first battle of Manassas. She wrote me last week, saying that the real killer had confessed on his death bed, and I am no longer hunted. It is a wonderful feeling to be free and not having to look over my shoulder. I am going home to ask Emily to marry me. I have written her to expect me in three weeks. I think we should sell the claims now."

Greg said, "I could not be happier for you. But it will take some getting used to calling you Leonard. We'll sell the claims as soon as possible."

"I thought you would agree. I have already made arrangements and the papers are ready for you to sign. I showed the claims to a fellow named Lord Cavendish and his geologist. They spent considerable time digging and sampling. They have offered twenty-five thousand dollars for the property. I think it's a good offer."

"There might be another fifty thousand in it, but it would take a year to get it out. We both know that the hard rock vein is very short. I think I'm delighted to get out. When do I sign?"

Leonard brought out a legal document and showed him where to sign. They hugged each other and sealed the deal with a drink.

CHAPTER 26

HOMECOMING

Travelling by stage coach to Salt Lake and to the rail junction in Kansas, and from there by train to Boston took fifteen days. It had then been twenty-two days since he had written Emily, telling her to expect him in three weeks. He hired a coach and looked at the changes in the city. Boston had really grown.

The Wilsons were expecting him. When he knocked at the door of his family's prestigious brownstone, the maid answered the door and asked, "What is your name and who do you want to see?"

"I am Leonard Wilson."

She was so excited that she forgot her proper behavior as a maid and ran to the dining room crying, "He's here! He's here!" The startled family looked up as the handsome Leonard walked in behind her. What followed was a bedlam of hugs, kisses, and tears. Finally, they sat down to finish dinner. His father said, "No more talk. Let him eat. We have a whole lifetime to talk and answer questions." Leonard was anxious to inquire about where Emily lived.

This was answered when his mother said, "Emily is a widow now, you know. She lives only four blocks back of us on Beacon Hill. I expect you will want to see her."

"Mother, you can't imagine how anxious I am to see her. I'm

going over after dinner to get reacquainted. It has been a long, long time."

The postman had delivered Emily's mail at the usual time. When she heard his whistle, she hurried to the mail box, hoping for a letter from Len. There it was, written in pencil, from Idaho City. She took it into the house and sat down in her rocking chair. Reading it, she started to cry and laugh. It said Len would be coming home, that he still loved her. She looked out the window and saw a tall man coming down the street. The doorbell rang. She opened the door, and he was there.

"Len, you have grown so tall and handsome."

"You are more beautiful than ever."

Whatever reservations either of them had about the possible change in the other dissolved. He sat down in a big chair, holding a joyful, tearful woman in his lap. They sat there, holding each other and catching up on the past, until her daughter, Mary, came home. Mary already knew all about her mother's lost love.

Len said, "Mary, you are as beautiful as your mother."

"You are even more handsome than she told me you were. You two have a lot to talk about. I'll fix a late dinner. We're having chops, yams, biscuits, and gravy. Momma made a pie for dessert."

Emily was intrigued at the prospect of living out West. They were married within a month and traveled to Boise, where Leonard set up his law practice.

CHAPTER 27

WINTER OF 1864

By September, the Chinese had accomplished far more than Greg had hoped. They were craftsmen. The fences and corrals were lined with precise straight fences, some with posts and wire, some with pine logs. The new two-bedroom log cabin with a fireplace, a stove with a stovepipe, and water piped into a kitchen sink, was snug and tight as the Chinese had hewed the logs until they fitted without any daylight showing. They showed surprising skill and ingenuity in fashioning furniture from logs and some lumber from the Salmon sawmill. The main canal was a success and they had run a satisfactory trial irrigation on the meadows.

Rosita was happy in the new house and had turned out to be a good cook. Greg taught her how to make a pie out of apples that the Lathams had stored. She was singing to her unborn child, due in November. Martha Latham said she could take care of the birthing.

A few colts and calves had been born, and Greg was pleased with the way his foreman, Raul, was training them. He was gentle with the colts and they would follow him around to be petted. They would be easy to break for riding.

Angus Latham and Greg thought highly of each other. Angus had proved to be very capable of supervising the ranch during Greg's frequent trips out for supplies. Greg realized that he needed him to stay. He offered to give Angus the forty acres that he had cultivated, their house, ten head of cattle, and their monthly wage if they would stay permanently. They were happy to accept.

Greg received notice from his agent that he had acquired six more brood mares. Greg no longer needed the Chinese, so he planned to escort them to Boise and bring the mares back, loaded with supplies for the winter. Some of the Chinese talked about prospecting along the Snake River. Others wanted to find work in Boise. They could not return to hostile Idaho City. He asked the tong leader what they wanted to do.

"Go to Snake, look fo gold." He spread his hands and made the motions of panning. "Much gold. Too small fo white man. Chinee make five dolla, eight dolla a day."

"Where did you hear this?"

"We make contact, shake hands, then Chinaman tell us."

Greg provided supplies for their back packs and regretfully watched their pigtails swinging as they headed south on the Salmon River, where they would cross Galena Summit and follow Wood River to the Snake. He would have liked to keep them. He had never known more honest, industrious, and skilled workmen. But he knew more than a thousand Chinese panned or placer mined the very fine gold flakes along a hundred mile stretch to American Falls. They had a town called China Town.

Greg packed Harry and his Appaloosa with the necessities for his trip to Boise to bring back the new brood mares. He needed supplies and would use the mares for pack horses on the way back. On the way, he stopped at Idaho City to attend a Masonic Lodge meeting and go to church, where he wanted to sing.

In Boise, he was pleased with the brood mares, settled up with his agent, and withdrew money from the bank for supplies and expenses for the current year. He spent a pleasant night with Marianne and asked her if she would marry him.

She said, "Greg, I love you, but I am not the wife for you. I had a miscarriage in Salt Lake and an infection, and the doctor said I would never be able to have children. Larry and I tried but without success. You need a wife who will give you sons to help you and to inherit your property."

Without a companion at his side, Greg turned his attention to his work. By tying the halter of each heavily-laden brood mare to the tail of the horse ahead, he was able to make them plod along. He was tired and dirty when he camped in the edge of the timber, a day away from home. After hobbling the horses and Harry, and eating a meal of beans, bread, and a grouse he had shot, he rolled in his blankets and was immediately asleep. He was suddenly awakened by the clanking of Harry's bell and the screams and stomping of the horses. He grabbed his rifle and ran toward the thrashing horses, who tried to get near him for protection. He thought it was a bear or cougar. If it was a grizzly bear, his fifteen-shot, .45-caliber rifle would be a questionable weapon. Evidently his presence spooked the beast away. He looked up at the sky and shouted, "Thank you, Lord. This is my lucky day!"

He built a fire and cooked coffee, bacon, and hardtack fried in the bacon grease for breakfast. He was not in a hurry, being only thirty miles from home. After catching each horse and tying it to the ring in the lead rope, he carefully cinched the pack saddles and loaded each one with about two hundred pounds of goods. He had included dress material for Rosita and Martha and boots for the men. The mares weighed near twelve hundred pounds and stood over sixteen hands high, meeting the standards for U.S. Cavalry horses.

The sun was just beginning to rise over the mountains to the west of him. Coyotes had finished their morning greetings to the world and birds were singing their territorial calls. The pack train had been climbing up a long ridge for nearly an hour. They were sweaty and breathing heavily. He stopped to give them a rest. There was a break in the timber ahead. He heard voices. He rode his horse to the clearing and saw two men skinning a cow. He thought it would be nice to take home some fresh meat and started down toward them. When they heard his horse's hooves clink on the rocks, they looked up, ran for their horses, and disappeared into the pines. He rode down to the dead cow. Its throat had been cut and it was half skinned. They had left a good, sharp knife. He picked it up and was looking at it, when four men rode out of the timber.

"Hello," Greg said. "I rode down to see what those men were doing and they took off like their pants were on fire."

"You're a damned liar. You're a cattle thief. Roll that cow over." Greg turned the cow over.

"It has the M brand, Mr. Mounce," a cowboy said.

"I didn't kill this cow. I have a ranch over by Spring Creek."

"So you are a damned nester trying to make a living on cattleman's range and stealing cattle." Mounce knew who Greg was, but he didn't let on. Greg's ranch had been a thorn in his side. Greg didn't have a very good appearance. His clothes were dirty, he was unshaven. Even his horse was gaunt from the long trip.

Mounce was a cattle baron. He had a relatively small holding on his home ranch, but claimed all the range around. He was notorious for running off nesters by any means, from burning out to murder. There was very little law in the territory.

Mounce said, "Tie him up." Greg could not resist as they had three guns trained on him.

"Take him over to that pine tree. We are going to hang him."

One of the cowboys remonstrated. "He might be telling the truth."

"Shut your face. I know what I'm doing. Jasper, you've been practicing tying hangman's nooses for months. Tie one now."

Thoughts raced through Greg's mind. This arrogant son of a bitch was going to end his life just as he was realizing his dream. He would never have his ranch or wife and children, never again enjoy the sun, sky, and joy of living. He watched as Jasper tied the hangman's noose with its many wraps.

Mounce said, "Do you have anything to say?"

"I didn't kill your cow. You are hanging an innocent man. I'll see you burn in hell."

"We are going to hang you no matter what. Anyone stupid enough to kill a wet cow and leave a calf to starve deserves to be hung."

Greg's hands were tied behind his back with a leather piggin' string. They took off his hat and slipped the noose over his head. A deep, guttural voice behind them caused them to turn around.

"No hang. No kill'um cow. Two go that way." There was a ragged Indian holding a double-barreled shotgun with hammers cocked. The cowhands were not unhappy about dropping their pistols, since they were not enthusiastic about hanging a man in the first place. When the Indian pointed his gun at Mounce, he turned and rode into the timber. His crew mounted and followed.

Greg's back was to his benefactor. When his hands were cut loose, he turned to see a tall, handsome, middle-aged Indian in worn buckskins. He heard a whimper, almost like a kitten in distress. The Indian took the pack off his back and held it out for Greg to see a crying baby. Greg noticed that the baby boy had unusually white skin for an Indian, and had blue eyes and curly dark hair. He pointed to the white skin. The Indian drew a picture of a covered wagon in the sand and said, "No Indian." The Indian indicated by signs that the baby was hungry. Greg knew what babies needed because he had taken care of the Fletcher's children when he was a boy. There was nothing in his pack string that would keep what appeared to be a four-month-old baby alive. He opened his palms and shook his head to indicate that he had no food. The Indian pointed to the cow, which was still warm, with a full udder. Greg mounted his Appaloosa, which had been standing patiently where it was left, motioned the Indian to stay with the cow, and rode back to his packstring. He brought them down the hill, and tied the lead to a tree. The horses were nervous in the presence of fresh blood. Greg noticed that the Indian had dried blood on his pants and shirt.

How to feed the baby was a problem.

Mother's milk was best for the baby and cow's milk could make him sick. But, it was the only choice. Greg had a bottle with a little whiskey in it, and he and the Indian drank, then Greg emptied the bottle into a cup. There was a little whiskey left in the bottle when he took it over to the cow. He was about to pour it out, but considered that a little stimulant might help the baby survive. The udder was full and in a matter of minutes the bottle was full of milk. Holding the whimpering baby and trying to feed it with a spoon didn't work out. Greg went back to his pack and brought out a smooth, new leather glove that he had bought in Boise. Quickly, he cut a small hole in the end of one finger, cut off the finger and slipped it over the neck of the bottle. Fortunately, it fit tightly. He was able to tilt the bottle, fill the glove finger, and let the baby suck it, which it did hungrily. The baby stopped whimpering, but was still uneasy and restless, and had an odor. Greg put him on his shoulder and was rewarded with a large burp and a bit of spit-up milk. He found a new cotton shirt in his pack and tore it up to make several diapers. The baby howled when they washed his bottom with cold water. The Indian was holding it and nodded approval as Greg dried him and dusted his bottom with flour. When he was wrapped in his blanket in the Indian's pack, he immediately went to sleep.

Greg noticed fresh blood seeping through the Indian's shirt. He motioned for him to take it off and examined his wound, which appeared to be made by a small caliber rifle. It had entered his side just below the ribs, and on his back was a dark, almost black spot, swollen and red. Greg poured whiskey on a piece of shirt and wiped his knife, then pierced the black spot. The bullet popped out. He then poured whiskey over the wound and bound it with a tight bandage torn from another new shirt, to stop the bleeding. He had only one of three new shirts left.

They started a small fire and cooked beans and bacon, which the Indian wolfed down. The last thing Greg did before leaving was to again fill the whiskey bottle with milk. The Indian, with the child on his back, brought up the rear of the pack train. He was keeping the pack train moving at the fastest walk they could make. After about three hours, they entered a long, narrow meadow that was bordered by a clear stream. The bloom of camas lilies looked like a waving ocean of white as they swayed in the breeze.

Greg was worried. Could they get the baby home in time? It would take at least ten hours. Would the mares hold out? How long would it take for the milk to sour? Would the Indian get sick from the wound? He decided to stop in this meadow and let the horses drink and graze for a needed rest. Chief, as he now called the Indian, handed him the baby, who was whimpering and fretting. The baby took five fingerfuls of the milk but didn't finish the sixth.

"I'm going to call him Jim," Greg said as they cleaned the baby, fastened on a new diaper, washed his soiled diaper in the stream, and hung it on a packsaddle to dry. "I'd sure hate for him to leave this life without a name."

Chief was getting weak from loss of blood and from fever.

Greg took the baby's pack on his back, barely able to wriggle into the straps, which were too short for him. He was able to feed the baby one more time from the milk before it became sour. Greg then filled the bottle with water. Chief refused to take anything but water.

They had been travelling almost steadily for nearly twelve hours, stopping only to water the horses, change the baby, and give him a drink of water. Chief was bent over, barely able to hold the saddle horn to keep from falling over, as they pulled into the ranch yard. The barking dog aroused Raul, who burst out of the door, pulling on his pants and carrying his rifle. He helped Chief get off his horse and took over care of the pack string.

Greg helped Chief into the house, and handed the baby to Rosita. Greg was astonished when she immediately opened her blouse and put a nipple into Jim's mouth. The response was instantaneous as he greedily nursed. Rosita laughed and said, "My son was born nearly two weeks ago. His name is Antonio. I have enough milk for both of them, even though this one is a pig. Where did he come from? He is not an Indian." Little Jim's background would remain a mystery.

When Greg woke up the next morning, Mrs. Latham was treating the Indian's wound. The night before, she had fed him a rich beef broth that she had prepared. She had removed his bandage and washed the wound with a mild solution of creosote and applied a bandage from the soft diaper cloth that Rosita had ordered. Now she again removed the bandage, and the Chief stoically endured the pain.

"Greg, look, it is already better. The redness is less and the swelling has gone down a bit. If we can keep him in bed and quiet for a few days, he will be fine. Luckily, it froze last night, and I have a little ice for a cold pack."

"Wouldn't a hot pack feel better?"

"It might, but heat would help germs to grow. Cold will give the body time to fight the germs and help stop the flow of blood."

"Martha, we're certainly lucky to have you."

Greg was anxious to find out about the baby. To his surprise, the Indian was able to speak English well enough to tell his story. He was a Nez Perce and had attended school at the Spaulding

Mission for a short time. His name was Tall Man and he was chief of a small band consisting of six men, their wives, and four children. They were on their way to Yellowstone to hunt buffalo for their winter supply of meat. On the way, they had come upon a wagon that had apparently been attacked by Indians, probably Bannocks. They found a baby who had escaped being killed, and Tall Man's wife wanted to keep him because they had very recently lost their baby and she would be able to nurse it. They had camped in a meadow by a spring to rest and hunt game for food. Two of the men took rifles and set out to try to find a deer or elk. Tall Man took a muzzle-loading shotgun to hunt for pintail grouse. They had seen a large covey a few miles back on the trail. Three men stayed at the camp as guard. The Bannock Indians had been trouble for the Nez Perce and they were constantly trying to steal their coveted Appaloosa horses.

After firing only three loads of powder, Tall Man had a bagful of birds and was returning with an empty gun when he heard shots from the direction of his camp. He arrived just as the Bannocks rode off with the Appaloosa horses. One fired at him, hitting him in the side. All of his tribe were dead or dying, including his wife, who was clutching the baby. With her last breath she asked him to take the baby to his own people. He promised her that he would do that. He abandoned the plan to go to Yellowstone and turned toward Salmon, where he came upon Greg and the Mounce gang.

Many events took place at the McKenna ranch in the winter of 1864. Chief Tall Man left for two weeks after he recovered, but returned to the ranch, taking up Greg's promise that he had a place to stay and food for as long as he lived. He made himself useful as he had no peer in training horses. Ten were broke to ride and ready for sale.

More than one hundred head of cattle grazed on McKenna land. Because the cattle Greg bought were bred at different times, they first calved all winter instead of May, and had to be taken care of in the barn for a few days. Raul Ortega proved to be a master in handling the cattle. Greg was surprised to see Raul take a knife and peel back the horn buttons, then carefully apply a white salve.

"What is that white stuff you're putting on?"

"It's lard and lye. It will keep the calves from growing horns, and when they are grown, they won't fight. They are also easier to drive. Soon we'll have a whole herd of cattle without horns."

"You sure know a lot about cattle. You know, the railroad is already started to the West Coast. Right now there's a good market to the mines, Indian reservations, and the Army forts. The market of the future is going to be shipping to the East, as the population there is increasing by leaps and bounds. If we can hold out until the railroads are completed, we'll have it made. So far, we are not in any trouble."

The land below the ranch had been almost completely homesteaded by new settlers. They helped each other with hay and grain harvesting. The shorthorn bull had sired twenty thick, blocky calves that were still leggy enough to be able to travel.

Angus Latham did an excellent job managing the farmland and irrigating. He also prospered, having ten head of cattle bearing his L brand. The McKenna cattle were branded with MC.

Happy Little Jim was growing fast. His big hands and feet indicated he would be a tall man. Greg spent time with him each day and took him for rides on his horse.

In the spring, Mounce still brought his cattle in to graze, harassing the settlers below the McKenna ranch. There was a very narrow trail down a creek into the valley. It was just wide enough in places for a cow or horse to pass. On one of his trips to Boise, Greg brought back fifty sticks of dynamite, caps, and fuses. Late in March, the snow was gone.

"Raul, how would you like to take a ride with me. I need your help."

"Sure. What are we going to do?"

"You'll find out when we get there. You're going to like it." They went up along the stream to the narrow Mounce pass. When Greg unrolled his pack, Raul saw the dynamite and caps. He slapped his thigh, remarking, "That will fix the son'a bitch Mounce good!" After thought, he added, "That's going to make trouble too. He'll have to go nearly fifty miles around and it'll keep him out of the valley."

"Raul, I've thought of that. We can handle the trouble. Chief

Tall Man can see or smell out any trouble before it occurs and warn us."

"Yah. He's always scouting. He's real talented that way. Can I light at least one fuse?"

Near the entrance, where the thirty-foot-high lava walls were about five feet apart, there was a deep gully that they could crawl into for protection from the blast. They gouged a crack in the wall with the crowbar until it was about three feet deep into the lava, and placed ten sticks of dynamite there. Greg carefully put the cap on the six-foot-long fuse which would burn a foot a minute, and pulled it into the dynamite. Then he added five more sticks.

"Dynamite has to be packed in to be effective. We need to fill the crack with dirt and rocks."

"We can carry the dirt on the canvas you had it wrapped in." When they finished packing the dirt, they piled on loose rock.

"Raul, you wanted to light the fuse. Now is your chance. I'll climb up with you so I can help you down in case you break a leg." Raul lit the match and scrambled down as if he thought it would go off immediately. They ran away and dived into the gully behind a curve in the wall.

"Don't raise your head at the blast. Wait until all the rocks stop falling." The blast shook the ground. Rocks of all sizes landed. When all was silent, they rose to look at their handiwork. There was a pile of rubble ten feet high and twenty feet long.

Raul said, "That fixes it up good!"

"That will do for a starter. Now let's blast the other side. That will block it for good." The dynamiting on the other wall was even more successful and the rocks in the pass were now more than twenty feet high. The stream still flowed through the large lava rocks.

"Hell, I never thought that we might shut off our water. Thank God we didn't!"

"Raul said, "We still have twenty sticks left."

Chuckling, Greg answered, "Let's use them all at once and blow down that big wall over there." That charge really blocked the pass with big chunks of lava.

"When Mounce sees this, he'll know that you did it and probably send that Jasper Snead gunning for you."

"Could be."

Jasper Snead was part of the Mounce spread. He never worked manually, was always well-dressed and seemed to have plenty of money for gambling, which he did with fair success. It was rumored that he was a gunslinger and responsible for the death, burning out, and disappearance of the nesters or settlers that interfered with Mounce's interests. But to date, there was no proof.

CHAPTER 28

ELLEN RYAN

Marianne Breckenridge was recruiting for her fancy house. It was indeed a fancy house compared to the other brothels in Boise. She was sitting in her buggy waiting for the stage to arrive from Salt Lake, remembering the time she had met Madam LeClerc in New Orleans. She was emulating Madam LeClerc in management of her establishment. The stage was the place to find girls who were down on their luck, who might want to take up prostitution as the easy way out. A tall, slim young girl walked down the street carrying a small valise and looking typically dejected. She sat down on a bench and took off her hat to fan herself. Marianne saw a head of curly black hair and very blue eyes with well-proportioned features. Marianne walked over to sit down beside her.

"Are you lost? Can I help you?"

"I am worse than lost. My landlady turned me out. I don't blame her as I was over a month behind in my rent. I haven't been able to find work that would pay enough for my board and room. I don't know what to do."

"You can stay with me for a few days if you like. Perhaps I can help you find work. What is your name?"

"Ellen Ryan. Thank you. That is very kind of you."

"Are you Irish?"

"Yes, originally. But I grew up mostly in England. I came to America two years ago."

"Put your suitcase in my buggy and we will have lunch at my house."

They drove along Warm Springs Avenue and into the drive of a very large two-story house. Ellen thought her new benefactor must be very wealthy and maybe needed a maid.

A man came to help them down from the buggy and take the horse and buggy to a carriage house in the back. When they entered the house, there were several attractive ladies in the living room, chatting and doing needlework. Ellen felt apprehensive. It occurred to her that this might be a brothel. Marianne introduced her to the women, then led her upstairs to a tastefully furnished room. It was nicer than the home of the late Lord Brelsford, where she had been the maid.

"Ellen, this is your room. There is water in the pitcher on the commode. While you freshen up, I will get some lunch." It was a good lunch for the very hungry girl.

"I am making a pig of myself," she apologized after taking her third helping of cold chicken and buttered rolls.

"When did you eat last?"

"Yesterday. I spent my last quarter for a sandwich and a bowl of soup."

"Take your time. When you finish, we will talk." After the maid had cleaned up the table, they sat facing each other in comfortable over-stuffed chairs.

"How did you happen to come to America?"

"I was the oldest of seven children. My father was tenant on the country estate of Lord Brelsford. We were very poor. The lord decided to spend the summer on the estate, bringing his wife and two children from London. Their maid became seriously ill and they asked for a replacement. I was given a trial. Those children were little hellions at first, but I played with them and won them over, and they tried to please me. I had a nice uniform to wear and received five shillings a month. I was sixteen then. Lady Brelsford was pleased as she didn't have to be bothered with looking after the 'brats' as she called them. She was surprised that I was able to teach the children to read and write. When they returned to London, they asked me to go with them.

The lord had acquaintances who made money by investing in the States, and he decided to go there. He had heard about the gold in California, and the fast-growing West. The lady didn't want to leave her social life and go to the wilds, but she was more afraid he would leave without her. They asked me to go with them. I wasn't happy about leaving, but he told me that the men far outnumbered the women in the West and it would be easy to find a rich husband. I had heard how wonderful America was, so I decided to go if they would pay me five more shillings a month. They agreed to that."

"What happened next?" Marianne prompted.

"I had a wonderful trip, with a nice room on the ship. The sailors were friendly when I took the children for walks and showed us around the ship, which delighted the children. The lady was sick the whole time and stayed in her cabin.

The stage from Kansas was horrible. The lord heard that there was gold discovered in Idaho, so we took the stage from Salt Lake to Boise. He bought a house and started investing heavily in mining properties. Being an English lord used to fox hunting, he got a pack of hounds and started chasing coyotes. He was in the midst of a chase when his horse stepped in a badger hole, breaking its leg and throwing the lord over its head. He died with a broken neck."

"I remember reading about the accident," Marianne said.

"The lady knew nothing about business and hired a lawyer who persuaded her to give him power of attorney. Apparently he sold the properties at ridiculously low prices and charged huge legal fees for settling the estate. When it was all over she had barely enough money to get back to England. She did not have enough money to take me, so she gave me twenty dollars and left me stranded."

Ellen relaxed under sympathetic remarks and questioning. She was surprised when Marianne asked, "Are you a virgin?"

"I was raped by the coachman in England."

"How did that happen?"

"The cook sent me to the stable to gather eggs. He had been after me for some time, but I'd managed to evade him. I didn't see him, but when I crawled back in the hay to get to a nest, he slipped up on me. I fought the best I could."

"Did he hurt you?"

"Yes. He really hurt me and I lay there all bloodied. I finally stood up and straightened my clothes. I took the eggs and started to leave. As I walked by the stable door, there he was, currying a horse and whistling. He didn't hear me pick up the pitchfork. He let out a terrible yell when I drove it deep into his buttocks with all my strength. When he turned and cursed, I tried to stick him again, but he ran. I was glad he had to sit on a pillow to drive and the doctor had to lance it."

"You were a very brave girl. You Irish are famous for your temper and your spunk."

CHAPTER 29

THE FIGHT

Salmon City was now the county seat and a supply headquarters for many of the mines in the area. A sawmill was busy making lumber from the abundant forest of large pine and fir trees. Greg had several things on his list to do. He was going to inquire about adopting Little Jim and get supplies for the ranch. Goods of all kinds were freighted from Salt Lake through Montana to Salmon City. He and Raul took the wagon and four horses to bring back a load of lumber.

"What are you going to do with the lumber?" Raul asked.

"Keep it just in case, to build another house or a schoolhouse, or something."

During the long drive, Raul noticed that Greg was wearing moccasins. He asked why.

"Those new boots wore a blister on my heel. I'm giving it a chance to heal."

It was almost dusk when they finished errands. They planned to stay all night at the hotel and load the supplies in the morning. Greg said, "Let's have a drink before eating."

"Go ahead," said Raul. "I want to buy a present for Rosita. I'll join you in a few minutes."

Greg was sipping his drink when he heard the bat wings of the saloon open. He turned to see if it was Raul. There was a large man, bigger than himself. It was Mounce. Mounce glanced at Greg and turned back to the bar, looked in the mirror, frowning. After a little while, he walked over behind Greg and said, "Do I know you?"

"You know me. You tried to hang me."

Mounce then realized who he was talking to.

"Too bad I didn't. You're the son of a bitch who blew my trail shut and I'm going to beat the living hell out of you."

Greg's answer to this remark was an overhand right to Mounce's face, breaking his nose and leaving a gap in his front teeth. A left hook split an eyebrow. Mounce had a reputation for being a very cruel man who had crushed a man to death and crippled several others. Greg was glad for the moccasins that helped him maneuver easily, and thankful for the boxing lessons that Moses had given him. The spectators moved the chairs to the wall when they realized a fight was starting, and were taking bets on the outcome. They hoped that Greg would win.

Greg kept circling to Mounce's left. It appeared that Mounce was pawing with his left and trying for the kill with a looping right, from which Greg swayed away, landing his own hard left jabs to the eyes. Mounce swung a hard right and missed, leaving himself open to a right cross that Greg landed with all his power behind it. Mounce appeared dazed and Greg threw a hard left hook to his midsection. To Greg's surprise, it was like hitting a solid wall. He didn't step back quickly enough and a right caught him on the jaw, causing him to stumble and fall. Mounce went in for the kill and Greg rolled away just in time to escape being stomped. He moved around to regain his balance.

It seemed this man was as tough as a bull. Then he remembered something Moses had told him about hitting the floating ribs a little on the backside, the liver shot. Finally, he got his chance. He feinted with a purposely slow left that made Mounce duck to the right, then drove a roundhouse right into the last floating rib. Mounce gasped in pain. Now Mounce was held up by the wall and hard lefts and rights were making his face a bloody mess. Mounce started to fall and Greg held him up with his left hand and continued to pound him. The sheriff, hearing the commotion, entered the saloon. Grabbing Greg, he said, "Stop. You don't want to kill him."

"Killing is too good for him."

There was a sharp crack and a thud. The sheriff turned and saw a man on the floor with a large gash in his head and whiskey all over the floor. Raul was standing there, holding a gun in his hand.

"What happened, Raul?" the sheriff asked.

"When this hombre walked in front of me, I grabbed the bar towel and the full quart of whiskey. When he reached for his gun, I conked him on the cabasa."

"Raul, you probably saved my life," Greg said.

"Greg, now there's all hell to pay. They will try to get even. Chief is going to have a lot to do. I can see him muttering to himself as he cleans that old Sharps."

"You're right about being careful and about Chief's shooting. I saw him shoot the head off a rabbit. I couldn't see the head as it was nearly one hundred yards, let alone hit the rabbit. But he could. The rabbit was flopping about without a head."

A few days, later Greg walked toward the barn, whistling "Buffalo Gal" and thinking about finding a wife. As he crossed the open space, he heard the resounding boom of a buffalo gun followed by the sharp crack of a smaller gauge rifle, whining as it went over his head. He rolled out of sight under a nearby wagon and looked through the spokes to see Chief waving his hat in a beckoning motion. He ran up the hill to where Chief was standing and saw a wounded man trying to stop the flow of blood in his thigh with a stick and bootlace tourniquet.

"Help me!" he whined.

Greg put his fingers on the ends of the severed artery, pressing hard.

"Who paid you to shoot at me, or I'll let you die."

"Mounce," the man gasped.

"How much did he pay you?"

"Five hundred." There was nothing they could do as the man's face was turning grey and he passed out in a few minutes. Raul joined them. He looked at the dead man with distaste and said, "It serves him right. What are we going to do with him? The easiest thing would be to bury him and nobody would know the difference."

"Raul, that would be the easiest, but we would know. We will take him to Salmon and let the sheriff take care of him. That will be following the law. If we don't follow the law, we can't expect others to."

Going through the dead man's pockets, they found twenty-five twenty-dollar gold pieces in a poke and a small black purse with nineteen dollars.

Greg said, "We'll keep these gold pieces as it was the price on my head. We will use it for building a schoolhouse."

When they took the body to the sheriff at Salmon, he said, "There will have to be an inquest." He went into the saloon and brought out six men. To Greg they looked like barflies. They all followed the sheriff to the courthouse, where the judge was sweeping out the courtroom. He put down the broom and took his place behind the desk, instructing the jury to elect a foreman.

"The court will come to order. The jury will be seated. It is your duty to determine whether a crime has been committed or whether the killing was a case of justifiable homicide in self-defense. Mr. McKenna, please take the witness chair."

The judge also acted as bailiff to swear him in. "Place your hand on the Bible. Do you swear to tell the truth, the whole truth, and nothing but the truth so help you God?"

"I do." As he told the story from beginning to end, he was frequently interrupted by the jurors asking questions.

"Did he have any money on him?"

"Yes, a small purse with nineteen dollars in it."

"How far was he from you?"

"About one hundred forty yards."

The judge asked the jurors time and again to keep still and let Greg finish. Raul was called to the stand and the judge asked, "Can you add anything to Mr. McKenna's testimony?"

"No, it was just like Mr. McKenna said."

"The jury will adjourn to the next room and reach a verdict."

"Your Honor, we don't need to adjourn. We have whispered among ourselves and we have decided the shooting was the right thing to do."

"You are saying the homicide was justified?"

"Your Honor, if you mean that it was all right to kill the bastard, that is our opinion."

The judge hammered his gavel. "The case is closed. Jury dismissed. Each juror will receive two dollars from the decedent's purse. The janitor gets one dollar, the bailiff gets two dollars, and the judge gets four dollars."

Greg asked the judge and sheriff to wait, as he wanted to talk to them.

"What about a warrant for Mounce because he hired a man to kill me?"

"We can issue a warrant and serve it, but I personally think it would be of little use."

"But there was a witness."

"True, but that witness was an Indian and a jury would be very skeptical of anything an Indian said. Any lawyer would be able to get him confused. They might say that the man was sitting there waiting for a deer, and the Indian killed him because he didn't like him."

"What do you think, Sheriff?"

"You are between a rock and a hard place."

Greg said, "I'm going to keep that telescope rifle he had anyway," and walked out with it. Greg and Raul agreed that in the future he would not ride alone in the woods and hills.

CHAPTER 30

ANOTHER TRIP TO BOISE

Greg was preparing to take twenty head of horses to Fort Boise to fulfill an Army contract. His plan was to leave in two days. His thoughts were interrupted when a small boy yelled, "Dadee, Dadee."

He picked up the child, who patted him on the cheek. He had been quite concerned about Little Jim's future when Martha Latham said, "It is too bad that it is so hard for a single male to adopt a child. Some couple would be glad to adopt him."

Greg said, "If anyone is going to adopt him, it will be me."

"Greg, if you were married, it would be no problem. You need a wife."

"Martha, I know that. I've been looking."

Two days later Martha and Rosita stood in the yard with Little Jim, waving to Greg as he left with Harry and the string of horses.

"Martha, I have a feeling he's going to bring back a wife," said Rosita.

"It would be nice to have another woman to visit with. If he comes back alone, leading that fool mule, I'll feel like beating him!"

"My grandmother had the gift of seeing into the future and knowing of happenings far away. She kept it a secret for fear of being thought a witch. She passed it on to my mother, and sometimes I have it, too. Last night I woke up from a dream. There was a wedding. I had only a brief glimpse of it. It was a wonderful wedding, with beautiful dresses. The groom was big, but had his back to me, the bride was tall and had black curly hair. It could have been Greg, but I couldn't see their faces."

"It would be wonderful if you are right."

The possibility of a marriage gave the two women a lot to think and talk about. They speculated about whether the bride would accept Little Jim. Rosita planned to move her family into the little house that had been built. They discussed the matter many times over coffee.

Meanwhile, in Boise, Greg put his horse and Harry in the livery stable after delivering the Army horses to the fort. He went shopping for clean clothes and found a good dark suit that had just come in on a shipment from Salt Lake. The outfit was completed with a white shirt and a new cattleman's hat with wide brim. The next stop was a haircut, shave, and bath at the barbershop. The barber cut his thick, almost red hair, exposing his ears, and shaved him clean with sideburns. He had not seen his bare face since he'd left Kansas, and decided that he was a fairly handsome man. To his surprise, there was a bathtub with claw feet and running water, hot and cold. The hot water came from a hot spring in the hills, for which Warm Springs Street was named. It was very hot and smelled like sulphur, but was wonderfully soft and sudsy. He soaked until the barber knocked on the door, saying, "Your time is up. Another customer is waiting for the tub."

He took the clothes that he had been wearing to a small Chinese laundry, then registered at the Palace Hotel. The bed with springs was a luxury, and he didn't awake until after the sun was up. After breakfast he walked down Main Street.

He saw lettering in gold on the window of a most impressive building, "Leonard Wilson and Associates, Attorneys at Law." He thought his former partner must be doing really well. The secretary greeted him with, "How can I help you?"

"I want to see Mr. Wilson."

"Mr. Wilson is with a client now. Would you like to make an appointment? He could see you at three o'clock tomorrow."

"Please interrupt Mr. Wilson and tell him that Greg McKenna is here."

"Mr. McKenna, I can't do that. It is against my orders."

"Orders be damned. You tell him or I'll walk through that door."

She got up and flounced as she opened the door and said, "I am sorry, Mr. Wilson. A Greg McKenna is here and insists on seeing you. I tried to stop him." Leonard threw up his hands, looked at the client and said, "I'm sorry, but we will have to finish this tomorrow after one o'clock." The disgruntled client left. The two men embraced after shaking hands.

"Greg, I'm so glad to see you. I've been missing you."

"Len, I've been missing you. I need your help on some legal matters and it is going to take some time for us to catch up. How about Wednesday afternoon?"

"Better than that. You haven't met my wife, and she's been dying to meet you. Come to dinner tonight." They had been corresponding and he knew Leonard had married his old sweetheart.

"I can't tonight. I have an appointment for dinner at half past five o'clock."

"I know where you are going—to see Marianne. We didn't find many safe women in the years we were together. It is wonderful to have a beautiful wife. You need to get married. Emily has inquired among the desirable women she knows. They were enthusiastic about meeting you, but none of them would consider moving out into the wilderness."

"Len, you are wrong about my meeting Marianne. She has arranged for me to meet a new nineteen-year-old girl. She said to be gentle because it was her first time to have a customer."

"You mean, she wants you to break in this filly. It might be a pleasant surprise. You never know what is around the corner. Come to dinner tomorrow night, then."

"Thank you. I'll be there."

It was just a few minutes before five when he pushed the button for the chimes at Marianne's house. A colored maid answered the door. She said, "We are glad to see you again, Mr. McKenna. Marianne's gonna be right happy. She is waiting for you in the parlor." Marianne greeted him with a kiss and an affectionate hug, saying, "I'll take you up and introduce you to Ellen. I know how she feels, as I went through the same thing in New Orleans."

Ellen answered the knock on her door, saying, "Won't you please come in."

"Ellen, this nice man is Gregory McKenna. I'll leave you two to have a good dinner and a very pleasant evening." She closed the door as she left. For a few seconds, they stood and stared at each other. Greg asked, "Are you as nervous as I am?"

"There is no way you could be more nervous, even though you are larger."

"I think we both could use a drink." While she poured the drinks, Greg gazed with pleasure at the beautiful hostess. What he saw was a graceful young woman with curly black hair and very blue eyes, and a face that showed strength and character. Her figure was lovely.

"Marianne mentioned you were of Irish descent. I thought the Irish were always redheaded and freckled."

"The story handed down is that my family took in a Spanish sea captain and hid him from the British," she laughed. "Actually, he probably was a cabin boy."

She was very impressed by the tall, well-built, handsome man before her, and thought how wonderful it would be to have a man like that for a husband. As they sat at the small table, sipping their drinks, he asked, "How did you happen to come to America?" She told him about herself, and he told her about his adventures. The maid knocked at the door and announced that dinner was ready, a choice of roast beef or goose. Almost simultaneously they chose the goose, which turned out to be delicious. Greg was hungry and really enjoyed the meal. Ellen was hungry but ate sparingly, remembering Marianne's admonition that an actress couldn't perform very well on a full stomach.

Greg was thinking that this girl was very like Marianne. It would be wonderful to have a wife like her. She probably wouldn't want to live in the wilderness. He was actually feeling guilty about going to bed with her. After the maid had cleared the table, Ellen, wanting to prolong the feeling of normal social amenity, asked Greg if he would like another drink, since she still had half of hers to finish. He accepted. She said, "You are from Idaho City?"

"I was there for several years. Now I have a ranch in the Lemhi Valley."

"Tell me about your ranch. How big is it?" To her a ranch meant something bigger than the five acres her father had farmed.

He told her about the ranch and his plans for the future. It took considerable time to tell about the Lathams, Raul and Rosita, and Little Jim. The story of Little Jim caused her to cry a little, and she dabbed the tears from her cheeks. She went over to him, gave him a kiss, and said, "You are such a wonderful, nice man. Your wife is a very lucky woman."

He pulled her onto his lap, held her, and kissed her. It was a long kiss, as neither seemed to want it to end.

"Ellen, I don't have a wife. I've been wondering if you would consider marrying me and living on the ranch?" She could not believe it.

"Marry you?"

"Yes, marry me. I've been wanting to ask you for hours."

"Oh, yes! Yes!" She dissolved in tears. They were both overwhelmed at the turn of events. "This is so wonderful. I was imagining how nice that would be, but I could not hope that you would ask."

"Could we get married tomorrow?"

"Tomorrow would be perfect."

"We have a lot of planning to do. Do you want to be married in church, with a white gown and flowers?"

"That is more than I would ever hope for. I can't believe that this is not a wonderful dream."

"It is no dream, this is for real. I will get up early and call on Leonard before he goes to the office. He will help me make arrangements. Do you want to wait until after the wedding?"

"Greg, that would make it more sacred." After they each had gone to the bathroom, Ellen said, "I will get into bed first." She dressed in a flimsy nightgown, turned the kerosene light down low, and waited. She could not help looking at the big, hairy-chested man wearing only light drawers. He blew out the flame in the lamp and crawled into bed, taking her in his arms. They kissed and cuddled, and the resolve to wait didn't seem to be important, but in fact pretty foolish. She helped him roll down his drawers and pull up her nightgown. He was careful and gentle, but she did feel some pain at first as he entered, then she was in ecstasy. Her sensation had almost reached the point of going out of control, when she felt the throbbing and spurt of warm fluid inside. He remained on top of her while they kissed with abandon. Soon she felt him harden again within her. This time they reached climax simultaneously.

"That was wonderful," she said, hoping he felt the same.

"It was incredible. Turn your back to me." He put his arm around her and both were asleep in a few minutes.

Ellen was still asleep when Greg rose the next morning at six o'clock. After washing and dressing, he woke her.

"You tell Marianne about our plans. I am going to see Len before he goes to the office."

He walked the few blocks to the Wilson residence and rang the doorbell. A lovely woman answered.

"You must be Emily. I am Greg McKenna." It ran through his mind that this was the kind of woman Len would marry.

"Greg, it is so good to meet you. You are a great friend and a hero to Len. Do come in. Len has gone to the office for an early appointment."

"Emily, I need to see Len real bad, as I need help."

"What is the problem?"

"I am going to get married today. I've met the most wonderful girl and want to have a church wedding, with a white gown and flowers and everything. There is so much to do and I don't know how to go about making the arrangements."

"Greg, I'm so glad for you, and Len will be overjoyed. He has been saying that you need a wife. Come into the kitchen with me and we'll have coffee while we make plans. I can help you more than Len. I can do a lot of arranging and I have friends who will help. They'll love it."

When they were seated at the kitchen table with coffee, she began to make a list.

"Do you have a ring?"

"Emily, we only met last night."

She wrote down, bride needs ring, gown, hair dressed, church.

"Do you want an organist and flowers? I hope we can get my church, the Presbyterian. It has a kitchen and dining room."

"I want everything. Price is no object."

"We'll have a dinner after the wedding, then. I have four couples, and the minister and his wife, and the organist. Is there anyone you want to invite?"

"Marianne Breckenridge." This caused a startled expression.

"You mean the lady that runs the fancy whorehouse down the street? Did your Ellen come from there? Is she one, too?"

"No, she isn't, and never has been. She was stranded in Boise. Marianne took her in and kept her from being hungry and on the street."

"Greg, you go ahead and bring her here and we'll see what can be done." It occurred to Greg that Emily might be giving herself an out. He went to fetch Ellen, who had just finished breakfast when he entered the mansion. They greeted each other with a kiss. "Don't ask questions. Just get your coat and come with me to meet someone very important who can help with the wedding."

When Emily met Ellen and talked with her briefly, she realized that the tall, beautiful girl was a special person, and no trollop. She said, "Greg, you are a lucky man. I'll take over from here and she will be ready for the altar. You go and see Len, get the ring, arrange for the minister, and see if we can get the church."

Leonard's client was just leaving when Greg arrived. Len was delighted to hear the news. He told his secretary to cancel appointments because he would be out for the day. When Greg showed Len the list, he said, "Let's try the church first."

"I hope my luck holds out."

"Don't worry, old buddy, this is your day and nothing can go wrong with Emily running the show."

The venerable minister was unlocking the church door. He told them the church would be available. Len said the organist would expect five dollars. The minister told him the dining room and kitchen cost seven dollars and fifty cents if it was cleaned up after.

"Cost is not a problem."

Patting Greg on the shoulder, the minister said, "You furnish the bride and the ring and I'll take over from there. You have to have a marriage license. You can get one at the courthouse."

"Is there a caterer that can serve a really great supper?"

"Yes. Three blocks north and one east is a new restaurant called Francois'. He is a Frenchman and his meals are the talk of the town."

Francois was in his kitchen. He knew Leonard.

"We want a dinner served at the Presbyterian Church at six o'clock this evening."

Francois threw up his hands and said, "There is no time to do a proper job of cooking. We can do it tomorrow for eighty-five dollars."

Greg opened his shirt, got into his money belt, and laid two one hundred dollar bills on the table, and said, "How about six o'clock tonight for this?"

The chef's eyes widened as he looked at the bills. "It will be difficult, but we will do it. I have a twenty-pound turkey that was ordered for another customer for tomorrow night. I can feed them leg of lamb." He pocketed the bills, snapped his fingers and began to give orders to his help.

As they walked out the door, Len said, "This is going to cost you plenty."

"What the hell? You get married only once. I sold horses for two thousand dollars yesterday, and we are able to sell the finished cattle for two hundred dollars a head. The area is just booming with miners swarming in and new diggings are being found every day. There isn't enough food, and until the other settlers are able to stock up, we will have a bonanza for the next few years."

"The ranch is paying its way?"

"Yes. We are showing a profit."

"Great. I'm glad to know that all those years we spent wandering around in the wilderness have paid off."

When they returned to the Wilson house, they found six women sitting around the table. Emily had sent her maid around to friends with a note asking for their help. They reported their accomplishments.

Emily said, "You are not so much more efficient than we are. We have the trousseau, and the wedding outfit is complete except for the shoes, which Ellen can get when she goes to the hairdresser. We are going to need flowers." Greg turned his back and got out another one hundred dollar bill.

"Don't you have anything smaller? There are a number of things to get and different people will be shopping for them." He dug out five twenty-dollar gold pieces.

"You and Len will have to get the ring. We tried ours on Ellen and this one fits. Take it to the jeweler and pick out one the same size."

The wedding went smoothly. Len was best man and Emily was matron of honor. The minister warned them that marriage was a sacred thing and one of trust, that it would die if they did not change with it as time went on, and that it would not continue to bloom unless there was understanding, consideration, and kindness on the part of both.

They said their vows and Greg placed the ring on her finger. They kissed. They were laughing as they went downstairs to the dining room. The women had brought their fine china and tablecloths. There were flowers on the table. Francois entered, wearing a tall chef's cap, and followed by two assistants wearing not-so-tall caps. The minister asked a blessing, and the caterers served a delicious onion soup with small, crisp croutons, followed by a fruit salad. They were surprised when the chef brought in a large turkey and placed it on the side table. For most of them, it was the first time in several years that they had turkey. Francois showed his dexterity in carving the turkey and placing the pieces on a platter, which he put in front of Greg, saying, "The groom can serve the turkey."

Marianne had attended the wedding dressed in a modest brown suit. At first the women who knew who she was were a little hesitant, but soon they warmed up to her pleasant personality and accepted her as one of them.

Ellen thanked them for the their generosity, saying, "Greg and I can in no way thank you for all of the wonderful gifts and for giving us such a wonderful wedding. We will remember it the rest of our lives."

The Wilsons had given them a complete set of china and silverware. Others had contributed items of cookware and linens. All in all, it would make quite a difficult bundle to pack.

"I'm glad I brought Harry along."

"Another surprise. Who is Harry?"

"Harry is a long-time faithful friend that has been with me for many years. We are practically inseparable. He is one damned smart mule."

"Greg, I don't know anything about mules."

"You will, darling. I hope he'll be around for a long time."

At eight o'clock the guests were saying good-bye. Emily asked, "Where are you staying tonight?"

"We are not telling. I've hired a cab. We'll take Marianne home and go on from there."

Marianne had put a "Closed for the Day" sign on her door at noon. When they entered the house, the ladies were all dressed in their finest and there was a table with candles, flowers and a wedding cake. They all sat down to cake and coffee while Ellen told them about the wedding. They had to open more gifts of household linens, blankets, and other items. At nine o'clock they happily climbed the stairs.

"What do we wear to bed tonight?"

"Absolutely nothing. Marianne says you have to be a lady at all times, but in the bedroom, anything goes!" He smiled and kissed her.

The prearranged cab was waiting for them when they finished breakfast the next morning, and after loading their loot and Ellen's clothes, they drove to the hotel where Greg had reserved a room. After bringing the gifts from the church, Greg arranged them in groups around the room, shifting some around.

"What are you doing?"

"I'm figuring out how to pack these things on Harry. It will be a bulky load, but not too heavy. I thought we would have to order these things from Salt Lake, which would probably take six months. We'll have to pack these dishes carefully so they won't get broken. Raul and Rosita will move into the small house and we will take the big one. The small house has everything the big one does, including a kitchen sink and a pump for water."

"Wouldn't it be easier if we just took the small house? They wouldn't have to move."

"I never thought of that. It would be easier for everybody, if you are willing to do that. Would you like to take a walk with me to see Harry?"

Harry was glad to see them and when Greg reached into his jacket and brought out a napkin, Harry nuzzled him impatiently, then carefully ate the piece of wedding cake from his hand. Ellen laughed. "That must be some mule."

"He's a mule to end all mules. Sometime I'll tell you all about him. We probably are going to need another mule for the trip. Harry can't carry everything. We have to get some supplies, too. Can you ride a horse? I'll get a nice, gentle one for you, and we can put a cushion on the saddle."

"I learned to ride as a young girl. The horse doesn't have to be all that gentle. Just a good strong horse that is broke to ride. As for the cushion, I am a little tender and sore. But not too sore," she added, giving him an impish grin.

"You'll need rough warm clothes, and a woman's riding habit."

"No riding habit. I'm going to wear britches, as we Irish say. Pants to you."

As they spent the day shopping for their supplies for the ten-day journey, Greg was continually amazed by Ellen's common sense and resourcefulness. She marveled at her great good fortune in having such a wonderful, generous man, so different from those she had observed in England who doled out pence and shillings grudgingly.

The next morning they rose before daylight and had a hearty breakfast before going to the stable, where the horses and mules were curried and tied to a rack, ready to be loaded.

When they were ready to leave, sun was breaking over the hills with cirrus clouds looking like waves of gold. Greg was riding his horse and leading Harry, who had "the mule" tied to his tail. Ellen was following the mule. Her job was to see that he kept up with Harry and to use a willow switch as a persuader.

The trail was very winding, as it took the route of an Indian and game trail, following the line of least resistance. Ridges were very close together, bordering the stream. The sun was still an hour high in the sky when they stopped for the night at Idaho City. In spite of numerous stops to rest the animals, to stretch and relieve themselves, Ellen was completely exhausted. She practically fell into Greg's arms as he helped her down from the black filly that she had named "Gerty" after Lady Brelsford. The stablehand knew Greg and his generous tips, and he promised to unpack the mules and curry and feed all. He would lock the gear in the granary for the night. Greg reached into his pocket for two sugar cubes, which Harry delicately lipped off his hand.

A warm bath in a big tin tub at the hotel refreshed both of

them. Shortly after they started eating dinner at the cafe, people began coming in to see them. Word had spread that Greg McKenna had a wife and she was a looker.

They retired early, and morning found them well rested and ready to travel on. Greg warned Ellen that they would be climbing steadily for almost four days, then the rest of the journey would be downhill.

"Since it is our honeymoon, we are going to take our time and travel only about twenty miles a day. You were such a good sport about the hard trip yesterday."

The day was almost perfect, slightly nippy in the morning and comfortably warm after the sun came up, with very little wind and only a few puffy clouds in the sky. Ellen enjoyed watching the numerous wild creatures. Ground squirrels scampered across the trail and scolded them for invading their territory. Marmots sat up and barked at them. A doe and her fawn ran across the trail, pursued by a coyote, which Greg scared away with a pistol shot. The spotted fawn ran a little way and curled up in tall grass beside the path. The doe ran on. Ellen cried, "Oh, the poor thing!" and started to walk toward it.

Greg said, "Don't touch it. If you do, the mother will abandon it because of the human scent. She'll come back to get it . We'll go into the timber and watch, while we take a rest break."

Soon the doe came back, nudged the baby and spread her legs so it could nurse. Then they both trotted into the timber.

They watered the horses and mules and ate lunch. Ellen watched an eagle glide around in spirals, rising higher and higher.

"How can it do that without moving its wings?"

"It is riding an updraft. The sun is warming the earth, and warm air is lighter than cold air, so it rises. The eagle is just riding the warm air up and up."

"I have such a smart husband."

"Honey, somebody else figured that out and wrote about it."

Ellen loved the small meadows with sparkling streams, and the abundant wild flowers that seemed to bloom in patches of various colors: the purple and blue of small flags, fields of tiny yellow buttercups, large yellow blossoms of the bitterroot, red-orange Indian paintbrush, and purple patches of wild lupine.

When they came to a cove with a little stream that made music as it cascaded over rocks, Greg immediately started to unpack and take care of the horses and mules. When he finished, he was again surprised at the resourcefulness of his bride. She had gathered wood, built a fire, and handed him a cup of hot coffee. Potatoes were frying in one skillet and the other was heating for the two steaks she had pounded and rolled in flour. Ellen curtsied and said, "My lord, supper will be ready in twenty minutes."

Not to be outdone, Greg bowed and said, "My lady, that will give me just enough time to circle the camp to see if there are any Bannock Indians in the area."

When he returned, the big log was spread with a tablecloth and dishes and she helped him dish out the steak, potatoes, and cabbage.

"Having you for a wife is one pleasant surprise after another. I feel that the Lord has blessed me."

"I am also surprised at my wonderful husband."

The sun was just disappearing as they prepared to go to bed. No tent was needed because there was no threat of rain. The birds were making their last evening chirping and twittering. Greg and Ellen had finished their lovemaking and were cuddled up half asleep when a loud scary screech came from the tree above. Ellen shuddered and clung to Greg in fright.

"What was that?"

"That is the great horned owl. He does that to scare the mice and rabbits and make them move around."

"Well, he certainly scared me."

The next morning, Ellen remarked, "Honey, that damned smart mule of yours barely tolerates me. I'm going to fix him, but good. You just watch and see."

Her program of giving Harry a biscuit with honey or jam on it each night after supper, and rubbing his long ears and talking softly, paid off. In a few days, Harry was her slave and showed his affection in a mulish way.

CHAPTER 31

ARRIVAL

Martha and Rosita were busy getting ready for the arrival of Rosita's third child. Martha said, "You said it will be a boy?"

"It will be a boy. I said boy, girl, last two times and it was boy, girl."

"You said the wedding was nine days ago. If you are right, they probably would start two days after the wedding and take their time getting here—ten days, maybe. This being Thursday, they will arrive Saturday afternoon."

On Friday they started looking to the west at the winding trail coming down from the hills. Saturday morning Rosita greeted Martha excitedly. "I had another vision. I saw two large people eating in the woods, and there were two mules and two horses grazing. They will be here tomorrow afternoon. I'll cook a big roast. You make a pie and you make the best bread. We will celebrate together."

Rosita from her kitchen window could see Martha popping outside every so often to look at the trail. Finally, Martha ran to the big house and threw open the door, shouting, "They are coming. He isn't bringing home a bride. It's two men. I can see from here. He's wearing a cowboy hat and pants." Rosita picked up the field glasses and looked. "The man has long hair down past his shoulders."

Everyone gathered to greet them. Latham took over care of the horses. Greg introduced Ellen to everyone, and Rosita grinned knowingly at Martha. "I'll never doubt again," Martha laughed as she hugged Ellen and playfully pulled a lock of curly black hair. Rosita winked back. Greg said, "Unpack Harry and put things in the new little house. Ellen and I have decided to live there and Raul and Rosita won't have to move.

The weary and dirty, but smiling couple were besieged with hugs and kisses. Little Jim yelled, "Dadee, Dadee," and was scooped up by Greg.

Ellen said, "I have heard so much about you nice people that I feel as if I know you. I'm going to love you and hope you will like me." Rosita took Ellen's arm and led her into the big house. The stove was covered with a big kettle and pots, all steaming.

Rosita showed Ellen how to use the water pump at the sink. It had to be primed before it would work, by pouring a pint or more of water into the top. Then you pumped on the handle until the water came up. She warned Ellen to save water each time for the next priming, keeping a pitcher by the sink for that purpose. If Ellen forgot to save water for priming, she would have to go over to the other house and borrow some.

"I know you want a good hot bath. Raul will fill the tub, as I must not lift too much at this time. Martha will go unpack your clothes in the little house, while you soak." She took Ellen to Greg's room, where a big tin tub awaited.

CHAPTER 32

BARBARA ELLEN AND MEGAN

Greg had just finished changing from his heavy longjohns to a soft flannel nightshirt. It had taken some persuasion to get him away from a twenty-year-old habit.

Ellen said, "Darling, if you will put it on, I'll show you just how handy it is."

He laughed and said, "I'm sure you will. Convince me."

She added to the bribe, saying, "We have been married almost a year. It is the first of January. If we start a baby now, it will be a Libra and that is the best sign. It will be a calm, considerate, levelheaded person."

After the lovemaking, they were holding each other.

"Honey, you were right about the nightshirt. There is something special about making a baby and that is maybe why it was so terrific. Do you really believe in those zodiac signs?"

"Of course I do. There is no question about it. The last thing I would want is one born under the sign of Scorpio. They are very willful and have very much a mind of their own, and resent any kind of suggestions."

"Ellen, isn't that just an old wives' fable?"

"It is not. I have read that it has been accepted ever since Greek mythology was written."

"Being Irish, I suppose you believe in leprechauns, gnomes, and foretelling the future."

"Of course I do. Foretelling the future has become a lost art."

It was the fifteenth day after her monthly flow and Ellen was sure she would conceive. She was surprised and disappointed when her next flow arrived. She had confided to Rosita and Martha that they were trying to have a baby, and they consoled her by saying that it often takes time, even years. Greg told her about the Fletchers, who had their first child after seven years. Early in March, Rosita greeted Martha with, "I had another vision last night. I saw a beautiful baby with a pink dress on. She was laughing as she was being held and looking over her mother's shoulder. I couldn't see the mother's face."

"Rosita, do you think Ellen's expecting?"

"Yes, I think the baby is already coming. Greg was gone for a few days early in February. Maybe the rest strengthened the little seeds. Shall we tell Ellen?"

"Let's do. She and Greg are getting quite concerned." They went over to Ellen's. She greeted them warmly and invited them in for coffee and a slice of the new cake she had made from a recipe in a cookbook from Boston. When Rosita told about her vision, Ellen laughed and said, "Guess what? It is three weeks past my monthly time. I'm going to tell Greg."

In telling Greg about Rosita's vision, she left out the pink dress. She thought he wanted a boy.

When the baby started to show signs of life, she let Little Jim put his head on her abdomen to feel the baby kick.

"Why does he kick?"

"He is exercising. He is impatient to get out and see the world."

Ellen and Greg knew that sometime they would have to tell Little Jim that he was adopted. He had been prepared that he was going to have a new brother or sister. Now the opportunity arose to tell him about the adoption.

"Mommy, did you carry me in your basket like my new brother?"

"Jimmy, it may be a girl. Little sisters are fun and you can take care of her and see that she doesn't get hurt."

"I can take care of a little brother, too. Mommy, did you carry me in your basket like the new baby?"

"No, Jimmy, we adopted you." His eyes widened in disbelief.

"Chief found you after your mother and father were killed by Indians. Your daddy brought you to live here. We adopted you. We loved you and went to the judge and asked him if we could take you for our son. We signed papers and you are just as much our son as the new baby will be, and we won't love you a bit less than the new baby."

Instead of reading him a bedtime story, Greg told him about how they found him and fed him with a glove, and how Chief had looked after him. After several tellings of his story, he seemed to be reassured. They took care to give him extra attention and affection.

The blond, curly-headed girl was born in late October at ten o'clock in the morning. Martha Latham assisted, and Ellen came through the delivery with no complications. When Little Jim first saw the baby, he said, "Will she always be that red?"

Greg did not seem to be at all disappointed in having a daughter. They named her Barbara Ellen. Two years later, another healthy daughter was born, named Megan. To Martha's disgust, a doctor was in the area and took over the delivery. Two days later, Ellen had a fever from childbirth infection, which was almost always fatal. The doctor's medications seemed to have no effect.

"Doctor, what are her chances?" Greg asked.

"She is a strong woman. It is in the hands of the Lord. There is not much more I can do. Her fever is going up slowly, which is unusual. It shows her body is fighting it and maybe her body will win."

Chief Tall Man listened to the conversation. A short time later, he was on his horse riding into the forested hills, carrying a tin bucket and a kettle. An hour later he was brewing a brackish-looking concoction in the large kettle. This mixture he let cool and strained through a clean towel into the tin bucket.

Greg was feeding the stock when Chief carried the bucket into the house.

"What on earth is that?" Martha asked.

"Indian medicine. Good for fever. Drink much all time. My

mother medicine woman. Show me. Drink cold all can hold."

Ellen heard the conversation. She said, "Tall Man is always saving people and I have faith in him. I believe this nasty looking mess will cure me."

"We have nothing to lose," Martha said. She fixed a large glass of the liquid, which Ellen drank, grimacing. "That stuff is horrible. It should kill everything from germs to tapeworms." The Indian indicated she should drink a glass every hour.

In the evening, almost ten hours after his last visit, the doctor's buggy stopped at the McKenna's. When he saw the partly filled pitcher of dark liquid by the bed, he asked, "What's that?"

Martha answered, "It is an Indian remedy for childbirth fever that Tall Man made."

"How do you feel, Ellen?"

"I am not any worse. Maybe I feel a little better." The doctor took out his thermometer, dipped it in whiskey, and shook it. After three minutes under her tongue, he held it up to the light. "Humph," he said. He shook it down again and put it back under her tongue. This time he waited five minutes. Martha and Greg waited for his comment.

"I'll be damned. Her temperature had been rising a degree about every twelve hours. It has been ten hours and I can scarcely see any difference. Keep on what you are doing. I'll drop by in the morning to check again."

Greg took over from Martha and Rosita to care for Ellen during the night and see that she had her hourly dose of medicine. About six o'clock in the morning, Greg had dozed off when Martha entered to relieve him.

"How is she?"

"I think she is better. She has been asleep." Martha woke Ellen to wash her hands and face. She pushed the hair back from Ellen's forehead.

"Look at that!"

"What?"

"Beads of sweat. That means the fever has broken. She will be all right."

Ellen said, "I feel all sweaty and I am hungry. I need some broth and a bath."

When the doctor arrived at ten o'clock, Ellen was sitting up and nursing Megan. He said, "Continue the medicine for three more days. Ellen, I'm afraid you won't be able to have any more children. Such an infection usually leaves considerable scar tissue."

After the doctor walked out the door, Martha remarked, "If that old fool had washed his hands properly, this wouldn't have happened. Doctors in England were very careless about keeping their hands clean, and we nurses had to clean up after them."

The McKenna ranch on the Lemhi, and in fact all of the Salmon area, was not really bothered by Indians. The warlike Bannocks had been diminished to small bands after numerous skirmishes with the whites. Gold was found at Leesburg, near Salmon, by a group of ex-Confederate soldiers from Georgia, Mississippi, and South Carolina, and there was almost no publicity when they almost completely wiped out a tribe of Bannocks. This left the area between the Salmon and Snake Rivers almost devoid of Indians.

In 1879, the Nez Perce Indians surprised and trapped a company of U.S. soldiers in the Whitebird Canyon, killing thirty-four and routing the rest, who left sixty-four repeating rifles and considerable ammunition and supplies. General A. O. Howard was assigned to capture, quell, and return the Indians to their reservation. It was a difficult task, as Chief Joseph proved he was more than a match in military strategy. For several months, he kept one thousand Indians, which included women and children, and more than one thousand horses from being captured. He decoyed the pursuers into false encampments, stole their supplies from the pack train, and furnished the Indians with ammunition and food. His warriors took a stand in a very strategic position to allow the rest of the band to escape. The Army could not overcome the Indians without heavy casualties. When the Army finally could move on, the tribe was two days' march ahead. The Chief was trying to reach a haven in Canada. He stopped when he thought he had reached Canada, but was still in the United States. He surrendered and vowed to fight no more.

CHAPTER 33

THE DRAPERS

Greg had innumerable stories of his travels to tell his children. When he told about Moses and how nice and helpful he had been, he added, "Moses' favorite saying was, 'Chickens always come home to roost.'"

"What did he mean by that?" Little Jim asked.

"There is a saying in the Bible that means the same thing. It means that if you do something bad, dishonest, or unfair, it will always come back to haunt you. Good things that you do are eventually rewarded."

When Little Jim was seven years old, he asked his father for a horse of his own, because Ramon Ortega, who was two years younger, had a Shetland pony. The Ortegas and McKennas each had three children, all of whom played together with few serious quarrels.

"If I get you a horse, are you going to look after it and take care of it every day?"

"He will be the best cared-for horse on the ranch." Chief Tall Man was present and raised an eyebrow. Greg winked at him.

"Your horse will be a mare. Stallions are too fractious and unpredictable for children to ride. Son, it's going to take a while to find a horse that fits you. Chief is breaking some young colts, but they are months away from being ready to ride."

Three months later, after school was out in May, the children were in the meadow gathering lilies and lupine for their mothers. They saw the men returning from a trip to Salmon. Following behind the wagon driven by twenty-year-old Darrell Latham was a small mare. She was almost three hands lower than the average thousand-pound saddle horse. Ramon Ortega said, "Look, they are bringing another young horse to break to ride." They all rushed to greet the riders and the wagon as they came into the barnyard. Jim at first thought it was a horse for him, but when he saw how small it was, he decided it was a colt. Chief walked up to the mare, blew in her nose, petted her, and with a gentle motion opened her mouth.

"Small horse for four years old." Little Jim looked at his father and saw the big grin on his face. He ran over to put his arms around Greg, saying, "Thank you! She is beautiful. Can I ride her now?"

"Not now. You must get acquainted with her first, so she knows you belong to her and she depends on you to care for and protect her. How do you plan to do that?"

"First, I'll blow in her nose. Chief says that is the way horses get acquainted. Then I'll talk to her and pet her, and rub her nose and neck gently. I'll give her a drink of water and a quart of oats. I'll put her in a stall in the barn and curry and brush her. If I give her one of Martha's cookies, maybe she will follow me around."

The Welsh pony became completely attached to Little Jim. No horse ever received more affectionate treatment. Greg told Ellen the small horse had been brought over from England to a Montana ranch, and when it changed hands, the new owner had no use for the little mare.

Several years later, it was late in November and the cattle had been rounded up and brought down from the hills to graze near the ranch. A neighbor told Greg that he had seen a steer in the hills with the MC brand on its left hip.

"That's one of our steers, Jim. What do you think we ought to do about it?"

"Dad, it's Saturday and no school," said the twelve-year-old boy. "If we go looking for it, and you let me use the 30-30, we might get an elk or deer, or shoot that wolf that's been bothering you. Besides, you need me to track because Chief is not feeling well."

"We'll take lunches and leave right after breakfast."

At ten o'clock the next morning they were up in the hills about four miles from the valley.

"Look, Dad. Tracks."

"They look like elk tracks."

"Dad, you know they are cow tracks. Elk tracks look like buns. Cow tracks are wide and pointed. These are at least a day and a half old. The tracks led downhill toward the valley. They followed slowly, looking for game.

About a mile further on Jim reined in his horse and said, "There are two people following the steer. One is a man on a horse, and one is a light weight, probably a boy or woman."

They were about a mile from the river when they heard the boom of a large-bore rifle.

"Son, we have to do some thinking and there are some tough decisions to make. Let's sit on that log and decide what we are going to do. Greg lit his pipe.

"Dad, I'll bet you are thinking someone shot that steer and wondering what to do about it."

"You are right, son. It is not only up to me. You are a McKenna and you must help make the decision. Let's suppose we find a dead steer and a man and boy butchering it. Most cattlemen hang rustlers on the spot. If we hang the man, what have we got? If we don't hang him, what do we have?"

"Dad, if we hang him, we'll have a dead man that we have to do something with. Then we have to do a lot of explaining to the sheriff. If there is a boy, he is going to be without a father and he is going to feel lost and terrible. If there is a wife and children, who will take of them? If we let him live, maybe we can get him to work out the price of the steer. We can always use another hand around the ranch."

Greg was very pleased with his son's reasoning. "You have said almost exactly what I am thinking. You know, I was almost hanged once, and it scared the hell out of me. Shall we scare the hell out of him?"

"Let's see what he is like. If he is a reasonable man, I don't think we need to scare him. If he is a smart-aleck, then we can treat him rough." They spotted the two people with the steer about a quarter of a mile ahead. They stopped, tied up their horses, taking their rifles. It was easy to slip up on the man and boy who were busily quartering the butchered steer to put meat into canvas bags. The man's gun was in the scabbard on his horse. Greg poked him with the gun barrel and said, "Put your hands behind your head. Sonny, you back up and sit down." Then he had the man put his hands behind his back and tied them tightly with a piggin' string. The boy started to cry, saying, "Don't hurt my father!"

"Son, you know that rustling cattle means hanging?"

"Don't hang my father. My mother and my sisters will starve." The man started to beg for his life.

"We was trying shoot a deer or elk. We are almost out of food, and the steer was too tempting. I knowed it was wrong. I never done anything like this before. Our cow has gone dry and the young'uns need milk. I'll do anything to make up for the steer. I'm a good worker. Please, for my family, give me another chance."

"What is your name?"

"Charlie Draper, and that's my son, Fred."

"You have the eighty acres below the bottom of the McKenna ranch. You came too late to get a crop in this year."

"Mr. McKenna, we got held up by sickness. I've got the plowing done, all ready for planting in the spring, and feed for my horses and milk cow. She won't freshen for another month."

"Jim, what do you think?"

"He said he would work it out. That boy needs his father. I sure would hate to lose mine." Fred came over and hugged Jim.

Greg said, "Draper, if you will agree to work out payment for half the steer by coming to my ranch every morning to help feed and clean stables, we'll forget this whole thing." Draper was beside himself with relief. "You won't be sorry, Mr. McKenna. I will work hard."

"Let's finish quartering this critter and put it in the meat sacks. Then we will go to your place. The half of the steer that you work for will be yours."

Greg was surprised at the appearance of Mabel Draper, who

was neat, clean, and young looking. The two other children were also neat and clean. He could see that Charlie was right proud of his wife. Seeing the McKennas and the bloody meat sacks, she was apprehensive.

"What happened?"

"We brought your husband home because he butchered one of my steers." Her mouth dropped open with a look of fear and despair. She knew how serious the situation could be.

"We decided to let him pay for it by working it out. We are leaving you half the beef. Your family is going to need some help to get through the winter and spring. If Charlie is a good worker, we will help out."

There were tears in her eyes as she said, "Thank you, Mr. McKenna. Charlie is a hard worker and you won't be sorry."

"We have a shorthorn heifer that has just freshened and we have to milk her as her calf can't begin to use all her milk. If you will drive your wagon over, you can bring her back and keep her until your cow freshens. If Fred can look after the smaller children, you both come. Ellen will be glad to meet you."

He and Jim rode ahead to tell Ellen what had happened. She said, "The boy and his father must have been terribly afraid. I'm sure Mrs. Draper is really upset."

When the Drapers arrived, they were invited in for coffee and a newly baked, iced cake. After taking one bite, Mrs. Draper wrapped hers in her napkin. "It's so good. I'm going to save some for my children," she said.

"Oh, you eat it. You can take the rest of the cake home for your children." Mabel gave Ellen a hug. The two women liked each other right away. During the conversation, Ellen learned that Mabel had been a school teacher. After the visit, they piled sacks of flour, beans, rice, potatoes, carrots, and cabbage from the cellar into the Draper's wagon. The men had gone to get the cow ready to follow the wagon. With profuse thanks, the Drapers drove away.

It worked out better than Greg expected. Charlie was a very conscientious worker, and Mabel and Ellen became close friends.

Greg was well aware of the feelings of an adopted child. However, he had deep and lasting memories and affection for the Fletchers, especially Helen, whom he regarded as his mother. They had corresponded occasionally. Carl was in poor health and promised Greg a farm if he would come back and manage his lands. Apparently, his own sons had been a disappointment to him.

Greg, like most parents, was concerned about continuing the McKenna name and who would inherit his property when he and Ellen were no longer capable of managing. With deep affection, he considered Jim to be his son and heir, because the daughters would probably marry someone not interested in or capable of managing the ranch. He wanted to turn the spread over to a McKenna. He and Ellen talked over the possibilities of the future.

"Childhood should be a pleasant period," Ellen said.

"It should be. Mine really wasn't. Helen was everything a mother could be, but she was dominated by Carl. His aim in life was to make money and accumulate property. My first recollection was doing chores and there were very few let-ups. He never asked me about anything, just gave me orders. I am not going to do it that way."

"I think Jim is happy and well-adjusted. I notice that you do ask for his opinion on problems, and I am surprised at what good judgment he has."

"I agree. Chief has had a lot of influence on Jim. He has taught him to fish, to track and stalk game. And he has counseled him about right and wrong and proper behavior."

Greg McKenna had acquired his holding of over thirty-two hundred acres and water rights none too soon. An influx of settlers in 1866–1867 took up almost all the desirable land. Some of the holdings were as small as forty acres of arable land, which was about all a small family could cultivate. Fortunately, there was plenty of water for irrigation. The land had been a favorite hunting ground for the Indians, where they camped to gather cattails, balsam, and salmon to dry. The settlers had crowded them out, and there was much resentment among the Bannocks and Nez Perce.

When Greg fenced off twenty acres of good pasture land adjacent to the stream on the McKenna property, it caused mixed feelings among the settlers. Some said, "That McKenna is encouraging those savages. He has even put out fire pits for cooking and an outhouse." Others thought it was a good idea.

The character of the different tribes varied from friendly by the Nez Perce to hostile from the Bannocks, who were aggressive and cruel. Fortunately, the once powerful Bannock tribe had been decimated.

When Jim asked his dad, "Why do you let the old Indians use our land, and even fix a place for them?" Greg realized that Jim was echoing the opinions he had heard at school.

"Jim, this was their land, where they hunted, fished, and gathered plants for food. The white man crowded them out and killed off all the buffalo. Now the Indians have to work hard to find enough to eat. No wonder they hate the white man. When you said 'old Indians' you were being disrespectful. They are people, just like you and me. They have their own rules and religion and they feel we have no right to impose ours on them. Remember, if it were not for Chief Tall Man, you would not be here."

"Dad, Chief is different."

"Sure, he is. But it just goes to show that Indians can care and help other people out. Do you remember when a large bunch of Indians rode up the valley and Chief went out to meet them? He told them about how Mrs. Latham had taken care of their sick and the way I had treated them, and they came in peace and said they would protect us."

"Dad, you gave them a steer. Did that help?"

"Every act of kindness and goodwill helps."

"When they get mad enough, they will still fight."

"I'm afraid you are right. They will fight, even though they know they can't win."

The doctor had been right. Ellen never had another child. This bothered her more than Greg. He consoled her by saying, "We are lucky to have three beautiful children. Jim is very intelligent, and he is so easy to get along with. You gave him a birthdate in July, because we figured he was three months old when we found him. I think he seems more like a Libra, like Barbara. She never has been any trouble. Megan, on the other hand, is a Scorpio and even at three years old she is stubborn and hard to handle. She can be cheerful and helpful, though."

When Barbara Ellen was small, she idolized big brother Jim. As she was growing up, Barbara Ellen almost openly showed her resentment when her big brother paid attention to other girls at parties and dances. However, there was always fun and camaraderie between them. She was diplomatic in hinting about the faults of his girlfriends. When her mother cautioned her about this, she said, "I was only teasing. He teases me about boys and other things."

When Jim had outgrown the little Welsh pony, it became Barbara's horse, and was her pride and joy. She often rode with him to do chores and herding.

The large schoolhouse a half-mile from the McKenna ranch house was the center of community activities, especially in the winter when the busy season was over. This was the site of dances, pot-luck dinners, school board meetings, and church services. The McKennas all liked to dance. Greg and Ellen almost always won the waltz contest. Jim, in spite of being a big boy, was a smooth, graceful dancer, and his sisters were very proud to dance with him.

The members of the community liked to gather for a special celebration of Thanksgiving by having the large dinner in the schoolhouse. School children decorated the schoolhouse with turkeys and other appropriate designs in colored chalk on the blackboards, and there were long tables with center decorations of fall flowers, candles, and nut boxes made by the children. It was a very festive occasion. Every family brought their special dishes, and there were several turkeys roasted by those who raised the birds.

Sometime between her twelfth and thirteenth birthdays, Jim became aware that his tall, fast-growing sister was changing rapidly. She was going to be a really beautiful girl and already her small, pert breasts were beginning to show. Although he knew that he was adopted and she was not really his blood relative, he felt that thoughts of attraction toward his sister were not appropriate and tried to turn his attention to other girls.

Barbara Ellen resented it. She had to visit the two-holer during a schoolhouse dance and saw him kissing Kathleen Denny. She left the party and walked home. For several days, she shunned him. Her mother noticed her behavior, and when she finally got Barbara to tell what was bothering her, Ellen said, "That was really none of your business."

"Mother, I don't care. She is really rough and crude. She swears and her table manners are terrible. It would be awful to have her for a sister-in-law."

Although Ellen secretly agreed with Barbara, she said, "Barbie, Jim will not be getting married for years, and it probably will not be anyone that he now knows. He will meet a lot of girls as he grows up. Kathleen can't help her manners; that was the way she was reared. Her mother was a mule skinner and driver of freight wagons. She came into Salmon with a load of freight from Laramie. Len Denny is a small, meek man who never had any attention from women. He met Lib in the hotel and she introduced herself. He was flattered that such a hale and hearty woman would notice him and he invited her to dinner. She learned that he had struck it rich at Leesburg and was in Salmon to spend the weekend. I'm sure she decided to marry him and he was gullible. They were married by the justice of the peace the next day. She wanted a cattle ranch and he was tired of mining, so they bought a spread four miles from ours. The neighbors said that he did the cooking and housework and she did the ranching. The three daughters were brought up as ranch hands. Kathleen is the last one at home, the others are married. Remember that she has had a very rough life, and be a little bit charitable."

CHAPTER 34

THE BANK

How Theodore "Ted" Williams happened to be in Salmon in 1870 was never revealed. He was a twenty-nine-year-old who set up a successful accounting business. He had worked in his uncle's bank since college. The businessmen were paying cash for gold and really gouging the miners. Williams received notice that his uncle had died and left him fifteen thousand dollars. He thought he would like to open a bank, but to get a charter, he would have to have twenty-five thousand dollars. In trying to locate a partner, he heard the name of Greg McKenna. The two men met and Williams pointed out the need for a bank and the profit it would make, not only from judicially placed loans at ten percent interest, but also from buying gold and selling for a profit after impurities and freight charges were deducted. It would take about six weeks from the time they sent the gold by stage to San Francisco until they would get their money, and that would tie up bank capital.

Greg agreed to match the fifteen thousand, which would leave enough for an iron door, frame, and combination lock for a foot-thick, fireproof concrete bank vault. He told Williams that he would have his lawyer draw up a contract and take care of getting the charter. In three months the Citizens State Bank of Salmon opened for business.

Ted married a nurse who had been working at a doctor's office in Salmon, and they lived in rooms above the bank. According to the charter, they had to have at least twenty-five percent of the total deposits in cash at the bank at all times. They could apply for ten thousand dollars in bills to be issued by the U.S. Treasury in the bank's name and signed by the bank's president and treasurer. However, ten thousand dollars in gold to cover was to be in the bank at all times and the bills could be exchanged for gold coins. The twenty-five thousand shares of bank stock were to be allocated as twelve thousand five hundred shares to the treasurer and manager, Ted Williams; twelve thousand shares to President Greg McKenna; and five hundred shares to Ellen Ryan McKenna.

The large concrete vault with its massive iron door and shiny bright trim, and the display of the money in the vault must have impressed the people touring the bank on opening day. Depositors, glad to find a safe place for their money, flocked in and kept Williams and his clerk busy recording deposits for nearly a week. They had nearly one hundred thousand dollars on deposit. Ted Williams' financial report at the director's meeting stated that all fifty safety deposit boxes were rented for one dollar a month, and that would pay the clerk's forty dollars a month wages. He reported that the bank had a loan capacity of seventy-five thousand dollars at the rate of ten percent interest. The bank would be cautious about loans for the first year, and would concentrate on buying and shipping gold to the San Francisco mint. Saloon and other merchants were allowing fifteen dollars an ounce for gold. The bank would pay sixteen dollars, and that would leave them about three dollars profit after paying Wells Fargo for freight.

Greg said, "That isn't very much profit."

"When you figure that if we ship only one hundred ounces at a time, we make three hundred dollars. We will ship at least that much every week. Over a year that would be fifteen thousand six hundred dollars profit, a conservative estimate, which is more than most small banks make."

The integrity of Williams was soon recognized and the bank prospered.

The change in the economy after the Civil War, from the lucrative manufacturing of supplies, guns, ammunition, clothing, medical, and other supplies to machinery and domestic needs caught up on the economy in 1873. Employment and wages were at low ebb. There wasn't enough work available or money to pay for it. Food riots occurred, and in many cities long lines gathered at soup kitchens. The government was short of money, having issued bonds to pay for the war, on which they were now paying interest. The government would buy gold and silver, issuing paper bills redeemable by silver and some by gold.

When the panic of 1873 hit, many banks closed, leaving depositors with little or nothing of their savings. It was the result of poor management and too much lending. People started hoarding their money instead of depositing it in banks. This did not affect the mining towns in Idaho, as the government was buying the gold and silver and paying for it with new paper money. New findings were causing the area to boom and build. Salmon was the supply point for a large area. Not only was the income from mines almost fabulous, but the ranchers and farmers were prospering. Wells Fargo still carried the gold to Salt Lake City, where it was shipped to San Francisco by train.

The Citizens State Bank of Salmon had bought considerably more than the usual amount of gold for shipping to the mint. When two miners brought in a large amount of gold and presented it for sale, the ever-cautious Williams feared getting into trouble with the impending visit of the bank examiner, since his cash reserve was low.

"We are not buying gold today," he said. "Come back next week." The disgruntled miners went to the saloon and told the patrons there, "The bank is out of money and can't buy any gold."

The rumor spread, and within an hour people were lining up, even out into the street, to withdraw their money. When the bank closed at three o'clock, Williams told the depositors it would open at nine in the morning, and assured them they would get their money. Two hours later, in a buggy behind lathered horses, he arrived at the McKenna ranch.

"Greg, there is a run on the bank. Some mad miners started it. If we can't raise about fifteen thousand dollars, we will have to close."

"I have ten thousand dollars in my safe we can use. I have two house guests who are here about the proposed railroad. As you know, the proposed railroad to Salmon is in limbo and hush hush. These men are not known hereabouts. If they and Raul Ortega get there early and first in line, and deposit the ten thousand between them, it just might stop the rush."

"Greg, you come up with the darnedest ideas. It might."

The three men were first in line. The first had five thousand dollars to deposit. He handed the banker several packets of bills in rubber bands. It took some time to count, and the depositors began to whisper along the line.

Next in line was Raul. He set a bag that clinked on the counter. "Rosita told me to get this deposited before the house burned down and left me with one big lump." The banker counted two thousand dollars in gold pieces. He and the next depositor were slowly counting the next five thousand when the line began to dwindle. Someone said, "I'm not going to wait all day to draw out my money. Looks like this bank is safe anyhow." By the time it all was counted and recounted, the last person wanting to make a withdrawal had disappeared. In another hour, the bank was accepting deposits.

CHAPTER 35

CATTLE AND SHEEP WAR

Trouble started brewing when the first bands of sheep started to graze on rangeland in south and central Idaho. Cattle had been grazing western range lands for several years, and the cattlemen thought they alone had grazing rights. They wrongly maintained that sheep ruined the range. Due to sheer numbers and being well established, the cattlemen had the advantage.

Sheep were very profitable. Lambs were ready for market in six months and there was a crop of wool every year. Cattle were ready for market in two years. Wool was much in demand in eastern mills and could be hauled, shipped, and stored for long periods of time.

Mounce was the most lawless and notorious of all cattlemen, as he led them in stampeding sheep off cliffs, burning herders' wagons, and even killing them. The Basques hired on as herders, and if they resisted, they got killed. All they could do was helplessly watch their herds destroyed. The sheepmen feared Mounce and tried to stay away from his territory.

The Department of Interior surveyed a road that almost divided the McKenna ranch. To protect his land from trespassing, Greg had the roadsides fenced. Whenever a band of sheep came through, he pointed out to the herders where his range was, and would tell them they were welcome to graze anywhere else. Very little was published about the raids on the sheep herds. F. R. Gooding, later U.S. Senator Gooding, was the most prominent sheepman in south central Idaho. His sheep were lambed out at his home ranch north of what became Shoshone. They were herded in the spring to the hills in the north as the season developed in the higher elevations.

The Basques were different from other nationalities. Some thought they were survivors of the lost continent Atlantis. They were usually short and heavyset, with extremely strong bodies and round heads. At first people thought they were stupid, because they came from Spain not knowing a word of English. They were unsurpassed in tending sheep. The Basques would pool their money, buy a band of sheep, and keep adding to it until they had one thousand head.

One of Gooding's bands got too close to Mounce. He shot the herder, Nicholas Asquena, burned the wagon, and drove the sheep over the bluff. Gooding was furious, but could do nothing about it. When Alonzo Asquena, Nick's brother, heard about it, he asked Gooding to arrange passage to the United States for another brother who was serving in the Spanish Army. This conversation took a long time, as Alonzo had very limited English. He pantomimed and drew out what he wanted to tell Gooding, that his brother Herando was a renowned sharpshooter.

Gooding filled out the papers for Hernando to enter the United States, but Hernando had to first defect or escape the Spanish Army and police. When the Army was maneuvering near Portugal, he managed to hide on a ship bound for New York and finally arrived at the stage depot in Shoshone, armed with an English language book. His ability to communicate with Gooding was limited, but each knew the other's interests.

After spending a week shooting and adjusting a new repeating rifle, he told Gooding, "I am ready."

He spent several days riding and looking until he found a suitable place, a large pocket bounded by a ridge of rough lava and a drop of fifteen feet into a gully of jagged lava rock. It was made to order for stampeding sheep, and not far from the Mounce ranch. Hernando found a spot that was well hidden, but would give him a clear shot at any part of the area. He settled in to wait.

At daybreak, his brother Alonzo brought a small band of sheep to graze. When he saw four horsemen approaching, he lay down on the floor of his wagon. The riders started shooting their pistols and yelling to stampede the sheep. There were four shots in rapid succession. Suddenly, all was quiet except for the crying of the sheep. The four horses were riderless. Mounce, his son, and two cowboys were dead. Hernando and Alonzo unsaddled the riderless horses and turned them loose. The saddles, bridles, and blankets were buried in the lava rubble back in a cave. Hernando purposely left the four brass shells on the ground.

Four days later, the federal marshal, the sheriff, and a deputy arrived on the scene to investigate. Upon finding the spent shells, the sheriff said, "We can match the firing pin and tell what gun was used. We just have to check the sheep wagons."

The experienced marshal said, "From what I can make out, this was carefully planned by a very good shot. He was shooting one hundred yards at men on horses and all four bullet holes almost matched."

They spent several days checking sheep camps. The herders had been crossed and recrossed and there was no way of knowing who the original herder was. None of them could speak English. They found only shotguns in the wagons.

CHAPTER 36

MOUNCE CATTLE

It was nearly two weeks later that the McKenna ranch received news of the shooting from the *Salmon Weekly* that Raul brought back. Everyone was relieved, most of all Ellen, who said, "If he had killed Greg, I would have shot him in the belly until the gun was empty, then watched him die slowly."

Greg laughed and said, "I believe you would. You are very hardheaded. Of course, in a nice way."

Mounce was survived by only one close relative, a sister in Texas. When an ad appeared in the paper that she wanted to sell the cattle, Greg had a conference with Latham, Raul, and the Chief. He thought it could be an opportunity to enlarge the herd. Raul and Greg decided to take along the Latham boys, who were good cowboys, in case they decided to buy.

Five days later, they were at the Mounce headquarters in Lost River Valley. The sister, Mona Wilcox, and her husband Jake, were glad to see them. They had a few buyers but all wanted only a few head, and wanted to give promissory notes or checks on banks in faraway places.

"How many head do you want?"

"One hundred or more, depending on the price, and we'll pay cash. If you'll have your hands show us the cattle, we'll take a look and decide how many we want, then try to get together on the price."

It was early June and because a late spring had delayed growth of forage on the higher elevations, the cattle were still close to the ranch. Many of the calves were over three months old and able to travel. After looking over the different herds, they had dinner with Mona and Jake Wilcox. Greg was aware that they were anxious to get on with the sale. He produced a tablet, pencil, and a large bag that clinked from his saddlebag.

"We will take two hundred head of cows and their calves. I hope you don't mind taking part of the payment in gold coins and the rest in one hundred dollar bills." He opened the sack and let some gold coins spill out onto the table. The couple couldn't keep their eyes off the coins.

"Cows are bringing forty dollars a head in Kansas City and that's a long ways off. We will pay forty dollars for cow and calf. We'll cut them out so the calves are old enough to travel."

"We have been getting fifty dollars a head." Wilcox said.

"How many have you sold?"

"Let's take his offer, Jake. That is eight thousand dollars and we can take our time about selling the other three hundred."

Greg was pleased with his good bargain. The cows were second generation from Texas longhorns with shorthorn and white-face blood in them. They were more compact and meaty, but they would require more winter feed and care. It took three days to sort out the two hundred cows and calves. Two of the Mounce cowboys were glad to be hired for three days to help drive the herd to the McKenna ranch. Mounce was miserly and had been paying them only twenty dollars a month. Greg kept them on to help rebrand, dehorn, and castrate the calves.

"Greg, do we have any money left after buying all those cattle?" Ellen asked.

"If we don't sell anything for three years, we will still have money left with Wells Fargo and the bank in Boise."

CHAPTER 37

HIGH SCHOOL

In the late 1880s, Salmon got its railroad connecting with the Union Pacific in Wyoming. This permitted the McKenna ranch to ship cattle to Chicago and added to its prosperity.

At fifteen, Jim entered high school in Salmon. The teachers were mostly women with only a year or two of higher education and they actually were reading the textbooks to keep ahead of the students. Jim didn't realize at the time how well-read and self-educated his parents were. He was able to get high grades with a minimum amount of studying, and graduated as valedictorian in a class of twenty-nine seniors. Kathleen Denny was in the same class and they had been intimate for over two years.

Steven Reeves, the principal and math teacher, was aware of Jim's intelligence and talked to him about going to college.

"Jim, going to college will open up a whole new world for you. What you learn there, no one can take from you. It will be like having a new, interesting book to read the rest of your life."

"Where do you think I should go?"

"There are many good colleges in California. I graduated from the University of California at Berkeley. They have courses in almost everything."

"I want to stay at home and run the ranch someday. I don't know if I need college."

"There is no reason why you shouldn't do both. They have courses in farm management, animal husbandry, chemistry, and biology that will be very useful to you in ranching. In fact, you need that knowledge to be a good rancher."

Greg was apprehensive when Jim reported this conversation, until Jim told him that he wanted to run the ranch. Then he was enthusiastic.

"Why not? College will broaden your outlook. The new friends you make will be valuable lifelong contacts. It will help you manage the ranch. Changes are so rapid—almost on a day-to-day basis."

"Dad, I'm going to learn everything I can. I want to do the best job possible when I run the ranch."

"Have you decided where to go to school?"

"Mr. Reeves said the University of California at Berkeley is excellent. That's where he went."

"Well, if you go to California, you can visit the Haines. Ellen and I visited them a couple of years ago, and they are anxious to meet you. They will welcome you with open arms. I think you have to apply for acceptance to the university and send in your grades. You'd better do that right away."

A few days later he took Kathleen to a dance. She was very amorous on the way home. When they came to their usual stopping place, the horses turned in as if they knew what was expected of them. He tied them to a pine tree, and held up his hands to help Kathleen down from the buggy. She jumped down into his arms, knocking him down. They both laughed and helped each other up. Jim took the lap robe and Kathleen followed him.

He told her about his plans to go to college in the fall. She was furious.

"I thought that now we was educated, we could get married. You bastard, you've been leadin' me on. You've been usin' me."

"I've never led you on. Besides, I'm not ready to get married. Anyway, who's been using who? You started this when you unbuttoned my pants a couple of years ago."

With a torrent of name calling and swear words, Kathleen got up and walked home. Jim felt depressed and perturbed at the loss of a companion with whom he had shared so many good times.

For days he was almost silent, keeping to himself. The family did not pry.

Barbara Ellen asked her mother, "What is the matter with Kathleen? She hasn't been around lately."

"I believe that Jim told her he was going to college. I think she expected him to marry her, and there must have been a terrible row. It looks like they have broken up."

"Goody—this makes my day!" Barbara said, clapping her hands. "She doesn't belong in this family."

"I feel the same way, but I feel sorry for both of them. It will take some time for Kathleen to get over the hurt, and Jim is not comfortable with it either."

CHAPTER 38

COLLEGE

Jim filled out the application paper for the university and was surprised to receive enrollment forms in two weeks. Fees for his dormitory and admission had been accepted. He was to take the small train from Salmon to Missoula, Montana, change trains to Ogden, then board the Union Pacific and ride in a Pullman car with a berth to San Francisco. Greg and Ellen had used this route two years before for their second honeymoon.

The month of August was a long period of waiting. Jim complained to his father, "It seems like the days just drag by."

"There is an old Arab proverb, 'All things come to he who waits.' Patience is a virtue and the more you cultivate it, the more content and better off your life will be."

The family went to Salmon to see Jim off on the train. They were sitting in the surrey waiting for the train, which was late as usual. Finally they heard the faint whoo-whoo of the whistle at a distant crossing. It was clanking, groaning, and whistling as it pulled into the station. There was only one passenger coach.

It was a tearful good-bye. "Be sure to write as often as you can. We are going to miss you," Ellen said. He shook hands and hugged his father and kissed his mother. Sixteen-year-old Barbara Ellen was last, and while she was hugging him, she gave him a vigorous kiss on the mouth and then winked at him. He winked back.

The little coal-burning locomotive had only two big drive wheels on each side and a smokestack that sloped up to three feet wide. The coach clinked, clanked, and swayed as it went over rail joints and around curves. It went through short tunnels and on the sides of mountains with streams hundreds of feet below. Every so often, it stopped for water and coal. The passengers could get out to stretch and get a breath of fresh air.

On his father's advice, Jim was wearing clean ranch clothes, cowboy boots, and a new wide-brimmed Stetson hat. He would change to a well-tailored tweed suit and dress shoes, but would continue to wear the hat.

The red plush seats soon became hard and uncomfortable. A cloud of dust rose from the cushions at the least disturbance. Open windows brought in cinders and smoke. The air was full of pipe and cigar smoke. Jim was a little reluctant to take along the basket of food his mother had prepared, but in time he was grateful for it. The train had only stale sandwiches and coffee available. In the evening, the conductor lit the gas lights.

The miserable ride took two days to reach Ogden. The conductor had a rather haughty expression when Jim handed him the ticket, probably because of the way Jim was dressed. When he saw that it was a Pullman ticket with berth, he called a porter. The black porter also looked at Jim's cowboy clothes with surprise. He took Jim's bags and showed him his already made up berth and the washroom. Jim's tip of a silver dollar brought a broad grin.

"Thank you, sir. Is there anything else you need?"

"Could you get me a sandwich and a glass of milk? I'm hungry. I am going to the washroom now."

When he returned to his berth, there was a large roast beef sandwich and a tall glass of milk. After eating, he soon fell asleep in the most welcome bed.

He woke at six o'clock as usual, washed and changed to his new suit, white shirt and bow tie. He looked in the mirror and remarked to himself, "You look mighty good."

Shortly after, the porter came through the car calling, "First call for breakfast in the dining car, three cars back."

Jim was surprised at the elegance of the dining room, even though his parents had told him how it would be. The waiter seated him at a table and gave him a menu. He ordered orange juice, a stack of pancakes, ham, and eggs. He was just beginning to eat when the waiter seated another couple at his table. After introductions, the wife asked, "Are you going to eat all that?"

"Yes, all that and possibly more."

The man, a civil engineer, told him about the miles of tunnels and snow sheds they would be going through, built by Chinese workmen who had blasted the way through solid rock. The train started the long climb over the Sierra Nevada mountains. Two big locomotives with four drive wheels on each side were added, one in front and one at the back to push.

After arriving in San Francisco, he took a ferry across the bay to Berkeley. The dormitory was open and he checked in. He was to share a room with Fred Cromwell, a sophomore studying law. Before registering, he met with his advisor, Dr. Gildow, who helped him map out a course of study.

"This is a heavy course and you will have to do a lot of studying.

At first, Jim had a difficult time. It seemed the professors piled on work to see how much the students could stand. It was then he was especially grateful for how well-read and self-educated his parents were, and how much they had trained him. For the first two months, all he did was attend classes, study, eat, and sleep. After that, the routine became easier for him.

One Saturday morning, his roommate remarked, "Jim, it is time you came up for air. They have a Saturday afternoon dance at the pavilion. It's a tag dance and the girls will ask you to dance. Get dressed up. It starts at one o'clock."

They entered the hall as the student band started to play. Fred walked out, took an attractive girl by the arm, and started to two-step. For two or three dances, Jim stood back and watched. He was surprised when a tall, beautiful blonde tapped him on the shoulder and said, "Do you waltz?" Jim held out his arms and they stepped out on the dance floor. They danced smoothly in perfect rhythm with each other. They exchanged names. Hers was Jennifer Hanford. She wanted to know where he was from, and said, "You are a real cowboy!"

"No, I'm not just a cowboy. I'm a cattleman."

At the end of the dance, Jim thanked her and was turning to leave, when she said, "No, you don't. I've just found you and we are just beginning to dance." Other girls began to cut in and Jennifer would cut back at the first opportunity.

Finally, Jim said, "This is getting too crowded. Let's go have a snack so we can talk." They were attracted to each other. At five o'clock she said, "I have to leave now to catch the trolley home. Why don't we have lunch here tomorrow?"

"That is a great idea."

The romance blossomed. They were dating steadily for school functions. Fred said, "Jim, you are very popular with the women, and the men are envious of you. Jennifer is the belle of the campus and has refused to date a lot of them. Her father is Charles Hanford. He owns a large insurance and real estate business and has a lot of property. It is said he is one of the wealthiest men in Berkeley."

After two months, Jennifer said, "My folks want me to bring you home to meet them. They want to meet the man their daughter is so crazy about. Will you come to dinner on Friday night? They are nice people and they are sure to like you."

"Well, I hope they will. But it makes me mighty nervous."

Jim was apprehensive when he rang the bell on the door of the large white mansion with its manicured lawn and tasteful landscaping. A colored maid answered the door and took his hat and coat. Jennifer appeared and took him into the parlor where she introduced him to her parents. He was awed by the thick Persian carpet, a huge crystal chandelier and oil paintings on the walls. Her father, a pleasant-looking man, heavyset with a round face, gave him a firm handshake and a big smile. Jennifer's mother was equally cordial. Charles soon put him at ease by asking questions about Idaho and the ranch. They seemed to enjoy hearing his answers and description of the McKenna holdings.

Jim was in a quandary about going home for Christmas. He was homesick, but the long train ride to and from would give only three or four days at home, and it didn't seem worth it. He received an invitation from the Haines to spend Christmas with them, and gladly accepted, saying he would be there December twenty-second.

Jennifer was most unhappy when he told her.

"My folks asked me to invite you to spend it with us. There will be a lot of parties and fun, and I need you," she pouted.

"I can visit with them for a week and then come to your house."

"But I want you for Christmas."

"Honey, I gave my word and we McKennas don't like to break promises, so I have to go there first. I'm sorry, but that is the way it is."

The Haines' visit was a delightful one.

The week spent visiting the Hanfords was one party after another. Jennifer was delighted with the ruby earrings he had purchased for three hundred sixty dollars, which took rather a large bite out of the one thousand dollars his father had given him. But, he still had plenty of cash to finance the rest of the year. Jennifer was slipping into his bedroom late at night. Her parents were treating him as a member of the family. Her father spent a lot of time talking about the insurance and real estate business and the great future it held.

"If you get a degree in business and finance, you will become a very rich man." Jim acted as if he were interested but didn't commit himself in any way.

When Jim returned to the dorm, there was a fat letter from Salmon, in the scrawly but readable handwriting of his father. It was a shocking one. The Ortegas were leaving to take over their family's old holdings in Mexico. An attorney in El Paso had been cleaning out his safe and found an envelope that Raul's father had left with him. It contained the original Spanish land grant giving the Ortegas the title. He had contacted the officials in Mexico City. The usurper of the Ortega ranch had been killed or driven off. Raul had been notified of the events by a cousin. The Mexican government said they would honor the grant, so Raul and Rosita could return to Mexico. Raul had been in complete charge of the cattle. Greg was handling the business but was involved in the bank, and had become involved in the legislature in Boise. He wanted Jim to finish the year at college, then to come home and take over Raul's work.

Raul was anxious to leave as soon as travelling arrangements could be made, probably in February.

Because of his interest in Jennifer and continuing his education, Jim had been considering going to college for at least another year. The Ortegas' leaving changed that.

When he told Jennifer, "I can't come back to school next year. My father needs me at the ranch."

Jennifer cried, "If it is money, my father would be glad to pay your way. We were talking about getting married and he said he thought you would fit in very well in the firm."

"We can still be married."

"Jim, you mean I would like living on the ranch way out away from everything!"

"It is nice and peaceful there. Getting away from the noise, hustle and hurrying people is wonderful."

"It may be like that to you, but we have gone up to our cabin in the mountains and two weeks of it was all I could stand." The two unhappy lovers continued to date, but it wasn't the same. They said good-bye with kisses and promises when he boarded the train in San Francisco. She promised to visit the ranch for a month in July.

There were many letters at first, but as time went by, they stopped. She never visited the McKennas.

CHAPTER 39

GOING HOME

To Jim, it seemed to take ages for the deluxe Union Pacific train from San Francisco to climb up over the Sierras. With the help of his waiter, Sam, and a generous tip, he was able to get a supply of sandwiches for the miserable ride from Wyoming to Salmon.

Barbara Ellen and Megan had driven the matched high-spirited black geldings to meet him. Barbara greeted him with a hug, a big kiss, and tears. Megan gave him a hug and a kiss on the cheek.

Jim was amazed at the change in Barbara Ellen. She had really bloomed. He held her at arms length and said, "My sister is really something to look at. You are gorgeous."

"Big brother, you like what you see?"

Without thinking, he said, "I more than like." That got him another hug and kiss.

It was mid-morning when the fast-trotting blacks drove up into the McKenna yard. A ranch hand took over the team. It was Sunday, and the Lathams were in a group with his parents, who had been watching them approach from a distance. It took several minutes of greetings before Jim could enter the house. His mother said, "Jim, you look like something the cat dragged in. Go take a bath and a nap. It is four hours until dinner."

Jim said, "Mom, there is something I have to do first." He went to the cupboard, took a handful of brown sugar, went out to the barn where he put a quart of oats in a bucket and walked out to Harry's pasture. Harry, like most mules, was stoical and seldom showed emotion, but he held his head with the long ears up for a better look. Then he cavorted a little and brayed a couple of loud hee-haws. Greg was watching and said, "That is one damn smart mule. The last time he brayed was to scare Indians."

After a bath, Jim crawled into bed, thinking to himself there was nothing like your own bed. He was asleep almost instantly. His mother woke him at four o'clock, saying, "By the time you wash, dinner will be ready."

Greg gave a short blessing, thanking the Lord for watching over them and the return of their beloved son, and said, "Let's eat before it gets cold. We'll have plenty of time to talk later."

After the table was cleared and the dishes washed and put away, the family gathered in the living room.

Greg said, "From your letters I gather you have learned a lot of ways to improve the operation of the ranch and cattle. The courses must have been very interesting."

Before Jim could reply, Barbara said, "What about this Jennifer you mentioned in your letters?"

Her mother admonished, "I believe you are jealous."

"Mother, I was just trying to find out if she is good enough to marry him."

"Barbara, you interrupted your father. Just be patient."

Jim then said, "Dad, there are a lot of possible new methods to talk over with you."

"I'm sure we'll have a lot to discuss. What course did you enjoy most?"

"I really enjoyed all the courses and looked forward to going to classes. The professors often digressed onto other topics. I guess the course in animal breeding was the one I enjoyed the most. There was a plaque on the wall behind the professor that said, 'Like begets like.' Dad, you would have enjoyed the devious way he supported Darwin's theory on the evolution of man. He had four of us debate Darwin's theory. He flipped a coin and my side got the choice. We took Darwin. I never will forget Reverend

Miller saying, 'Darwin will burn in hell for his theory.' I said that the Bible was a book of stories retold many times before it was written. That's what you told me a long time ago. I also told them about Chief Tall Man who told me that the Great Spirit made three images of man and three of woman out of white clay and put them near the fire to bake. The images on the outside didn't get baked enough and remained white. The inside set baked too much and were black. The middle set baked just perfect and were red. The class laughed so much that it took nearly five minutes for the professor to get them settled. My partner said, 'You can go to the zoo and see your ancestors in cages. To support evolution, scientists say man can and has changed wild cattle from scrawny small beasts to large, meaty animals. Fossils show that the horse was just a small, dog-like creature with four toes.' Of course the other side countered with the sin of contradicting the Bible. Mrs. Henderson, our grade-school teacher, would have had fits. She maintained that it was a cardinal sin to contradict the Bible."

CHAPTER 40

BARBARA ELLEN

One evening Barbara was unusually quiet, as if she were worried about something. When she was alone with her mother helping with the dishes, Ellen asked, "Barbie, what is worrying you?"

"Mom, the girls were talking about people in the valley about how several of the women met their husbands while they were working in, I won't say the word, one of those houses."

"Let's sit down here at the table and we'll talk about this. What you said is true. Not all, but most of these women had been orphaned, abused at home, without money, and hungry. The only way they could keep from starving was to go to work in those houses. There was no other work available. When this country was first settled, there were at least a hundred men to every woman, and the only unmarried women were in those houses. I know many of the women the girls are talking about, and they are good wives and mothers."

Barbara was silent for a while, then said, "I know you met Dad in Boise."

"Yes. I was penniless, hungry, and had no place to stay. Marianne Breckenridge, who was a madam of a fancy house, met me on the street and took me home with her. She fed me and took care of me, and since I could not find work anywhere, I decided to stay there. Your father was to be my first customer. We fell in love immediately. It was like a wonderful dream to meet that kind, understanding, and handsome man. I still have trouble believing how it all happened."

"Mom, you are wonderful, too!" Barbara gave her a hug and kiss.

Barbara Ellen was very popular in high school. School dances were held at the high school, but everyone was invited to attend the twice-monthly dances on Saturday night. While Jim was in high school, he would drive his sisters to the dance, unhitch, water, and feed the horses, dance one dance with each of his sisters, then go to the saloon to play penny ante poker. He would have the team harnessed, hitched up, and waiting for the dance to close at eleven o'clock. Barbara insisted that he be there to dance the last waltz with her. He acted like he was doing a chore, but secretly he looked forward to the dance.

One of the teachers, Florence Winn, gave Barbara special attention, perhaps because she was a pretty and bright student, a possible Mormon convert, or because she had a very attractive, eligible brother. Miss Winn said, "I certainly would like to meet your folks and see your ranch." Barbara finally arranged for her to have a weekend visit. Jim followed up with a few dance dates, then stopped. Sometime later Florence confided that she was going to marry a prize, a returned missionary from a prominent Mormon family. Barbara felt very much relieved and the friendship continued to blossom.

Miss Winn persuaded Barbara to go to college at Provo, Utah, to get a diploma for teaching grade school. She liked the school and the very friendly Mormon classmates. There was considerable study of church doctrine, as well as many social functions, especially dancing, which Barbara loved. She started dating a senior from a very important family. She thought she was falling in love with him. After a few dates, he said, "You should marry me. We will be married in the temple, but you will have to join the church first."

She said, "I need time to think about it."

On a later date, he asked, "Have you made up your mind?"

"Not yet."

"I've talked it over with my folks. We can have a temple wedding and you will be sealed to me."

"What do you mean, sealed?"

"Wives are sealed to their husbands for all eternity. All three of my father's wives are sealed to him."

"Your father has three wives?"

"That's right. But don't worry. I wouldn't take another wife for at least three years."

"I don't want that kind of life." She walked alone back to the dorm.

She was one of the top students in her class and her practice teaching grades were excellent. Leonard Wilson was chairman of the school board in Boise. When he heard that Barbara would receive a teacher's certificate in December, he wrote to the McKennas saying that they would have a vacancy in January because the second-grade teacher was leaving to have a baby, and Barbara could have the job.

Barbara was elated. The Wilsons were alone as their daughter was married and they invited Barbara to live with them. The only thing that bothered her was that she would be unable to go home for Christmas and start teaching in Boise on January second. She decided to go directly to Boise.

She was to receive thirty dollars a month. The Wilsons refused to let her pay for board and room. She helped with the housework, dishes, cleaning, and cooking. Emily remarked to Leonard, "She is such a jewel. It's like having another daughter in the house."

They included her in their social activities. She was very engrossed in her work and loved the class of eager children, which she had charmed. She had written Jim several times but received no answer. Finally, she received a letter from him telling her of happenings at the ranch and the valley. In the last part of the letter, he said he had been missing her very much and was looking forward to seeing her funny face again. It was signed, "Love, Jim."

The McKennas were talking in bed, as they often did. Greg was talking about his concern as to the heirs and the future of the McKenna ranch. He had been fretting more as time went on. He said, "Jim should be over that Jennifer by now."

"Honey, he is. He has been wrapped up in making the changes

on the ranch and you must admit he has done a remarkable job. He just hasn't time. You must have noticed that he has dated a few different women lately."

"He seems to be very particular."

"You wouldn't want a grandson from just anybody."

"No, but...."

"I have some good news and I'm sure it will all work out."

"Good news from whom?"

"You know Rosita has been writing to Martha and me. We got a letter written to both of us. The Ortegas are well established on the ranch. Her letter was about one of her visions or dreams and it was about a wedding. She couldn't see the people, but there were mountains and trees in the background. A few days later, she had another vision and people were standing around looking at a baby boy with a lot of black curly hair."

"Ellen, dreams like that are just from wishing and are fantasy."

"Rosita foretold about her baby being a girl, our wedding, about my having Barbara Ellen, and that Megan would be a girl. You can't say she was just lucky."

Greg gave her a hug and said, "I hope she is right."

"Of course she is. People for ages have had people who could foretell the future. In fact, one of the reasons I came to America was because of Meg."

"Who is this Meg? Did you name Megan after her?"

"I did. Meg was a medicine woman. She was old but spry and lived in a neat cottage by herself. She gathered plants for healing and treated the sick. She was sought after and very much respected. The poor paid her with food or an occasional penny. Business men consulted her for advice, because she could foretell the future, and they paid in money."

"What did she have to do with your coming to America?"

"My friend and I were carrying a basket of turnips to pay on our bill at the store. Meg was sitting out in the sun when we walked by. She said, 'Would you like me to tell your fortunes? I will do it for four turnips.'

Marge thought it would be fun and said, 'Let's do it.'

Meg took my hand, looked at it a long time, closed her eyes

and said, 'I see a ship, lots of water—the ocean. There are tall trees and mountains. You are a lucky girl. There is a big man, a nice man.' This made me feel good. Then she looked at Marge's hand, closed her eyes for only a little bit, and said, 'I will not read your fortune.' This ruined Marge's day. Three months later, she was fishing with her parents when a sudden storm came up and they were all drowned. Their bodies were never recovered."

Greg held his hand over the kerosene lamp and blew it out. After a kiss, he said, "Let's go to sleep and dream."

Barbara Ellen's school would be out in early May. Although she had enjoyed the teaching and the warm and pleasant hospitality of the Wilsons, she was just plain homesick. Report cards were passed out and fond good-byes took most of the morning. Another teacher, Janet, expressed Barbara's sentiment when she said, "I love them dearly and will miss them, but right now I'm glad they are gone!"

The railroad did not go through Boise, bypassing it several miles to the south. Emily Wilson drove Barbara to the depot to catch the east-bound train, which came to a screeching, grinding, bumping halt at seven o'clock in the morning. The train had barely stopped, a few passengers got off and a few got on, when there were two short blasts of the whistle and the pistons hissed out steam as the train began to gain rhythm and speed. Barbara forced herself to eat a hearty breakfast in the diner. She soon became tired of watching the endless sagebrush plains and began reading.

It was not practical to get a berth since she had to change trains at Pocatello and again at Missoula to the Salmon City Express, as they called the slow train of less than ten cars pulled by a very small locomotive that huffed and puffed uphill and squealed its brakes downhill. She did have a pillow and was able to lie down across the seat and doze. The train seemed to stop at every crossing to pick up a passenger, and by the time it was slowing down at Salmon, she thought how heavenly it would be to have a hot bath and sleep in her own bed. As the train pulled into the station, she waved at her parents and Megan. She wondered about Jim but was glad he wouldn't see her so disheveled.

The family greeted her with joy. She asked, "Where's Jim?"

Her mother said, "Meg put up such a fuss about not seeing

her sister for a long time, he agreed to stay home and finish surveying the ditches for the new irrigation system."

On the drive to the ranch she realized how much she had missed the hills, the mountains, the trees, and her family. When they stopped at a clear stream, they all had a drink upstream from the thirsty horses. Barbara pulled a bunch of fresh watercress and tasted its minty flavor. She remarked, "This is better than candy."

As they drove past Harry's pasture, she yelled, "Hi, Harry!" He picked up his ears and stretched his neck toward her, as if to greet her.

Greg started to say, "He..." and the family, in unison, said "He is one damn smart mule."

A hot bath and a four-hour sleep did wonders for Barbara. She took great pains in preparing herself for dinner, as she wanted to surprise Jim. She did. When she was walking down the stairs to the dining room, Jim rose from his chair and walked over to the foot. He reached for her and they came together solidly as she kissed him heartily. With his hands on her shoulders and holding her away from him, he said, "You are the most beautiful young woman I've seen in a long time—or ever. You have really grown up in the last year. The Mormons must have been good for you."

"They were, Jim. They made me appreciate my folks more and the ranch more, and maybe you just a little bit more."

The next morning, Barbara expressed a desire to ride in the hills. Jim said she could help him check the fence lines. They took a lunch which they ate while riding, as they found several head of cattle had wandered through a break in the fence.

Barbara knew that Kathleen had lost her husband in a mine cave-in, and asked Jim about her. He said, "We had a couple of dates, but it wasn't the same. I know you thought she was crude, but that wasn't her fault. How that battle-ax of a mother and mouse of a father had such a good-looking, fun person for a daughter, I'll never know."

When they were unsaddling and taking care of their horses, Jim said, "Would you like to go to the homecoming dance Saturday night?"

"Jim, are you asking me to go with you?"

"You're fishing. The answer is partly yes and some no, but mostly yes."

The homecoming dance was the big event in the spring. There

would be at least a hundred couples on the dance floor at one time. In the past, the McKennas all attended. That evening, during the washing of the dishes, Barbara mentioned to her mother that Jim had asked her if she wanted to go to the dance.

Ellen said, "Your father and I have been thinking about going, but I am afraid Megan is coming down with mumps. She has been complaining about swelling behind her ears. A lot of the high-school students have caught it during the past month."

That night she told Greg, "Barbara and Jim are going to the homecoming dance. Meg can't go because she has the mumps. Maybe we should stay home with her as she is going to feel bad about missing it." Greg looked at his wife, wondering if she had some other reason for not going.

"You're right," he said. "It won't hurt us to miss the dance."

Jim and Barbara agreed that it would be nice to go early. Because of the long ride over the dusty road, she wanted to change clothes at a friend's house in Salmon. They could eat dinner in town. When they discussed about where to eat dinner, Jim said, "The new Chinese restaurant is really good."

"No cats or dogs!"

"The reports are they are very particular about the food they buy and some of the women have complained when they refused to buy their parsley and vegetables. Besides, they will go all out to please us. Their names are Wong and Ching Li. They used to work for Dad and his partner twenty-five years ago in Idaho City."

It was nearly three o'clock when they arrived in Salmon. Barbara's Basque friend, Dorothy Asquena, was delighted to see her. Dorothy and her boyfriend, Jess, were planning to go to the dance. Jim said, "I'll leave you now, but I'll be back to take you to dinner. Dorothy, why don't you and Jess have dinner with us? It will be on me. I'll pick you up at half past six o'clock."

Barbara looked at him and said, "I'll bet you are going to play poker until then."

"Barbie, you are so right. Don't worry, I'll be here on time. I have a very beautiful dance partner."

"I am so thrilled that my date isn't going to dance only the first and last dance with me and play poker all the time between like he used to do."

"That was because you were a little girl and not a grown-up lady."

The dinner was a big success. When Ching Li, who was supervising the dining room, saw them enter, he went to the kitchen to get Wong to greet them. They shook hands and bowed.

"We glad you come to us. We make special dinnah, chop chop."

It was a very special dinner with a variety of Chinese dishes. Dorothy remarked, "You two make such a handsome couple."

"Barbara was always a very pretty girl, starting when she was a baby," Jim said. "And she got prettier as she got older."

"Jim, you never told me that. You always delighted in teasing me."

The New Year's dance, the homecoming dance, and the Fourth of July were the biggest events in the valley. Everyone dressed in their best for the homecoming dance. Jim was wearing his best dark blue suit with a white shirt and the new style tie called a cravat. Barbara had splurged on a new dark blue silk dress that had cost a month's wages. The seamstress had tailored it to bring out perfectly her straight carriage, wide shoulders, modest pointed breasts, and thin waist which blended into well-proportioned hips and long legs.

There were over a hundred numbers painted on the floor. When the band—piano, banjo, trombone, and drums—stopped playing after each dance, the dancers stopped and stood on the closest number. The band leader would spin a bicycle wheel attached to the wall with numbers painted around it. If the pointer on the wheel stopped on your number, you won a prize donated by businesses and merchants. Prizes ranged from free dinners, shoes, dresses, hair cuts, liquor, groceries, and meat. Dorothy hugged Jess, her escort, and said, "We really could use that beef!"

Barbara asked, "You mean..."

"Yes. We haven't got around to telling everybody. He just proposed last night."

The announcer held up a box, saying, "In this box is what I consider the grand prize." He reached into the box and held up a small white furry ball. "This little lady is some kind of terrier. I never could speak French. She is housebroke at two months old."

He put the scared, white pup with the pointed ears and square nose on the floor.

"I want her!" Barbara said.

"Maybe you will be lucky. I feel this is going to be a very special lucky day for us." The pup started to squat.

The grinning band leader said, "Well, she is almost house-broke," and quickly put her in the box where she stood up with just her head showing.

"Hold your breath, Jim, and wish with me." The wheel stopped and the announcement was, "Number 47." The two couples laughed and patted each other. Jim held the box with the pup while Barbara petted it.

"My new shoes are just killing me," Dorothy said.

"We haven't missed a dance," Barbara replied. "I'd like to get my shoes off, too. The pup needs company. Let's leave." Jim and Ralph agreed that they were ready to quit. After feeding the pup a saucer of milk at the Asquena home, the McKennas left their friends.

Barbara was holding the small pup in her lap, where it immediately went to sleep, and snuggled up close to Jim. "I'm so sleepy. If you don't mind, I'd like to take a short nap. Then I'll be all awake."

About an hour later, she awakened when he stopped to relieve the horses.

"Jim, the pup and I have to go as soon as they stop splattering."

"I do, too."

Instead of helping her back into the wagon, he picked her up and put her on the seat. "Thank you, Jim. That was a fun way to get into the buggy." When he went around and climbed into the seat, she reached over and taking his face in her hands, gave him a long, hard kiss.

"That was not a sisterly kiss."

"I hope not. In the first place, I'm not a sister." He grabbed her and said, "I'll show you," and gave her a longer, hard kiss.

She laughed and said, "I'll show you" and gave him a passionate kiss with her tongue searching and finding his.

When they finally came up for air, he said, "That does it."

"That does what?"

"We can no longer live in the same house unless we are married."

"I agree."

"Barbie, do you mean you will marry me?"

"That is just what I mean. There is no reason why we can't marry. We are not related to each other."

"Finally, I can think about you rationally. Ever since you were fifteen I have wanted to hold you and tell you I loved you. I just would not let myself consider it. I was always so jealous of your boyfriends."

"Jim, I died a thousand deaths when you went with other girls, especially Kathleen, and that Jennifer you wrote about."

He was letting the horses set their own pace, since they knew the way home from their many trips over the years. When they came to the break in the timber, the horses slowed and started to turn off. Jim reined them back.

"See, they tell on you."

"What do you mean, tell on me?"

"That's where you stopped with Kathleen."

"You know about that?"

"Of course I do. I checked the buggy and the lap robe, which had pine needles all over it. I even found a garter and a dried-up handkerchief with a little blood on it."

They continued to be affectionate with each other and both were quite aroused. He said, "The lap robe is clean."

"Lover, and I do mean lover, I am going to be like Dorothy Asquena who follows Basque women's beliefs and conduct. Dorothy always told the boys, and now Jess, that marriage is sacred and for a lifetime. It is the most important part of a woman's life and the first man I go to bed with will be my husband and nobody else. It will be hard for us to wait, but that is the way I want it. Please help."

"Darling, I'll see that your husband will be the first man in your life."

With that, she pounded on him and said, "Boy, are we in for some fun!"

"What do you mean, fun?"

"It's going to be fun when we wake up the folks and tell them we are going to get married as soon as possible, or sooner."

"How do you think they will feel?"

"They will be overwhelmed with joy. You know Daddy hasn't said anything to you about getting married, but he has been really fretting about not having a McKenna to inherit the ranch. We can furnish that."

"My love, there is a half-pint bottle under the seat with just enough Old Crow in it for two drinks. It's been there for about a year. We need it to get our courage up." After they finished their drinks, they sang songs all the way home.

She helped him put the horses away and they entered the house, holding hands. The parents were asleep and they hesitated for a short time. Then they both knocked loudly on the door.

Greg sleepily said, "What in hell is going on?"

Barbara said, "You and Mother have to get up. This is an emergency. Something has happened!"

"Ellen, are you awake? Barbara says there is an emergency. I'll light the lamp and we'll put on our robes." When he opened the door and saw both of them, the anxiety on his face turned to a grin.

"Just what are you two troublemakers up to?"

"Dad and Mom, we are going to get married."

"What?"

"We are going to get married as soon as possible and we want your blessing."

Ellen held out her arms and said, "Of course, you have our blessing." She winked at Barbara.

Greg said, "It's too bad you are too old to be spanked. You nearly gave me a heart attack. Let's go to the kitchen. This calls for a drink or two."

In the kitchen they discussed wedding plans, deciding that they could be ready in ten days. They wanted to be married in the schoolhouse on the ranch.

Ellen said, "You should take a month and go to California for your honeymoon. The Haines will welcome you and there is so much to see in San Francisco."

Greg said, "We will invite all our friends and neighbors, could be nearly one hundred. There is a fellow in Salmon that can barbecue a half beef. We'll get Wong and Ching Li to cater the rest of the food. I will take care of all of the arrangements. You ladies will have enough to do."

The family was late having breakfast on Sunday morning. Talk was all about the wedding. Jim said, "Barbara should have an engagement ring to wear for the next ten days." Barbara replied with a hug, saying, "You are beginning to behave like a proper husband-to-be." Greg laughed.

"What's so funny?" Ellen asked.

"I was thinking that we'll have to go to town in the morning to do the shopping and get the ring and license. I thought about Hellfire and Damnation."

They all knew that he referred to the county auditor and recorder, Grace Northrup. She was a fixture as she kept good records and no one else wanted the tedious job for thirty dollars a month. Greg went on to say, "She believes that every word in the Bible is true, and that any deviation, such as swearing, or talking about sex, is a cardinal sin. Rumors are a salesman selling kitchenware persuaded her to have dinner with him. When he reached down to pick up his napkin, he accidentally touched her hip. She jumped up, glared at him and shrieked, 'You filthy sex maniac!' and walked out."

Ellen remonstrated, "Shame on you, Greg."

"She is going to have a fit when she hears that brother and sister want a license to marry. After all, a lot of people do not know that they are not blood relation. We will take Jim's adoption papers to show her."

When they drove into Salmon, Greg and Jim tied the horses in the livery stable to rest. They agreed to meet at Ching Li's restaurant for lunch. Jim took Barbara's arm and said, "Honey, let's get the engagement ring first."

"It's like you're not my brother any more. Rather, you are the loving, considerate man that I will trust my life to and marry."

"Barbie, I feel the same. You are my bride-to-be and lover."

The jeweler had an almost perfect white diamond of nearly a carat, set in a ring that needed only a little adjustment to fit. When the alteration was done, Jim took the ring and slipped it on her finger. The wedding band in its velvet-lined box made the total cost five hundred seventy-five dollars. As they left the store, Jim said, "Now we will have fun confronting the old battle-ax."

"How can I help you?" asked the county recorder as they approached her counter.

"We want to get a marriage license." She handed them forms to be filled out, and they sat down at a table and completed them. When they were handed back, she started to read and her face reddened. She sputtered and finally said, "I'll not issue you a marriage license. You have the same parents. You are brother and sister. That is incest and punishable by a jail sentence. The Lord will punish you by hell fire and you deserve it. Get out of my office or I'll call the sheriff!"

It took considerable time to convince her, even with the adoption document, that Jim was adopted and no blood relation to Barbara. She said, "I still don't think it is right. I'll ask the prosecuting attorney if it is legal," and left to go upstairs to his office. She was back almost immediately, saying, "I'll issue the license, but I still don't think it is right."

When they met for lunch at Ching Li's, Jim and Barbara told of getting the license, causing hilarious laughter. Wong and Ching Li were delighted to be chosen to cater the wedding dinner.

Before heading for the ranch, they stopped at the newspaper office to place an announcement, with an explanatory note at the end informing people that Jim was adopted and no blood relative. This revived the stories about how Greg had been saved from hanging by the Indian Chief Tall Man, who had the white baby that he had found.

Ellen insisted that the groom should not see the bride on the day of the wedding until she walked in and joined him at the altar. Jim took his clothes and spent the night with the Lathams. Barbara declared that this was a joyous occasion, and the school bell should be rung before the ceremony started.

Ellen's wedding dress fitted Barbara perfectly. Jim was almost speechless at the radiant beauty of his bride as she walked down the aisle with Greg and stepped to his side. He whispered, "You are so beautiful. I can hardly believe you are going to be my wife."

"Jim, this is like a wonderful dream."

The ceremony went off smoothly. When Greg joined her in the front row after giving Barbara away, Ellen whispered to him,

"Now you can stop worrying about a McKenna taking over the ranch after you."

"Ellen, I actually believe Rosita was right."

The women were crying and the men shaking hands as the new man and wife walked down the line of people to the reception area, where the sumptuous barbecue and long tables laden with food, a pile of gifts, and a beautiful wedding cake baked by Martha Latham awaited. The crowd was still celebrating when Jim and Barbara slipped away to their buggy to drive to the ranch house and change clothes. The buggy was already packed with their suitcases for the trip to California.

As they entered the room to change, Jim said, "Honey, we are not in a hurry, are we?"

"Jim, if you mean in a hurry to get to Salmon, no." She started to unbutton his shirt.

As they drove past the waving crowd at the tables, Harry let out a loud series of brays. Greg laughed and said, "That is one damned smart mule!"

"Not so smart," Ellen replied. "You forgot to give him his oats and brown sugar this morning."